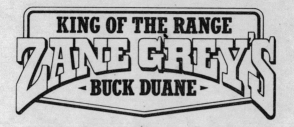

KING OF THE RANGE

ZANE GREY'S

◄ BUCK DUANE ►

ROMER ZANE GREY

LEISURE BOOKS   **NEW YORK CITY**

A LEISURE BOOK®

July, 1999

Published by
Dorchester Publishing Co., Inc.
276 Fifth Avenue
New York, NY 10001

ISBN 0-8439-4597-4

CONTENTS

KING OF THE RANGE

The rider was loose in the saddle, rocking a bit with the pace of his scrubby range mustang and keeping his seat more by instinct than anything else. The raw frontier whiskey in his gut kept him warm against the biting wind out of the north, and he was tunelessly chanting tag ends of a popular ballad of the range.

He never really felt the heavy lead slug from the old Hawken buffalo gun when it smashed both lungs and cut through his heart. The shock of impact lifted him slightly so that he came clear of the saddle and tumbled, rag limp, onto the frost hard ground. He was dead before he hit.

When his friends found him in the morning he was already frozen stiff and hard, blood crusted in icy crystals on the front of his patched wool jacket. His own frontier hog-led Colt was still holstered and unfired.

"Bushwacked," Ben Reedy said and spat onto the ground. "Less we go down and clean out all that scum, they'll bushwack every last rider we got."

"You better leave them ideas to Mr. King," Slim Taylor said. "He'll know what to do, you can bet, and when the time's right he'll tell us. Now wrap this one in a blanket and we'll take him home."

"Bitter weather for digging graves," Ben Reedy said then. "Bitter work for any weather I say."

In the one roomed soddy under the lee of Long Butte the scrawny, bitter-faced woman watched her man clean his rifle.

"Killin' agin'" she said. "Ain't there never gonna be no end to this?"

"Not never while the King sits so high in the

saddle," her husband said. He looked around the single room. It was eight by fourteen feet, windowless and walled with dirt and squares of piled up prairie sod. The door was rawhide on a sapling frame and let the wind come in as it pleased. There was a fire on the rude hearth, and a bedstead and a saddle in the corner. His wife was frying meat in a bit, three-legged iron spider on the hearth.

"The King rides high," the man said bitterly. "He's ridin' on the backs of folk like us. It's to stop, Mary. It's to stop if it means killin' or no."

"You're a fool, Jud Ballew," his woman said. "You were born a fool and grew worse. It's not killin' will make you wise nor rich. The King has men and his men have guns. It's my mind that the man to die will be yourself, and soon."

"I left no trail," the man said suddenly.

"There's a trail in their minds," the woman said. "It's you and them like you that kills with long guns. They'll know and come riding. You mark my word."

In the comfortable big room that served for office and parlor at the King's Crown Ranch House, big Jared King might have been reading the woman's mind.

"Of course we know who killed him," Jared King told his foreman, Slim Taylor. "Which one makes small difference. It could be any man of that range scum. Ranchers they call themselves! It's hatred and envy that chews their guts, Slim, till they get so full of bile that they have to kill."

"The dirty bushwacking rats," Slim Taylor said. "What will we do, Mr. King? The men are nervous. They see a rifle back of every bush when they ride out as it is."

"I know," Jared King said heavily. "I'm already doing what has to be done. I sent Sam down to San Antone to bring Miss Georgia home. I gave him orders to hire fighting men and bring them back when he comes. He's got a letter on the bank. He'll show gold eagles and hire the best. I said enough of them to do the job. There's a nest of rattlers on this range, and we'll clean it out for sure."

Slim Taylor said, "The boys will be happy to hear. Them rustlers and the soddy scum will never stand to regular guns."

"Don't look so pleased," the ranch owner said. "There's nothing to smile on in killing, Slim. It's bitter business and I wish need not be done. If it weren't for the herd—"

"Ah yes," Slim Taylor said. "The herd. The King's own herd."

Winter came early to the high West Texas plains that year. The winds flowed like a bitter tide down off the roof of the world where the white bears stalk the seal and the vast ice mountains grind each other's flanks and jostle in the sullen Arctic sea.

The winds whooped and moaned past the lonely lodge where a Cree family crouched and feared the lobo wolf and heard the wind voice as wailing demons in the night.

The winds came across the high broken hills, down over the Nebraska plateaux, scouring the tilted plane of Kansas and the territory of the Indian Nations. They came down in waves of cold and fury onto the Llano Estacado. Everything bowed to the winds.

Even in San Antonio, far to the south, they rattled windows, pounded the loose-hinged doors in crazy frontier clapboard false-fronts, and woke a whole legion of cold dust devils to dance in the streets.

The building that housed the San Antonio office of the Texas Rangers dated back to Mexican days. It was solidly built of adobe brick, and the office of Captain MacNelly boasted a fireplace burning mesquite and scrub oak logs. It was a little warmer

6

than the street outside and a little quieter than the saloon next door, but that was all the anyone could say.

Both the captain and the man who faced him across the rough board table on the particular evening wore their heavy wool overcoats and kept on the wide-brimmed high-crowned hats that marked a Texas man. A couple of candles guttering in tin illumined the map spread out on the table.

The wiry, weather hardened captain hardly noticed the cold. He was tracing some lines with a pencil on the map in front of him.

"It's wild country, Buck," he was saying. "You go in on your own, and there's little or no help we can give you when the trouble starts."

"I'm used to that," the tall Ranger replied. "Don't worry. Just tell me what side I'm supposed to be on."

The tall man's name was Buck Duane. He was known as an outlaw, a killer and a king of the owlhoot trails. For almost twenty years the law had hunted him like a rabid wolf. Almost no one knew that he had been a Ranger and a confidential assistant to Captain MacNelly in more than one desperate and bloody affray. He wore no badge and asked no public praise or glory for what he did. Because the outlaws saw him as one of themselves his value to the captain was immeasurably enhanced. Peace officers avoided him, grateful that he made no depredations in their territories.

Men on both sides of the law knew his name and dreaded his lightning guns. "The man who outdrew the rattler's strike," they called him.

Now he sat quietly and waited for his commanding officer to explain.

"That's simple enough," Captain MacNelly said. "Simple, but makes no sense. You're on both sides this time, Buck. Both sides or none at all. You kill anybody you need to stop him killing someone else."

7

A grin split Duane's lean, usually impassive face. "You're right this time," he said. "It makes no sense at all."

Captain MacNelly poured two glasses of whiskey from the bottle by his right hand, and pushed one over to the tall, deadly man he called friend.

Duane drank some of the whiskey from his glass and settled back in his chair.

"You've got to have heard of Jared King," Captain MacNelly said. "He has the biggest spread on all the high plains, with water and grass for twenty thousand critters if he wants to hold them there."

"The King's Crown brand." Duane nodded. "Every rider knows that one. British money bought it for him."

"That's right. He was an Eastern man to begin with and educated abroad at a place called Oxford. Money of his own and friends who are dukes and earls and with money of their own to burn. When he saw the west and decided to settle here he went back and persuaded his friends to invest. That's one reason they call him 'the King' as well as the pun on his name.

"For ten years now he's built that spread and sent his herds up the Chisholm Trail every spring. He's an educated man, Buck. He knows about things like cost accounting and markets. He knows horseflesh and cattle. That big ranch has prospered. He's taken out gold like it was a mine and not a ranch he has."

"What need has a man like that for me?" Duane asked.

"You wait and I'll spell it out," MacNelly said. "Perhaps it's not King that needs you, boy. More like it's Texas' need.

"You know what our range cattle are, Buck. Bred out of the longhorn brush-poppers. Wild as wolves and tough as wang leather, till they get fattened in

8

Kansas or Illinois. King knew the fat cattle of Europe. They carried meat for three or four of ours. He set to breed beef cattle he could raise and drive and sell with fat meat still on their bones."

"I remember talk of that," Duane said.

"It's more than talk now, Buck. He brought in stud bulls from Spain and England. He bred and cross bred. Now, this year, he has the King's Own Herd. Only five hundred head as yet, but cattle of a sort that Texas never saw before. Why man, if our ranchers raise and drive these steers it'll triple the price they can get at the railhead market.

"That one herd, Buck, is the seed for the wealth of all the Texas cattle country."

"Go on," Duane said when the captain paused.

"That is," MacNelly continued, "if all goes as planned. The work that King has done in breeding those steers is wealth in the pocket of every man in Texas, if the herd lives and is bred and cross bred."

"There has to be a joker in the deck," Duane said drily. "Go on and tell me why the herd won't live without a Ranger to ride midwife for its birth."

MacNelly pointed to the map. "You see the King's Crown there," he said and placed his finger. "The one big spread for a hundred miles. Nothing else up there yet but the little ten cow and loose rope outfits. Riders with a few steers, rustlers, buffalo hunters scratching for a dollar on the high staked plains. Little men with little minds, Buck. They hate the King because he's big. They hate his herd because it's better than anything they ever saw before. For years they've raided his stock for beef and spat in the tracks his horses made."

"Nothing new about that," Duane said. "All the big outfits are bothered that way. Isn't this feller man enough to hold his own?"

"Of course he is," MacNelly said. "At least he thinks he is. His brother's been here in town hiring guns. They'll fight and men will die. Range war. That's where you're going, Buck."

"To fight on which side, Captain? But I asked you that."

"I gave you the answer. You fight both sides. You go to stop the war. Somebody's behind it, Buck. Somebody wants the King spread smashed and, worst of all, the King's Herd all destroyed. We don't know who he is, but we know he's there. He's stirring up the little men to wipe out the new cattle breed.

"If the range war isn't stopped it'll happen too. King will wipe out the little men, but they'll get to his herd before they die. That's why I'm sending you out, Buck. You know the Rangers can't go in officially before the trouble starts. If we wait till fighting begins, there's little chance we can get there in time. I've got confidence in you, Buck."

"By God but you must," Duane burst out. "You send one man to fight both sides of a war. Why, the Seventh Cavalry or the whole Comanche Nation could hardly do that job."

"I've got confidence in you, Buck," Captain MacNelly repeated.

That same night in San Antone not more than half a mile from the spot where the two Rangers conferred, the Honorable Sam King, member of the State Legislature and younger brother of Jared King, sat at his ease before a roaring fire in the most expensive suite of the town's finest hotel. There was a glass of the best imported Scotch whiskey in his hand and a silver case of black Havana cheroots. His shirt was freshly laundered Irish linen and his boots the triumph of a master leather worker's art.

Sam King—"Judge" King as he was called, although the title was purely honorary—had the same sandy-red hair, gray eyes and big rawboned frame as his brother Jared. In matter of fact there

10

wasn't an inch in height or three pounds of weight difference between the two. Glimpsed at a distance and in a crowd, one man could easily be mistaken for the other.

Seen side by side though, there was no possible doubt which brother wore the title of "The King". Jared was big and strong, hard-handed, steely-eyed, with an inner strength that radiated to all about him.

It was that inner strength which Judge King lacked. That, and a general, indefinable slackness of fiber stood him apart from and a step below his elder brother. It didn't show too much this night. Warmed by the whiskey and the fire he radiated a fine content with life.

At least it seemed that way to the younger woman who sat with him before the hearth. She was a tall girl, beautifully formed, long-legged and high-breasted with clear blue eyes and long, light brown hair.

"Father," she was saying quietly, "your real reason for coming here wasn't to meet me."

"Of course it was," Sam King said, but without conviction.

"Oh no it wasn't," his daughter said. "Don't think because I've been away at school in New Orleans for two years that I've forgotten everything I learned all my life before that. I haven't. I can look at the sky and tell when a Norther's blowing up just like I always could. I can smell a different kind of wind too when it blows men instead of the tall grass."

"I don't know what you're talking about, Georgia."

"Oh, of course you do, Father. I'm talking about those ranch hands you've been hiring all week."

"Nothing unusual about that," Sam King assured her. "You know the new herd will need careful attention and the drive next Spring will be the most important we've ever made. I'm sure your Uncle

11

Jared has written you all about the new cattle breed."

"Of course he has. The King's Own Herd, the breed that will make Texas the greatest cattle state in the Union." Her voice was low, almost awed as she spoke. "Yes, Father, I can hardly wait to see those wonderful cattle critters."

"Well, then . . ."

"But that's not what I'm talking about and you know it. Those men you've been hiring aren't cattle hands or trail drivers. You can't fool me about that."

"You're mistaken," Sam King said.

"I'm not mistaken, and I'm not some silly little Eastern girl. One of those men you hired is Pecos Red. Don't you think I know who Pecos Red is? He's a gunny. A killer for hire. If you want plain speaking, he's a professional paid murderer. Now why do you suppose the King's Crown Brand needs hired guns to ride winter herd. Why?"

"There's been trouble," Sam King said.

"Trouble? With who? The Comanches haven't recovered from their last whipping yet. Big rustlers leave a spread as large as ours alone. At least when the King rides to defend his, they do. So who?"

Sam King shifted in his comfortable chair. "We didn't want to trouble you, Georgia. It's been building up. The soddys. The little loose rope ranchers."

"The foothill men?" she said incredulously. "Those saddle tramps. You need thirteen hired gunsels against those miserable rats? You know we've always let them kill a steer now and then to eat. We expect it. Now all of a sudden we need an army!"

"I said you didn't understand," her father told her. "It's worse than you know. They've taken to shooting horses, shooting steers and not even butchering them, killing men. Georgia, honey, we've had two men bushwacked and killed."

12

"Oh no," Georgia King said with genuine concern. "Killing our boys! We never harmed them. Why would they do anything like that? Why, Father? Why?"

Sam King finished his drink. "I know you think it's strange, dear. You're a woman. You don't know how men are." He paused again for a moment, seeing something in the leaping flame on the hearth. "Sometimes I think hatred and envy are the strongest emotions a man can know."

There was something in his voice that chilled the spine of the girl sitting beside him.

Early next morning Sam and Georgia King rode out of San Antonio on the first leg of the long road north and west to the high reaches of the King's Crown Ranch. Altogether they had quite a caravan for company. There were three big, lumbering mule drawn wagons full of gear and winter supplies for the ranch, their mule-skinners and the two riders who had come down with Sam King. In the van rode the thirteen gunmen Sam King had hired while staying in the City.

Mostly the men rode quietly, hunched down against the cold in their heavy wool coats and with broad hatbrims pulled down over their eyes.

The only one who rode close to the big Sam King and his niece was the man called Pecos Red. He was still a young man but his face showed the lines of constant consciousness of danger and death. He was cadaverously thin, with the pink flush of the comsumptive already touching his cheeks.

His eyes were feral, restless, darting from side to side with the alertness of a hunted animal. He was watching the laughing, eager girl who rode just ahead. He wore a short overcoat, cut back so as not to cover the two big revolvers hanging from his belt.

The party rode slowly, held back by the difficulty of moving the heavily loaded wagons along. A few miles north of the last straggling city shacks the King caravan was overtaken by two riders going in the same direction and at a much faster clip.

The older of the two was a tall, lean-flanked man riding a magnificent specimen of the frontier horse. His clothing, boots and saddle were all perfectly ordinary but he rode with an air that marked him as an unusual man in any company.

His steely eyes swept wagons and riders without betraying emotion as he passed. He wore two guns, tied down but under a long coat, and a .44 Winchester carbine in its saddle boot. He rode easily, parallel to the road where the wagons struggled along. His face was hidden by a neckerchief tied over mouth and nose against the bite of the winter wind.

His companion was a younger man, slender, with merry, laughing eyes for the other riders and particularly for Georgia. The two kept a fast steady pace and outdistanced the King party in a matter of minutes.

"Who was that man?" Georgia asked her father.

"I don't know," Sam King replied, rousing from his own thoughts. "Just some saddle tramp I guess."

"Oh no," Georgia said. "No saddle bum rides the way he did. The man rides like a king of the range. I wish I knew who he was."

At just that moment Pecos Red had dropped back to ride beside one of his friends. "I seen that big hombre some place, Charlie," he said. "He's one of us, but I can't put a name to him. You know him?"

"I didn't see his face," Charlie said.

The big man was Buck Duane and the other was his friend, the Jackrabbit Kid.

Buck Duane and the Kid rode fast and hard. They wanted to get up in the King's Crown country before snow came to slow their pace. On a ride of this sort

Duane usually camped in the open. It was a habit bred of long years of running from the law, when a roof and a smoking hearth had signaled danger instead of shelter and a welcome.

This time, however, there was no necessity to avoid the few ranches, saloons and little border towns they found, and the Kid was far less used to winter camps than was Duane. They slept under roofs every night but one.

Duane had recognized the King party. He knew several of the gunmen Sam King had hired by sight and rightly interpreted their presence as a sign of imminent bloody violence on the high plains.

"Looks like the King's raising himself an army," the Ranger told the Jackrabbit Kid. "That means it won't be long before real trouble starts. Every hour we can be there before that lot rides in can be important now."

"Isn't there a chance things'll simmer down?" the Kid asked his big friend. "I'd think the little fellers'd think twice before they go up against so many hired guns. Was it me I'd pull in my horns and lie mighty low before I took on Pecos Red and his boys."

"That's because you got brains enough to get in out of the rain," Duane said. "The men you're talking about probably don't. They got hunger and hate and envy instead of brains."

"They're stupid then."

"Sure they're stupid," Duane said. "In the long run they can't fight an outfit like the King's Crown and win. Maybe they even know that, but it won't stop them. As soon as that crowd rides in the word will go round. In a matter of days the killing would start even if Jared King didn't want it to.

"If the rustlers don't start it, Pecos Red will anyhow. He gets his pay and bonus for something besides eating beans and sowbelly in a bunkhouse all winter. He'll want to do his job and get out of there."

"I can see how he'd figure that," the Kid said. "He's hired for a war so there'd better be one. If it's still simmering when he gets there, it will be to his own advantage to bring everything to a boil."

"That's right," Duane said. "There's bound to be somebody up there who's already brought suspicion on himself as a bushwacker. Red and his boys will burn that man's place, run off his stock if he has any, and put him and his family out in the winter to starve. The soddy will fight back of course and get killed.

"About that time the rest of them will decide to gang up on the King spread. They won't have the chance of a snowball on a hot stove of course, but they won't be smart enough to know that. They'll go for Pecos and his boys."

"Yeah," the Kid agreed, "and that'll be like a run of house pets tangling with a lobo wolf pack. Amateurs can't stand against the professional guns."

"Exactly."

"Then why are we going up there, Buck? Are we supposed to keep them dumb soddys from gettin' massacreed? Is that what Captain MacNelly wants?"

"Not exactly," Duane said. "You know a Ranger can't take sides, and if he did it would have to be with the Kings. They stand for law and order. At least they do till Pecos' boys actually murder somebody. After all the little hit-and-run-boys have been cutting up King beef and bushwacking King riders. No, we aren't rightly standing up for any underdog this trip."

"What are we doing then?"

"Right now we're trying to get there before a big snow makes us hole up. After that we're supposed to stop the war. Captain MacNelly figures somebody on the soddy side will be bright enough to know Jared King can be hit worst by killing or stealing his prize herd. He can. So can the rest of the State of

16

Texas. That's what we've got to prevent and the captain and I figure the best way is to keep the war from breaking out at all. I don't know quite how we can do it yet, but that's the job."

The Kid hunched his shoulders against the steadily rising cold North wind.

"Fine," he said. "Just fine. You and me fight the bushwackers *and* Pecos Red all at once. Just like that. Can't old King look out for his own cow critters?"

Jared King was saying to his foreman, "When Sam gets back here with his war riders I want you to take charge of them. I want them held on a real tight rein. If there's to be more killing, I don't want it to be our men that start it."

"You know what Mr. Sam will say," Slim Taylor protested. "You were at Shiloh and Vicksburg same as the rest of us was. He'll say hit your enemy first. He'll want to burn out them saddle bums and harry them over the rim of the hills. He'll be all for attack and so will the gunnys he hires. They like to do the job, get their pay and go back to the women and cards."

"I know all that," Jared King said. "If there has to be a war, that's what we do. Till then I give the orders and not Sam or any gunhand. You know as well as I do, Slim, once the killing starts they'll go for my herd. We can't barn up five hundred steers. If we could they'd put fire arrows on the barns.

"Those five stud bulls can't be replaced. Their lives are worth more than any man to Texas right now. We have to guard them first."

"I know," Slim Taylor said. "You're right. Jud Ballew is a breed himself and there's more out there with Injun blood. Once they get a mind to it there's no sentry line can keep them from the herd. Special not in winter. Come a big snow they could stampede

17

the lot to freeze and die."

"The rest of the range stock we can replace," Jared King said, "but we can't replace the King's Own Herd."

Jud Ballew met his friends in a rickety abode and wattle house a good twenty miles back in the foothills from the rich grazing land of the King's Crown Ranch. The windows of the place were shuttered tight against the wind. A meagre open fire and a couple of sputtering beef-tallow candles gave them enough light to see each other. In that bare room there was little else to see.

They drank raw whiskey and conferred.

"The word come through," Ballew told the others. There were six of them beside himself, and they represented the leadership of the group that called itself "West Texas Independent Ranchers' Association." The title was a personal conceit of Ballew's. In his mind it somehow cast a cloak of legality and legitimacy over the activities of his group to have so high-sounding a title.

Now they looked at Jud Ballew expectantly.

"The rider I been waitin for come through last night," he told the others with a note of triumph in his voice. "He got the word for me from my friend. The time to strike for our liberties has come."

A couple of the others greeted his pronouncement with a note of approval, but it wasn't by any means unanimous.

"Just hold on a minute now," one of the older men said. "Ain't you talkin' just a mite wild, Jud? Sure we've had our differences with old Jared King. It's always that way between the little spreads and a big one, but that don't mean nothing that says we have to fight no battles. When men have differences, there's no reason they can't be settled reasonable like. That's what I say, and it makes sense to me."

There was a stir amongst the other men.

Jud Ballew didn't give anyone else time to speak. "You don't think we have to strike for our rights, Jim Wills? Well, I think old Jared King believes we should. Why else would he hire thirteen paid killers down to San Antone? I ask yuh all. What does he need thirteen gunmen for, lessen he means to wipe us out?"

There was a growl of assent.

Jim Wills wasn't cowed however. He was one of the more prosperous of the small ranchers. Over the years he'd built up a herd of close to two hundred steers to wear his J-W brand. In most things he spoke for the other more responsible small ranchers in the area.

"Let me speak," he said. "It may be he don't like the beef killing and the bushwacking that's been going on. Just like some of us don't like the killing of riders neither. It may be his thought in hiring guns—that is if he has hired guns—is just to protect what's rightly his own. I say we go and talk to him before there's any more killing."

"You're crazy in the head," said a voice from the edge of the circle.

"I say reasonable men can settle things a reasonable way," Jim Wills repeated stubbornly. "Me and my people ain't about to take to guns withouten we know that we must."

"You must alright," Jud Ballew said. "What must be done to convince you? Must you see your place burned over your head and your childer hungry in the snow. What else would the King hire him them killers for?"

"I haven't seen killers yet."

"I tell yuh, Jim," Ballew said, "my friend he sent a rider by to bring the news. Sent a man who was going on west and moving fast. Yuh can trust that word. There's killers hired, and their trade is to kill. When they get here, yuh'll see for yerselfs. You and yuh friends think you be better than us, but you'll go under them guns like the rest."

"How do we know we can trust this mysterious friend of yours? Who is he? For that matter how do we even know a rider came by your place? We know you hate the King, but ain't that all we really do know."

One of the others backed Jim Wills this time. "That's right, Jud. Who is this friend? What does he want out of a range war here?"

"I can't tell you his name," Ballew said. "I tell you this though. He's a man who hates the King for his injustice like we all do. He wants to help us little men."

Jim Wills pushed his advantage. "Why don't this mystery feller show his hand? He wants war. You want war. What about the rest of us? Who is this friend?"

Ballew said, "I'll show you is he a friend. His rider brought this to help us out." He pulled a deerskin pouch from a pocket of his filthy greatcoat and poured out its contents on the floor.

"My God!" One of the men said. "That there is gold."

Buck Duane and the Jackrabbit Kid made much better time than the Sam King party could possibly with their heavily loaded wagons. The big Ranger and his companion got into the high plains country a good two days ahead of the small army Sam King had recruited.

They headed straight for the little town of Kingston which had grown up as a trading center for the King Ranch riders and the small ranchers and nesters in the adjoining area. It wasn't much of a town, but it did boast a branch post office, general store, hardware "Emporium," stage office, half a dozen miscellaneous and not very successful minor business enterprises and a couple of saloons.

A few miles outside of town Duane and the Kid split up according to plan. The younger man swung wide around the town and made directly for the King's Crown headquarters. They had planned that he'd hire on there as a rider. Since the Kid wasn't known to Pecos Red and his crowd he could keep an eye on their operations from the inside.

As it turned out the Kid was hired off-hand to replace the rider who had been bushwacked. Slim Taylor was glad of the chance to add another hand to his working crew.

Buck Duane headed straight on into the little town where the frame buildings huddled forlornly against the rising blast of the late autumn winds from the North. He didn't ride into the single commercial street until late afternoon. Dusk was falling and the bare branches of the winter-stripped cottonwood and scrub oak trees fringing the narrow stream along which the town had been built rattled an aimless drum beat in the wind.

Kerosene lamps had already been lit in the more pretentious stores to signal a welcome to any possible customer, but there were few people abroad.

Duane located the combined blacksmith shop and livery stable easily enough. The forge fire was only coals and the proprietor gone home to early dinner, but a stableman took his money and opened a stall for Duane's magnificent mount, Bullet.

There was no real hotel in the town of course, but the man said there were rooms for hire on the second floor over one of the saloons. "That is if you ain't too perticular."

In the winter cold Duane knew perfectly well he couldn't afford to be fastidious about the quality of quarters available. His own prime requirement was a shelter from the winds and snow. He left his saddle at the stable, but lugged his bedroll over his shoulder as

21

he walked up to the saloon, just in case there was already insect life in the beds to hire.

The saloon keeper, a burly Irishman by the name of Thomas Ryan, was happy to take the rider's money. "All them rooms is empty now," he said, and tossed Duane a key. "This'n is the best. Corner in front to yer right at the top of the stair. Ye'll be wanting to eat, I suppose."

"The biggest steak you've got for the fire," Duane agreed, "and a whole pie if you have one. Any sort of pie. I've been a long while on the trail."

"We've got dried apple pie and canned termaters," Ryan said understanding the trail man's hunger for fruit and green stuff.

"That's fine," Duane said. "I'll put my stuff in the room and be right down."

He found the room easily enough. It was larger than he had expected and a great deal cleaner. He lit a candle and made a close inspection of the big brass bed. The blankets had been recently washed. Besides the bed there was a straight chair, a rough wood chest to hold his things and a black oak washstand. The big crockery water pitcher on the stand was empty.

Just about the time he made that discovery there was a knock on the room door. Duane still wore his long wool overcoat, but he'd unfastened the lower buttons so that he could get at his holster guns in case of need. He checked that they were loose in the holsters before he went to answer the door.

The woman in the hallway was bundled up in a big overcoat much like the one the Ranger wore, but her head was bare. She stood so tall that her eyes were almost level with his own. She was young, big-boned and big-breasted, with blue eyes and a wide mouth. She was toting a hooped wooden pail of steaming hot water in each hand.

"For a weary man to wash himself with," she said

as she stepped past Duane into the room. "Mostly lodgers uses the pump out in back and breaks the ice in the pail to suit themselves. It's in my mind that a man fresh into town needs something better than that."

"You've got a good mind," Duane said, "And a fine warm heart to match."

She gave him a level stare. "Now don't be exciting yourself about the warmth of my heart, mister," she said. "It's sister to Tom Ryan who owns this house that I am, and not one of your fancy border women."

Duane smiled at her. "It wasn't that which I meant. Just that only a woman of kindness would have thought to bring so much hot water without my demanding it. I assure you that was every bit of my meaning."

Then she smiled back. "Sure and I think you mean it, so pardon the bite of me tongue. I can see now that you're no saddle tramp at all, but a gentleman of quality indeed."

She put out her hand to him like a man after setting down the still steaming buckets. "I'm Molly Ryan, and most pleased to make your acquaintance to be sure. And who might you be indeed?"

Duane took her hand in a strong clasp. "Just call me Buck. I'm happy to meet you too."

For a moment he thought she was going to ask his last name. It was in her look, but she let it pass. "I'll go see that your meal is in order by the time you come down for it," she said.

Duane stripped down to the buff when the woman had left and gave himself a thorough, all-over sponge bath which refreshed him immensely. When he dressed to go down to eat he left the overcoat across the foot of the brass bedstead. He wore two pairs of socks—one cotton and one woolen—under his high heeled ranchero boots, a suit of red flannel "long johns," wool pants and shirt and an old wool

23

short suit jacket. A voluminous blue neckerchief was knotted about his throat. He wore only his right hand gun, tied down to the leg. The other gun and the rifle he left tied in his bedroll. His hair had grown rather long on the trail, but he brushed it back as well as he could.

Dressed as he was Duane could have been anything from a travel-worn man of substance to a gambler or traveling professional man. This was by design. On this assignment he didn't want to appear as a saddle tramp.

Darkness had already fallen by the time he got down to the bar again, but it was still late afternoon rather than evening. There was only one other customer, a booted rider in close conference with Ryan at the bar.

Buck Duane sat down at one of the small tables in the room. Molly Ryan appeared almost at once from the kitchen to bring him a candle and a big mug of steaming coffee. Within minutes she turned carrying a big, blue and white china platter on which reposed a two-pound steak, six fried eggs, and a dozen biscuits hot from the oven. There was butter and cane syrup for the biscuits and an opened can of tomatos for a side dish.

Duane pitched in like the hungry man he was. When the last savory smear of steak juice and egg yolk had been mopped from the platter with the final biscuit Molly appeared again. This time she carried a whole dried apple pie still smoking in its tin baking plate and a crockery pitcher of what proved to be cold milk. When she put these down on the table she didn't leave again but pulled up another chair and sat opposite him.

"You don't mind?" she asked.

"Of course I don't mind," Buck Duane said. "Glad of the company."

She watched him finish the pie and milk. He took

24

a long cigar out of the breast pocket of his jacket. She nodded assent to his smoking, and he lit the cheroot at the candle flame.

"I don't mind saying," he told Molly, "that's one of the finest and tastiest dinners I've ever had. For a man who's been long on the trail there's nothing that could have been finer."

She gave him a curious glance. "Why, thank you," she said, "And will you be here to eat more of them?"

"I may indeed," Duane said. "It's late in the year for traveling to the North, and besides I'm looking for a place to settle for a while. That is, I am if I find the one that will suit a man of my sort."

He could see both that he'd caught her interest and that she was trying not to show how much her curiosity had been aroused. That was just what Duane wanted. If he could get her talking he might well pick up plenty of useful information. After all she probably knew anything her brother did—and the saloon keeper was usually the best informed man in any town of this sort.

"Can I buy you a drink?" he asked Molly.

"Only a beer," she said. "I'm not a bar girl. Or did I say that once already?"

"You did," Duane smiled at her. "A beer will be fine for me also."

She went behind the bar and came back with two tall, foaming mugs. Her brother, still deep in his conversation, let her draw the beer herself. No other customers had come in yet.

Molly said, when she sat down, "You were about to tell me what your business is in Kingston."

He put his head back and laughed at her over the cigar and beer. "Young lady," he said. "I was about to do no such thing, and well you know that. Are you new to this part of the State of Texas, that you ask a stranger questions to his face?"

"I know," Molly said. "People don't ask questions

out here. It wasn't that sort of question in my mind, not the sort of question would harm a man. I mean—you seem like a decent man and you talk about settling here. You did, didn't you?"

"Another question," Buck Duane said, and then laughed at her expression. "It's all right. I may have let slip something of the sort, but it was only a thought in my mind. Nothing but an idea. I only rode in a couple of hours ago."

"I know that," Molly said. "Still it takes no wise woman to see that you're an uncommon sort of man. The way you carry yourself. It's like the old King out to the ranch."

"The King?" Duane asked. He wanted to get her talking.

"Mr. Jared King, that is. Him that owns the King's Crown spread and the fine, wonderful herd that he's bred. Not that you look like him, you know. Just the way you walk and the way you hold your head as you sit. A man like you can make ripples in a country like a big rock in a pond."

"Would something be wrong with that?"

"It might, Mr. Buck. It surely might. You don't know this pond, you see. In the winter of the year 'tis like everything has set here. Like thin ice on a pond. A big enough rock could make more than ripples around here. It could smash up everything."

"I begin to see that," Buck Duane said. "I may even have heard just the whisper of a talk of trouble on my way here. Still you mustn't worry yourself about me, Miss Molly. I can look out for myself."

"I see the way you wear your gun," she said. "Should you settle here though you might find yourself in the middle of two bands of angry men. Then it could be you would choose sides for your own safety, if for naught else."

Duane drank some of his beer. "And if I did—"

"Then it comes to my mind," she said, giving him

that level, alert look of her eyes once more, "that you could be a mighty fighting man for the side you choose. For many poor folk it could be a great thing. The side you chose for your own could be a matter of life and death for folks you don't even know."

Duane said, "Tell me, Molly. If I chose a side, which one do you wish me to pick?"

"You'll pick for your own," she said. "A man like you won't go by a woman's word. Besides it's not for me to say the word. Here comes himself now."

Her brother and his single customer had left the bar and were walking over to the table where they sat. Buck Duane watched them impassively.

The man walking with Tom Ryan was a square-built, steady looking fellow. He was middle height, middle aged, rugged, with an open, friendly face. He wore the warm, substantial clothing of a small rancher and a gun at his right side. Duane noticed that the holster looked rather new and the man swung his right leg a bit as he walked as if he hadn't habitually carried a side arm and was still getting used to its feel and weight.

The saloon man stopped by Duane's table. "Mr. Buck?"

"Just Buck," Duane said. "Would you gentlemen care to join me in a beer."

"The beer's on the house," Ryan said. "Mr. Wills here would like a word with you. That is if you don't mind. No offense meant, you understand. It's just that these hard times in a small country, and you a stranger, don't you see?"

"Miss Molly was saying somewhat of the sort," Duane said. "Are strangers so great a matter in this town, Mr. Wills?"

"Jim Wills," the man said. "Just call me Jim. No not always they aren't, but as I said this is a troubled time. Let me ask you one question, Buck. Did you ride here in the pay of Jared King?"

"I came in no man's pay," the tall Ranger said quietly. "I'm no man's man but my own. Not that I might not hire to your Jared King if it should suit me, but I came riding my own man."

"Ah, then," Ryan said, "and might I ask what sort of thing you do?"

"You might not, Mr. Ryan," Duane said. "I do whatever suits my mind. I might be looking for a small ranch to buy. Of course I only say I might."

The two men across the table exchanged glances. "And why would you expect to find one here?" Tom Ryan asked.

Buck Duane smiled at them both. "I only said I might be looking," he said. "I've had a bit of good fortune, so to speak, and a man likes to think of settling down."

"King didn't hire you?" Molly pressed him.

"Woman, be still!" her brother said. "You heard Buck tell us not."

"I never spoke to a King man," Duane said honestly. "If it interests you though I passed a herd of them on the road out of San Antone."

He saw that his words startled the two men by the glances they exchanged. "You mean Sam King and the winter supply wagons, I take it?" Wills asked.

"Sam King I don't know. Wagons, yes,—and horses wearing the King's Crown Brand. Drivers and a young woman. An older man well dressed and a lot of riders."

"And would you say the riders were ranch hands?" Ryan asked. "You'll pardon me, but it's important."

Again the Ranger decided to be honest with these men. "Why, no. They were a mangy lot and more like some of the wild bunch, if you want the truth. I noted, for it startled me to see such men ride with the King wagons. He must be short of men indeed, I thought."

"Gunmen, by God," Wills said and slapped his hand down on the table top. "That damned Jud was right after all. Now what do we do."

"Hold your tongue," Ryan said. "Buck here has no interest in that."

"He will," Jim Wills said, and hit the table again with his hand. "Every man and woman in this country will."

"Come on," Ryan urged him. The two men left the table, and a little later Molly followed them. Duane drank alone for an hour and went up to bed.

In spite of the weather, which continued cold and blustery, Buck Duane spent the next two days riding Bullet in long, apparently erratic sweeps and loops across the range outside the town of Kingston. The hard cold of winter wouldn't set in until after the turn of the year, but the big Ranger was afraid of the coming of a big blizzard out of the Canadian tundra.

His weather sense, sharpened by years of life on the outlaw trail when his very survival had depended on being able to "smell out" a storm and find or improvise shelter before it arrived, was warning him. This would be the year for one of those early storms which sometimes bring deep blankets of wet, heavy snow. Once such a storm struck movement about the range would be seriously impeded.

Duane meant to get his bearings and learn the country before that could happen. His mission— indeed his life itself—might hinge on his knowing his way about.

What any watcher might have mistaken for aimless riding was far from that for the big ex-outlaw. He saw and stored in his memory the salient features of an apparently boundless range. He learned the courses of the rare little streams, the roll and direction of valleys and draws. He looked at and memorized the silhouettes of each low hill and butte and the location and relation to each other of springs and the clumps of trees about them.

Almost casually he spotted smoke and horse tracks to locate the homes of soddys and small cattle men, noted the brands and the condition of the steers he passed. He was careful to leave as little "sign" of his passing as possible, but after noon of the first day was sure he was being followed.

An ordinary rider would never have detected the trailing watchers, but Buck Duane was no ordinary man. Like an Apache he could sense the men who hung upon his trail.

For the time being he gave no sign that he knew of their presence. Let them follow if they pleased. They'd learn nothing that would help them from his actions, and sooner or later they'd send Jim Wills or someone like him to ask questions again.

Duane was sure it was the small cattlemen faction that trailed him. A big outfit like King's wouldn't even be curious about a lone rider—unless they knew who he was, of course. Duane was positive they didn't.

It was early in the afternoon of the second day that the Ranger got his first look at the famous King's Own Herd of specially crossbred beef cattle. Unlike the rest of the King steers, these weren't allowed to roam completely at will across the vast range.

The King's Own steers were herded on the best grass flanking King's Creek, which came down through a long valley to the west of the ranch house itself. They were watched night and day by a special detail of riders. The guard was relieved at regular intervals night and day by fresh men riding out from the main bunk house.

Duane had picked up this information from casual conversations in the town. He was interested to see that the townspeople were about equally divided between pride in "our breed" and a jealous hatred that said: "Them steers will ruin every little rancher in the State. Only the big cattle kings can afford to breed them and once they get common an ordinary steer won't be worth hide and tallow."

He could see now why someone might feel it worth his while to organize an attack on the herd. The Ranger had no difficulty locating the prize herd. He stayed a long way off, back of the rim of the valley so the herders wouldn't spot him, and used the special German made field glasses which were one of his prized possessions to get a clear look at the grazing cattle.

"My God," he thought. "No wonder men will fight for these cattle."

They were big, heavy-bodied steers, still fat and glossy hided from the summer grazing. Each one must have averaged almost twice the poundage of the longhorns with which Duane had been familiar since his childhood. The breed bulls themselves brought an awed whistle to the big man's lips. In all his life he had never seen such magnificent beasts.

"Those are indeed kings," he said softly to himself. "Whoever holds those beasts is cattle king of all this country and no mistake." He had a moment of hightened respect for Jared King. The man who had the foresight and the purpose to conceive and breed this herd truly deserved respect.

He put the glasses back in their leather case and walked the few rods to where he'd left Bullet standing near the crest of the gentle hill. As he did he saw a brief flash of movement in the grass at the swell of another rise almost a half mile distant. Someone had been watching him even as he glassed the steers.

Duane mounted Bullet and sent the big horse in a long looping curve behind the spot he'd watched. The spy, whoever he was, was too quick to be trapped. Duane found his tracks and that was all. The man had been riding a small mustang, unshod like an Indian pony. He was no Indian though.

Duane found the mark of a boot heel on the ground where the fellow had dismounted. The heel had been badly worn down by long wear and the protruding iron heel nails made a distinctive pattern in the dirt that the Ranger knew he'd easily recognize again.

He didn't try to track the fellow. Dusk would be falling soon, and even Buck Duane couldn't find sign on hard ground in the dark. He would only run the risk of being bushwacked, in any case. Besides he had a rendezvous of his own to keep, so he rode on back to town.

As they had arranged before separating outside of town, he found the Jackrabbit Kid at the livery stable, picking up a new bridle for his horse.

"We didn't get here none too soon," the Kid told his big friend. "The war party from San Antone's expected at the ranch tomorrow or next day. The hands are jittery. They say Sam King, old Jared's brother, is bringing gun hands to clean out this country. Some of them don't like it. They're cowhands, not killers, and they figure some of them will get killed too. Likewise they figger something has to be done. There can't be no more bushwacking. Sort of a damned if we do and damned if we don't way of looking at it."

"The townsfolk don't want a war either," Duane said. "They figure nobody wins in a hassle like that and it's real bad for business."

"I think that's in Jared King's mind too," said the King. "We all know he's spooky as a hungry lobo about that herd of his. Has riders out watchin' them day and night. They say he'd rather not fight unless he has to."

"Nobody wants it, but everybody expects it," Duane said. "That's the way trouble brews with fighting cocks and dogs and men. Both sides strut around stiff legged wanting peace and hunting blood. When Pecos Red gets here, it'll be like a match to a bomb."

"Allright then, Buck. What do we do?"

"There's only one thing we can do," Duane said. "Was it a bomb, I'd pull the fuse. With men, it's find the ringleaders and pull their fuse. That means take Pecos for one. There's a couple soddys named for bushwacking too. I got them on my list too. That'll be rough enough, but even then it ain't all."

"What do you mean by that?"

"I mean that ain't the whole list. There's one more man, and I think that's the most important one of all. The ranny who smoked up this here whole war right from the start. Captain MacNelly said there was somebody behind the scenes, but he didn't know who. I thought it might be Jared King, but from what you say it ain't. Might be this Jud Ballew the bushwacker, but I don't think he's got the brains. Mean enough but no brains. Anyway that's the man I want to meet."

"And then—" the Kid asked.

"He can throw in his hand or go for his gun."

When Buck Duane left the Jackrabbit Kid at the livery stable and walked back to the shelter of Ryan's Saloon he noticed that the streets of Kingston were unusually crowded. There were horses and some rigs at the hitching posts, lights were on in some of the shops, and the loud sound of men's voices came from the saloon itself.

Of course it was a Saturday evening. Nesters and small ranchers and their wives had come into town for the purpose of buying groceries and dry goods. Hands from the ranches—at least from those large enough to employ riders—were looking for whatever measure of excitement the little town could

33

offer. All of that was natural enough on a frontier Saturday night.

There was more to that than just Saturday bustle, though. Duane had lived for too long by wits and instinct not to know when there was extra tension in the air. He could almost smell the mood of a town and the people in it.

On this wintry night the mood of Kingston was not good. There was excitement and anger in the air, these and tension and fear also.

For one thing there was a crowd in the town's other saloon. This was a disreputable place called a barrel house because the fiery spirits which it dispensed—a mixture of raw spirits colored with tobacco juice and watered down to the limit the proprietor dared attempt—was not sold from bottles but from a keg set on boards across two saw-horses. It was called Lew's Place and generally avoided by the townsfolk. Tonight there were rough looking, loud talking men inside. Duane heard angry voices as he passed the door.

Ryan's was crowded also. Instead of the usual three or four late afternoon drinkers there were at least twenty men bellied up to the bar when Duane walked in. Duane went up to his room just long enough to wash, shed his overcoat, and belt on his second big .45 revolver. Only a fool went unarmed on such a night.

Back in the downstairs bar he took his usual table with his back against the wall and a clear view of the big room and the men in it. The customers at Ryan's place were a long cut above the men Duane had seen at Lew's. These were the merchants and men of business in the little town. The riders at the bar were for the most part solid, respectable men. Jim Wills was there.

The men were gathered in tight little groups,

talking earnestly and heatedly. They were drinking whiskey for the most part and tempers were sure to mount as the evening wore on.

When Molly Ryan brought Duane his regular steak and trimmings he could see that the woman was obviously eager to talk. She needed no second invitation to sit down at his table.

"What's going on tonight, Molly?" the Ranger asked. "Seems like a lot more excitement than usual."

"You can bet your life there is," Molly said. "The word come through about midday. Sam King and his party have been scouted. They'll be in sometime tomorrow or next mornin' at the latest."

"Oh."

"Maybe you can sit there and grunt, Buck. It ain't so easy for the rest of us. Old Sam—he's bringing in a regular army. Professional gunmen from San Antonio, they say. Enough of them to kill us all if we let them."

"Who says all this, Molly? And how can you be sure? Who is it that scouts a party just bringing supplies to a big ranch?"

"I'll tell you who it is," she said excitedly. "The West Texas Ranchers Association; that's who. They been watching the roads ever since the word come that Jared King was hiring men to wipe us out."

"Then that's who's been tailing me too?" Duane asked.

Molly looked taken aback. "Oh, Buck, I hope not. That'd mean they suspect you of being a King man. You ain't, are you?"

"I'm my own man," Duane said. "Don't you worry about that."

"I sure am glad you say so, Buck. If they thought you were a friend of King's you'd be in danger."

Just at that point Tom Ryan himself came over to the table. "Go tend the bar, Molly," he said, and then, politely enough, "If you don't mind, mister, there's a couple of us would like a word with you quiet like in the office."

Then, as Buck Duane hesitated, Ryan added: "It could be important."

Duane stood up and picked up the half eaten steak on its platter. "In that case let's go. I'll just bring this along and finish eating there."

Inside Ryan's office back of the bar the ranger found Jim Wills waiting for them. "I'm going to get right to the point," the rancher said. "You know you've come to our town at a mighty difficult time. You must know by now too that there's talk of a war between the King's Crown spread and the rest of us folks."

"I've heard it," Duane said, "but I don't quite rightly know why it has to be."

"That's because you don't live here," Ryan said. "How'd you feel if killers was riding in against you?"

"Why are they coming?" the Ranger asked. "Isn't it because King men were killed first. Who's responsible for that?"

"Are you a King man?" Ryan burst out.

"Of course he ain't," Jim Wills said. "Mister, I wish I knew who started that killing. Jud Ballew maybe, but nobody ever said. It ain't just that though. You know that herd King has bred. Them cattle are beautiful, plain beautiful. I know that—but when they're bred up enough to go on the trails north—then what becomes of the rest of us? Who'll buy my rangy steers when they can get King beef? It worries me."

"I'd think," Duane said, "that you'd breed up your steers too. Buy breeding stock. I saw those steers. In twenty years there'll be some of their get on every spread in this state."

"I know," Wills said. "But what do folks like me do for that twenty years? The State will belong to the

36

Kings and the other big ranchers by then."

"Get back to the point, man," Ryan said. "It's twenty days we got to think about, not twenty years. We brought Buck in here to ask him something. Get about it."

Wills said, "I'll be brief. We don't think you're a King man, Buck. We see the way you wear those guns and we think you can use them. If there's a fight, we want you in with us."

"I'm my own man," Duane said.

"If you mean it's no skin off your tail," Wills said, "we can pay you. Jud Ballew has gold. We need every gun we can get, and we can make it worth your while."

"I'm not a gun for hire," the Ranger said. "I just don't know that I ought to take sides. I'm not against you, mind. Not a paid man of King's."

"Mister," Wills said. "We're just plumb desperate. We need every man we can get. Or is it that you think we're bound to be beat so why risk it with us? Don't be too sure. We may be townsmen and riders, but all of us were in the Secession War. Before we ourselves get massacred, we'll fight."

"I know you will," Duane said. "It's not that."

"Well then?"

"There's some questions I'd want answered before I ride the war trail," Duane said. "I rightly would. I'd want to know who pushed who into killing. I'd want to know what's been tried to stop the war—and who wants it to happen. Most of all I'd want to know where the likes of Jud Ballew gets gold to buy a man like me and what he wants to buy me for."

The silence lay heavy in the room—so heavy that the listeners crouched outside the window lifted a bit to peek through the crack around the shade and make sure that the three men were still there.

"By God," Jim Wills said at last, "I never thought of it quite that way. Too busy worrying, I guess."

37

"You better think that way," Duane said. "Who hates Jared King and his herd bad enough to risk your lives for it?"

"You mean there's somebody else stirring up this fight?" Wills demanded. "I better talk to the boys about this."

He never got the chance.

The shot from outside smashed the window glass and the heavy slug struck Jim Wills right shoulder with enough impact to knock him out of his chair onto the floor.

Ryan yelled and jumped to his feet.

The man outside began to cut loose through the window with a forty-five. He couldn't see much through the shade but he fired anyway.

Buck Duane snuffed the single candle on the office desk with a sweep of his big left hand. His right pulled his own forty-five and he made for the door leading out into the alley behind the bar.

It was locked. Duane raised one big foot and kicked the lock out of its flimsy panel. When the door flew open he dived through, landing full length in the snow. Over by the window a dark form spun and snapped a shot through the opened door. A second man behind him jumped for cover past the corner of one of the sheds behind the bar.

Even from the prone position and shooting by instinct into the dark the big Ranger was deadly. His first shot hit the man by the window. It was a body shot. The man lost his footing and went down, dead before he hit the ground.

A second man Duane hit savagely before he could go for his gun. Behind him, a third prowler took to his heels. The fight was over.

By this time the men were running from the bar itself.

"Somebody get a doctor!" Buck Duane yelled. He

grabbed the leg of the man he'd shot and dragged him into the light spilling out the rear door.

"Who's this?"

"It's one of Jud Ballew's pals," Tom Ryan said. "He's dead. He shot Jim Wills through the window."

"There was another one with him," Duane said. "Probably Ballew himself. He got away. If it's Ballew, he'll be back. You better get that doctor in a hurry 'fore Wills bleeds to death."

"There ain't no doc in Kingston," Ryan said. "Molly's tending Jim. She's good at it. What do you mean Ballew'll be back?"

"I mean you men better fort up this bar," Duane said. "Wills got killed because he believed what I told him. Ballew ain't going to let you stop his range war. Not while there's gold for him in it, he's not. He'll shoot up anybody who wants to argue that just as soon as he gets his boys here from Lew's."

"There's more of them than us," Ryan said. "What can we do?"

"The one thing you can't do is what he thinks you will do," Buck Duane said. The Ranger was thinking in terms of a professional fighting man. "He figures you'll wait here and make a stand at the bar. He's got you outnumbered two to one and with the wind howling like it is, he'll fire the bar. It'll go up like a torch. When the heat drives you out, he'll gun you down like rabbits."

"We got to make a stand," one of the other men said. "If we run, that gang of soddys will loot the town. Rape and kill maybe. What you want us to do?"

"Whether I like it or not I'm in this now," Duane said and reloaded his Colt's. "I'm going to do the only thing that has a chance of working. I'm going down to Lew's and take Ballew himself before he gets organized. Any man has the nerve to fight can come along with me."

39

The big man left his topcoat unbuttoned so he could reach the butts of his two Colt's revolvers without trouble. He set his big Stetson firmly on his head, limbered his fingers and started for the front door of the bar.

Ryan grabbed up a sawed-off shotgun from behind the bar and started after Buck Duane. A half dozen other men, all but one of them ranchers and friends of Jim Wills' followed him also. The rest hung back, caught by indecision in the moment when decision had to be made. This was life and death and the townsmen knew it and hesitated. In time perhaps they could summon courage, but the time was all run out.

Buck Duane took in the situation with a glance. He knew he couldn't fight a stand-up battle with the few men backing him. There must be at least fifteen or twenty of Jud Ballew's friends inside Lew's bar, and all of them were hardy, desperate fighting men.

The big Texas Ranger spoke urgently to Tom Ryan and the others. "You men spread out around Lew's place and take cover. I'm going in after Jud. They won't expect one man alone, and I think I can get the drop on him and bring him out. Anybody comes out of there except me, you shoot him down."

It was a desperate play. Perhaps no other single man in all of Texas except for Captain MacNelly himself would have had the nerve to make it. Even Buck Duane himself wasn't sure he could carry that off. Sure or not, he had to try.

Speed and nerve were his only weapons, and he put them to the best use possible. Duane was right in one respect. Ballew and his crowd didn't imagine for a minute that he'd dare to come in alone. They were still yelling, drinking, checking their guns and getting ready to attack Ryan's place.

Duane came through the swinging doors to Lew's place with an icy wind at his back that set the kerosene lamps on the crude plank bar flickering. For a minute the men didn't see who the big man in the doorway was. By the time they did, they were covered by the muzzles of two big forty-fives held in rock-steady hands.

There was a moment of sudden, incredulous silence. Duane gave them no time to recover their wits. "Just everybody hold steady," he said. His grim voice sent an icy shiver along the spines of the half drunken, hate twisted soddys. "I come for Jud Ballew and I'm taking him out of here. Everybody else just stand real easy."

They were stunned. Ballew was the first to recover.

"You're crazy," he said. "You can't get out of here alive."

"If I can't, Jud," Duane said, "then neither can you."

One of the men in the background went for his gun. Duane's right hand Colt's boomed like a cannon in the narrow room. The man yelled like a catamount and collapsed,—his arm shattered.

"Take him!" Ballew yelled.

No one else moved. The Ranger swept them with a scornful glance. "Any taking to be done, Ballew," he said in icy tones, "you're going to have to do it yourself, seems like. You think you're man enough?"

Ballew was holding his rifle near the muzzle with his left hand. There was no way he could get it up and fire before Duane killed him. He could still have tried for his knife or a hidden six gun with his free right hand. In his shoes, Buck Duane would have made the move.

Jud Ballew wasn't quite man enough to try.

When the rest of them realized Ballew wasn't going to make his try, there was an almost tangible release of tension in the room. Duane felt it and knew he'd won.

If Jud Ballew had gone for a gun, his friends would have backed him. The Ranger could have gotten Ballew and a couple more before he died himself, but that would have meant he'd failed at his job. Whoever was backing Ballew would still have been able to launch his range war at the King herd.

"Come on, Jud," Buck Duane said. "Leave that gun of yours where it is against the bar and keep your hands in sight. Any of the rest of you so much as belch or blink I shoot him first and Jud second. Let's go now."

Ballew followed orders. He came quietly enough to the door. Duane held it open and let the soddy step through. Then he followed him into the street.

Before he let the door swing to, he spoke to the men inside. "This place is surrounded by armed men," he said. "Anybody sticks his nose out for the next half hour gets it shot off. Stay where you are till then, and nobody will be hurt."

Duane stepped out into the street and let the door swing closed. The men inside must have believed him. They stayed quiet. Duane motioned Ballew to walk the long block over to Ryan's saloon.

They didn't make it. Both of them heard the thud and clink of hoofs on the hard ground and the tearing squeal of tallow greased wagon wheels.

The column of riders, hunched down into their coat collars against the wind came into the street from its eastern end. In the wind and gloom they looked at first like a troop of cavalry all together. Then they saw the two men walking, Duane with his guns out, and started to rein in. Behind them the big covered wagons came into view.

Sam King and his killers had hit Kingston a day ahead of schedule. King himself in a buffalo coat and eared beaver cap was riding a big sorrel in the lead. His men fanned out to block the street.

Buck Duane looked at the crowd of Pecos Red's

42

hired guns. He looked and dropped his own guns back in their holsters.

"Good evening, gentlemen," the tall Ranger said.

Sam King sat his big horse in the middle of the street and looked down on the two men in front of him. Obviously he wasn't entirely sure what was going on, and equally obviously he was trying his best not to show it. It had been a long hard day on the road. Just one in a series of long hard days. He's been pushing the supply wagons to the limit of the endurance of teams and men in an effort to get back to the ranch ahead of schedule.

Sam King was tired. He felt tired and looked it. "What's going on here?" he said finally. "Do I know you?"

"No," Buck Duane said. "No, you don't."

Behind him the big Ranger was aware of Tom Ryan and his friends drifting away from their posts around Lew's Place and getting up on the long board sidewalk at the North side of the street. At the same time the men who had been inside of Lew's, also sensing a change in the situation, were watching through the front doors.

Both parties were armed to the teeth. So were the men who rode with Sam King. Pecos Red and his boys were professionals. They could smell trouble clearly but they weren't yet sure exactly what was happening and what sort of trouble it might be.

They took precautions though. Carbines and Winchester lever-action rifles were slipped quietly from their saddle boots. Overcoats and pea-jackets were unbuttoned and big forty-fives unobstrusively loosened in the oiled leather holsters. The men spread their mounts in a line from one side of the street to the other in back of Sam King and made ready to ride for the buildings or dismount and shelter behind their horses when the shooting started.

It was as if the whole street crackled with a deadly static electricity—ready to erupt in violence and death at any second.

"I said what's going on here?" King demanded again.

"I'm taking this man into custody," Buck Duane said.

"Custody?" Sam King was puzzled. "Who are you anyway? Has this town hired a marshal while I was gone?"

"He's no marshal," Jud Ballew said. "Just a crazy saddle tramp too fast with his guns. Make him let me go, Mr. King."

"Who are you?" King said. "What's he holding you for?"

Buck Duane didn't give Ballew a chance to answer. "This man shot and seriously wounded a rancher named Jim Wills," he said to Sam King. "Shot him in the back through a window. The honest citizens of this town want him to stand trial."

"Shot Jim Wills? That's an outrage. You turn this man over to us. We'll hold him at the ranch till a marshal or a judge can be sent for."

"We can hold him," Duane said.

"You can, can you? I'll be the judge of that. Who is this man, and who are you?"

"This is Jud Ballew," Ryan called from the board sidewalk. "If we turn him over to you, what guarantee do we have he won't be shot out of hand?"

"Ballew?" Sam King spurred his horse forward to look more closely at the prisoner in the dimly reflected light. "So it is. So it is. We'll hold this one for sure."

His riders moved a little, resting rifle and shotgun barrels across their saddle horns. It was plain they meant to back him up.

King turned his face again to look at Buck Duane. The Ranger stood immovable. "Who are you? Who did you say you were?"

"I didn't say, Mr. King."

Back of Sam King one of his riders moved his horse beside that of Pecos Red. "I've seen that big guy, Pecos," he said. "I don't know where, but I'll remember. I do know this. He's poison with a gun."

"He can't take us all no matter who he is," Pecos said. Then, in a louder voice directed to Duane, "You there. You heard Mr. King. We're taking that man. Unless you're a marshal, get out of the way."

Buck Duane was thinking fast. If he made a fight now the men with Pecos could possibly bring him down. Certainly there would be very little to gain. Ryan and some of his friends would be killed and nothing important gained by their deaths. Just at that moment another rider came up from the wagons in the rear. Even bundled against the cold Georgia King was a beauty. She sat her mount and looked at the Texas Ranger for a long moment. Then she spoke to her father.

"Whoever that is, he's no common man. Don't push him too far."

"Don't interfere," Sam King said brusquely.

"That's right, Miss Georgia," Pecos Red said. "Get out of the way. There may be shooting here."

Buck Duane stepped back. "There's been too much shooting already this night. I'm no marshal. You all take this man if you want, but remember the people expect him to stand trial."

He stepped back beside Ryan on the boardwalk. One of Pecos riders got Ballew's horse from the hitching rack and made him mount. Then the whole group went off towards the ranch. Ballew's friends had made no move to rescue him. Now they got their own mounts and rode out of town. With their leader

45

in custody the fight was temporarily gone out of them.

Buck Duane, Ryan and the rest of their party went back to the saloon. Jim Wills had recovered enough to sit up in a chair, and Molly Ryan was just finishing bandaging him.

"Jim will be okay," she told them. "He's got a smashed collarbone, but the slug went on through. I don't think it touched either heart or lungs."

"Thank God for that," Ryan said.

"What do we do now?" Wills asked weakly.

"We get some sleep to start with," Duane said. "Leave a guard, if you like but I don't expect any more trouble tonight. With Ballew a prisoner, his people will lay low for a while. He was the real he-rattler in that crowd."

"Doesn't that just leave old Jared's hired guns free to settle with the rest of us?" one of the ranchers asked. "At least Jud Ballew and his boys would of fought them fellers. I don't see but we're worse off right now that we was."

"There may not have to be any fighting now," Buck Duane said. "In the morning Ryan and I and a couple of you men will see if we can't have a talk with Jared King. Ballew was the real troublemaker, and he's out of the picture now. Let's try and see if we can't make a peace instead of a war."

Duane himself was dead tired by the time he lay down, fully clothed except for boots and overcoat, on the bed in his room at Ryan's saloon. In spite of that he didn't go right to sleep. There were things that bothered him.

For one—he's expected Sam King to order Jud Ballew killed at once in the streets of the town. This was the man who had bushwacked and killed two King's Crown riders. Everybody knew it, proof or no. It wasn't like a man like Sam King to talk about waiting for a marshal. Frontier justice was more swift and sure than that.

Ballew would have known that too, yet he'd made no effort to call on his friends for help. In the face of sure death it wasn't natural for him to submit to being turned over to his mortal enemies. There was something not quite natural about the whole incident. It left the Ranger with an uneasy feeling. He wondered if there was something he could do about it.

By now Buck Duane was beginning to suspect who it was that really wanted the war—the man who had sent gold and information to stir up Jud Ballew. After a while the Ranger drifted off to sleep.

He woke before dawn to the sound of hoofs pounding as a hard driven pony ran down the frost hardened street and pulled up in front of Ryan's hotel. A moment later a familiar voice hailed the sentry inside the saloon.

Buck Duane was out of the blankets and pulling on his boots before he heard the Jackrabbit Kid knock on the door to his room. "Get up, Buck," the Kid was calling. "There's all hell to pay for sure."

When Buck Duane opened the room door the Kid came bursting in. "Whatever your idea is you better get at it," he said to the Ranger. "There's nothing but trouble out at the big ranch."

"What happened?" Duane asked. "I figured things would be quiet for a while what with Ballew locked up and all."

"That's just it," the Kid said. "Ballew ain't locked up. He's loose and yelling for blood. Your blood first of all."

"What happened."

"I ain't quite sure," the Kid said. "Sam and Pecos and that crowd got in very late at night. Nobody was looking for them. Old Jared had gone to bed. Sam and the girl went up to his room to talk to him.

47

"Late as it was, Jared didn't come down to see Ballew. They locked him in a shed by one of the big barns and put one of the regular riders to guard him. Claimed Pecos' men were too tired to do guard duty. Maybe they was. I don't know.

"Anyway I got up before dawn and went by the shed. Wanted to see what this Ballew gent looked like. I was too late. The guard was down on the ground with his head busted open by a gun barrel. The door to the shed was broke open and no sign of Ballew. Gone with the winter wind he was."

"What did you do then?"

"I didn't have time to do a thing. Right then a couple of Pecos' boys came round from the bunk house. When they seen me at the door, one of them yelled I'd let Ballew loose and went for his gun. I was faster. I shot him in the arm. The other one ducked into the barn and started shooting at me through the door. From the yelling and hooraw up by the bunk house I knew the rest would be after me but quick, so I ran for it.

"Lucky for me one of the night guards had just rid in to call the relief. His horse was saddled at the hitch rack by the cook shack. I climbed leather and headed right for here."

"That's fine," Buck Duane said. "Now they're after you for horse stealing. On top of that they got somebody to blame for letting Ballew loose, and that somebody is us since you rode straight to town. They got their reason to let Pecos Red loose on us now. The war can start right now before we have a chance to talk peace."

"What could I have done, Buck?"

"Nothing different than what you did, I reckon. If it hadn't been you found Ballew gone, they'd still have blamed it on our side. When they let the soddy run it was done just for one reason, to start a war."

"You think they let him go? I figured maybe a

48

couple of his friends sneaked in and busted him out."
The Kid was honestly puzzled.

"That's not the way I figure it," the big Ranger said. "There was something funny about the way he went with them so easy last night. Like he knew he needn't be worried. Ballew had a friend at the ranch who let him loose. That gave an excuse to start the war and it set Jud free to do what he's been paid to do right from the start."

"Start a war?"

"No,—finish a war. Finish a war that'll set this State of Texas back a good twenty years, just as it's supposed to do."

"What will happen now?"

"I can tell you that," Buck Duane said. "Pecos and every man the ranch can spare will be riding for town on your trail right now. We've got to get out of here before they come."

"And not make a fight? That ain't like you, Buck."

"They expect us to make a fight here, Kid. They want us to make a fight. With us boxed in these buildings Pecos and his boys can keep us here a year. A day'll be long enough."

"We can hold them," the Kid said.

"Sure we could. They want us to."

"I don't get it, Buck. I don't see."

"Sure you don't," Duane said. "That's because you've forgot the wild card in the deck. That's Jud Ballew. The whole point of this here range war was just one thing, to give Jud a chance to do his job."

"What job?"

"To wipe out the King's Own Herd of course. That's what it's all about. There's big men in the State don't want that herd to ever walk to railhead. Old Jared's ten years ahead of them with his new beef and they know it. Who'd send gold to a soddy like Jud? Somebody big, that's who. Somebody who wants to see those cattle killed so he can breed up a prime herd of his own, now that Jared's proved it can be done.

"Now they got their chance. The townsmen and the men like Jim Wills will be fighting Pecos here. While everybody's busy, Jud Ballew and his friends go in and kill the guards and run off that herd. If they can't get it clean away, at least they kill the bulls and the best of the breeding stock. That's what they really want."

"You mean to let them do it?"

"Of course I don't," Duane said. "Come on."

Ryan and the riders from the small ranches were already gathered in the bar downstairs, roused by the Kid's arrival.

"Pecos and his gunsels, and probably Sam King with most of the King's Crown riders are already on their way to town," Duane told them. "Wake up the townspeople. Put barricades of wagons across both ends of the street. Don't let them in. They'll ask for Ballew and the Kid here. Tell them they aren't here. Parley awhile and then offer to let Sam King in to see for himself. Stall for as much time as you can. I'll need it where I'm going."

"You're going?" said a suspicious voice. "When the fighting starts you're pulling out?"

"Yeah," Ryan said. "Suppose they rush the town and kill us all. We aren't soldiers."

"They won't rush this place," Duane assured them. "Pecos is a killer and a fighter, not a fool. What they really want is just to keep all of you pinned down for a while. Both sides are going to be stalling for time. So why should he get even a couple of his boys killed? Besides Sam King doesn't want a massacre that would force the Governor to send the Texas Rangers in. Both sides will put on a fireworks show and that's all. The real fighting will be where I am."

Buck Duane picked three of the riders to go with

him and the Kid. One was a wild boy who looked to be good with his gun. The other two had fought with Hood's Texas Brigade. There were no more seasoned veterans anywhere in the world.

The five men rode out of town into the gray, icy dawn. A dull red sun glowed like a smoking coal just at the eastern horizon and masses of ragged, dirty grey clouds drove south before a bitter wind that rattled the dry strands of grass and drove the tumbleweeds in frenzied flight before its force.

The men tied kerchiefs over nose and mouth and huddled into their heavy wool greatcoats. The Ranger led them in a long loop clear of the road to the town.

"The last thing I want right now is to tangle head on with Pecos' crowd. Let them go by to the fireworks show at town."

"It's a cold day to fight," Jackrabbit said.

Duane laughed. "Name me good weather for dying," he said. "What sort of day did the Alamo fall?"

"Where are we going, Buck?"

"Use your common sense, Kid. It'll have taken Ballew a while to get his crowd together, half of them are still drunk and scattered everywhere. As soon as he does, they'll go hell for leather for the King's Own Herd.

"Old Jared King will guess something like that. He'll try to get the herd into the big corrals at the ranch. That's his only chance to defend them. He'll look around and find his brother Sam took most of the riders to town and maybe he'll send to order them back, but it'll be too late. The herd will be driving fast for ranch headquarters right now with Jud Ballew after it."

"We try to get between them then?"

"We do not. With twenty-thirty soddys and roughs Ballew would ride over five of us just like he

51

would the three herders and the two or three people Jared can bring out from the ranch."

"What then?"

"For now," Buck Duane said, "save your breath for riding."

The five men were well mounted and skilled horsemen. Duane had scouted the ground after coming to town. He knew exactly where the herd would probably be with the time factor involved and just how he wanted to get there.

In spite of that they were almost too late. They came up to the top of the low ridge edging the valley through which the stream flowed down to ranch headquarters and saw the herd stretched out before them. The magnificent beasts were strung out as desperate riders pushed them along at a run.

Duane could see old Jared King and mark him by his towering height and air of command. The three night herders were with him, and two men from the ranch, and a slender figure with long flowing hair who had to be Georgia King his niece.

The seven of them were pushing the herd, trying to keep them bunched and moving. A half mile back—and coming up fast at a pounding run—was a long, ragged crescent of riders on smally shaggy mustangs. Jud Ballew and his wild men rode like Comanches and were using the same battle tactics. They'd overtake the herd in a long line. The men in the center would hit and down Jared King's rearguard while the two long wings would circle the herd and drive it off.

With the herd to watch and the few men at his command, King hadn't a chance. He hadn't until Buck Duane and his party got into the fight.

Ballew and his center knot of fighters were within three hundred yards of the rear of the herd. Already Jared King and two of his riders had halted their mounts and faced to the rear. Guns out, they were

52

ready to make a brave but hopeless stand to gain even a few short minutes more for the racing herd.

A wild, keening whoop of blood-hungry triumph came up the wind from the charging Ballew men. At the precise instant Buck Duane and his four comrades hit the right flank of the charging wild men. The soddys didn't even see them come at first. There were shots and men fell. Riderless horses shied into the center of the line.

Some of the soddys turned and tried to fight. They were facing battle hardened veterans. Duane and his men shot the nearest fighters out of their saddles. Ballew's boys were no heroes. The change from rabbit chase to bloody and fearful battle was more than their courage could endure. Their ponies wheeled and they fled over the icy plain.

Only one small bunch of six or eight men held together. These rode at full speed around the far side of the still running herd of cattle. Led by Jud Ballew himself, they were making for the van of the herd where the magnificent breed bulls were running. If these great studs could be killed, Ballew would have accomplished at least a major part of his mission.

Jared King and his herders saw what was intended but were powerless to stop it. Ballew was already past them and on the far side of the herd. They had no chance at all of catching him before he could draw alongside the bulls and shoot them down as the Indians had shot running buffalo in the past.

It was then that Buck Duane leaned forward over the saddle horn and spoke to his horse, urging Bullet to a burst of speed. The big horse fairly flew across the prairie, parallel to Ballew but on the opposite side of the herd. He was far faster than the mustangs the wild bunch were riding, and gained on them rapidly.

As Duane drew abreast of the head of the herd,

and then pulled out ahead, he turned Bullet to the left and urged the faithful horse into a final burst of speed which carried him across the path and barely ahead of the now thoroughly stampeded cattle.

As he cleared the herd he found himself squarely in front of Ballew's charging bravos. The soddy tried to slide down on the off-side of his pony in the old Indian war trick and at the same time fired his rifle at Duane. The pony staggered and tried to shy out of Bullet's path, and the rifle shot missed Duane's face by inches.

His own forty-five roared and the heavy slug took Ballew right between the eyes. The soddy leader let go his saddle horn. His pony holted, dragging its owner's lifeless body by a foot still tangled in the stirrup. The rest of the men with Ballew bolted for their lives, not even stopping to recover their leader's lifeless body.

Within moments the men with Buck Duane had joined Jared King's riders in turning the running herd and setting the cattle milling in a circle. From now on there'd be no point in forcing the prize steers to run off weight and risk broken bones or death in a headlong dash. They were far too valuable to risk, and would be driven at a slow pace the rest of the way to the ranch corrals.

Only when the herd was under control did Jared King take the time to ride over to the big Texas Ranger. The two men sat face to face and took each other's measure. Each was a leader of men, the rancher's authority buttressed by wealth and prestige and the easy manner of a man born to command and Buck Duane with the surety of a man who has proved his right to respect on the hard battlefields of life.

Georgia King came and joined them. The boss of the King's Crown was the first to speak.

"I owe you thanks," he said frankly. "You saved more than just a few cow critters and an old man's life."

"I know," Buck Duane said. "There's a big slice of the future of Texas tied up in this herd of yours. To tell the truth that's why I was sent here to begin with, sir. I'm a friend of a friend of yours in San Antonio. His name is Captain MacNelly."

"MacNelly of the Rangers," King said with surprise in his voice. "No wonder you came right in the nick of time. But what does MacNelly know about our troubles up here?"

Buck Duane gave the rancher a long, level look. "I think it best if you wrote and asked him that yourself," he said. "For now just let it be that I'm a friend of his—and yours too if you'll have me."

Jared King returned the look in kind—then reached his own decision. "Let it stand at that," he agreed. "I know there's things the captain can't do officially at times, and I've heard that he has ways of getting them done anyway. I suppose you are one of those ways."

Buck Duane just smiled in answer.

"This is the man who passed us outside of San Antone," Georgia said then. "He's also the one who was holding Ballew at gunpoint in Kingston last night."

"Oh, that was you?" Jared King said. "Tell me, why didn't you hold Jud Ballew when you had him? There's dead men on the ground back there would still be alive if you had."

"Would they?" Duane asked gravely. "I'll give you question for question, Jared King. Which of Ballew's friends came into your ranch at dawn and let him free to raise his men?"

"There was no sign of raiders," King said. He didn't add: "Ballew had a friend on the ranch." But the unspoken words were in both their minds.

"The little men Ballew led hated your power and your herd," Duane said. "There are big men in Texas who can be envious and greedy too. Had they a friend who envied you, had they such a friend in the King's Crown. I say, what is easier than a cattle war?"

He saw by the big rancher's eyes that he knew there was only one name to name—his brother, Sam King. Neither of them would name it then or later. In the manner of the Texas border they would leave such things to a lesser breed of men. Then realization came to Jared King. He remembered Pecos Red and the men who's guns his brother had bought.

"So it's not over yet," he said half to himself.

"I don't understand," Georgia King said. "What isn't over? Oh, look, Uncle Jared. Here comes Father now."

The two men followed her gaze. Sam King was riding toward them across the prairie at a gallop. There were three men with him. One of them was Pecos Red.

"He's come to see if the herd is safe," Georgia said.

Her uncle and the Texas Ranger knew better than that. Sam King rode to make sure that Jud Ballew had smashed the herd.

"I'd better go meet him," Jared King said.

Buck Duane said, "That won't be necessary, Mr. King. This is still part of my job today."

He turned Bullet's head and rode to meet the four men riding with the bitter north wind in their faces. They saw and recognized him. Sam King gave an order and then pulled his mount away. This man let others do his fighting while he watched.

The others spread out and pulled their horses down to an easier pace. Pecos rode in the middle with a man to left and right. When the range closed enough, they'd spray lead at the Ranger all together.

Buck Duane put up his head and pulled the

kerchief from over his mouth so they could see his face. His great horse came fast and easily. Duane kept watching Pecos Red. The gunman was confident. Three to one were good killing odds. He closed up fast.

The man on the right said: "Pecos, that's Buck Duane." His voice went up to yell and he wheeled his horse away in fear. "That's the man outdrew the snake!"

The other two went for their guns together.

Buck Duane had the hard cold knot in his stomach that always presaged a killing fight. The cold of grim and ice hard resolve. He dropped the reins and a gun seemed to leap into each big hand.

To the men watching at the herd the gunfire came like a rapid, brief tap of a drum. When it was over Pecos and his man were down on the sod, broken and dead. Their horses ran free. The man who had recognized Duane bent low over his horse's mane and rode for his life to join his friends near Kingston. They would ride out of the country.

Sam King sat his horse, with his face gray and hard. His brother would not punish him, but Sam King was a broken man.

The morning sun broke through the clouds and shone on Buck Duane where he sat Bullet's back. It shone on Jared King, white maned and tall, and on the great stud bull that led the herd.

The Texas sun poured golden rays down on the kings of the Texas range.

TRACK THE MAN DOWN

I

The tall rider sat his mount and watched the cattle come up out of the ford to the northern bank of the Brazos River, west of Fort Worth.

They came in a seemingly endless stream, tossing long, wickedly pointed horns, shaking, and endlessly bellowing a meaningless protest against the men who drove them. They came like a living tide of wild and shaggy brutes, a tide of life driven north against its will to a fate it neither foresaw nor desired. Its ultimate destination was the stockyards of Chicago and the dining tables of the East. Its present emotion was protest and anger.

The men who rode the flanks of the long, bovine river of cattle seemed no more important than the gnats that circled each individual steer. They were a few and scattered, dust caked and weary.

The men themselves and the shaggy, jugheaded, tireless ponies they rode were almost as wild and undisciplined as the steers that bellowed and pounded up the muddy banks out of the river ford.

The watching rider too was a natural and normal part of the Texas scene—as much a part as tumbleweed or scrub mesquite or the bleached buffalo skull not far from where he sat his horse.

He was a tall man for his time, more than six feet of bone and muscle, sun tanned and lean flanked. His eyes, like an Indian's, noted at one glance the line storm riding darkly at far horizon and the flickering tongue of a sun-basking lizard only feet away. Long years of lonely riding under conditions of endless danger had made him as alert as the gray wolf or the keen sighted pronghorn antelope of the plains.

He wore the flat, wide brimmed Texas Stetson hat, the heavy wool shirt and the pants tucked into high tooled leather boots that best suited the needs of the horse nomad of the American West. His mount and saddle, his bedroll and weapons were all he possessed in life.

If anything actually set this man apart from his fellows it was the weapons he wore and the way he wore them. The Winchester rifle on his saddle boot was of the latest model, cleaned and oiled and fitted with a modern tang-mounted aperture sight that was screw-adjustable for both elevation and windage. The two Colt's heavy caliber revolvers suspended from crossed cartridge belts were tied down in cutaway to make possible a sure and swift draw. So armed, and skilled as he was in the use of his weapons, this man was one of the most efficient and deadly fighters that the world had ever seen.

The man's name was Buck Duane, and he was a Texas Ranger.

He raised his head suddenly and turned his head towards the east. The city of Fort Worth was thirty miles away. Neither sight nor sound could possibly have reached out to the rider on the Bank of the Brazos.

Yet, without being in the least conscious of how he knew it, Buck Duane knew without any shadow of doubt that something of importance to him was happening there.

With the keen instinct learned in years of riding lonely, dangerous outlaw trails, Duane knew better than to doubt or dismiss the premonition he felt now. He turned his horse's head and rode away from the cattle crossing towards the distant city in the east.

*   *   *

At that precise moment in Fort Worth a young man who went by the somewhat improbable name of The Jackrabbit Kid moved his head closer to the butt of his holstered Colt's and spoke in a voice that carried clearly in the suddenly hushed Red Aces Saloon.

"Don't make no mistake, Lefty," he said to the man standing at the far end of the bar. "I said I want to have a talk with you, and that's just what I mean to do. You can do it the easy way or the hard way. Suit yourself about that. But talk you will do."

Lefty Linkett had a stubble of black beard and a mean expression. His body and clothing were equally unwashed. He was small and shifty and everything about him was no-account. In spite of that he was more scared of talking than of Jackrabbit's threats.

Lefty Linkett went for his gun.

The Jackrabbit Kid made a smooth, fast draw that would have delighted Buck Duane—he'd taught it to the boy a year before. He fired one shot and broke the bone of Lefty's left arm a few inches above the wrist.

He could have killed the cowering man easily then, but he didn't fire again.

"You shouldn't ought to have made me do that, Lefty," he said. "I don't want to hurt you now, and I never did. You come along nice and easy now, and I'll let you see a Doc while you talk."

Lefty Linkett snarled, "I got nothing to talk about and you know it. Git away from me now. Git away from me. I'll call the law. So help me I will."

The owner of the place bobbed up from back of the bar, where he'd ducked when the shoot-out seemed imminent. The other patrons began to relax a little.

"Leave him be, Kid," the saloon man said. "Or leastways take him out in the street. Shooting in here

60

ain't no good for my business. Git along with you now."

"All right," the Kid said. "You walk ahead of me now, Lefty, and don't make no run for it. Leave your gun right on the floor where it is. You can come back for it. Now get going."

Lefty Linkett turned reluctantly towards the door. Under the dirt and beard stubble his lips trembled as if he wanted to cry.

"I can't," he said in a whining voice. "I can't talk to you, Kid. I'm dead if I do. Besides, I don't know nothing."

"All I know is you're going to answer some questions. Maybe you'll be dead if you do, but I can promise you right now you'll sure be dead if you don't."

The Kid was still young and an inexperienced fighting man. Lefty Linkett could never have made his next move against Buck Duane, and probably wouldn't have dared to try. With the Kid he almost got away with it.

Lefty Linkett had a forty-four caliber single shot Derringer hung down his back inside the shirt by a cord looped around his neck and tied to the trigger guard. He tried to yank it up by the cord and get off a fast shot.

His good left arm was broken and he had to fumble for the cord with his right hand. It slowed him just enough so the Kid woke up just about the time Lefty got the deadly little gun in his palm.

Jackrabbit made the fastest draw of his life. There wasn't time to fool with aiming or shots to wound. As the Colt's muzzle cleared leather and came forward and up, the Kid grabbed his right wrist with his left hand as Duane had taught him to do. The big forty-five stuck out in front of his body at a little over waist height held level by the two-hand grip. He aimed, or rather pointed, it by swinging his body and loosed off the shot by instinct.

This one took Linkett right where a rooster packs its wishbone. He was dead before he hit the floor.

There was a moment of stunned silence in the crowded bar. Then the saloon owner spoke.

"He was right about just one thing," he voice said into the sudden quiet. "He sure ain't gonna answer no questions. Not now nor never he ain't."

Miles away to the West Buck Duane touched hand to the neck of his big horse, Bullet, and rode with sudden urgency.

II

When Buck Duane rode into Fort Worth just after dark that night he didn't even know his friend The Jackrabbit Kid was in town.

He rode first to the Alamo Hotel, where a room had been booked in his name. He turned his horse over to the hotel hostler, dropped his saddlebags in his room, number twenty-two, removed the trail dust hastily with water from the big earthenware pitcher on the washstand in the room and went out again.

He crossed the street and went down the block to the Lone Star Hotel. The desk clerk told him "Mr. Mellick" was in the front corner suite on the third floor. Duane climbed the stairs and knocked on the heavy door.

"Mr. Mellick" was Duane's Ranger Officer and longtime friend, Captain MacNelly—small, tough, intelligent and a deadly shot with either hand.

The captain led Duane into the room. He had a table pulled up near the corner windows with maps and papers spread out across its top. There was a whiskey bottle and a couple of glasses. Duane poured himself a thin two fingers of the brown fluid and downed only half of that. He liked to keep his

62

mind clear when he worked.

"The word was passed you wanted to see me in a hurry," Duane said. "I was clear down in Brownsville when I heard, but I came as fast as I could."

"Didn't expect you for a couple of days yet," Captain MacNelly said. "Even for a ranger, you cover ground faster than any man has a right to expect. I'm glad you did, though. There's trouble. Big trouble, Buck. Something we have to be mighty careful how we handle."

He poured himself a good half tumbler of whiskey and drank it down as smoothly as if the raw spirits had been coffee from the pot. For chaser he wiped his mouth with the back of his hand. Duane almost laughed at the familiar gesture. When Captain MacNelly drank like that he meant there were problems, for a fact.

The big ranger didn't let his feelings show though.

"I take it then we can't just take a company and ride in and clear up whatever this mess is?" Duane asked quietly.

"By God I wish we could," MacNelly said. "It wouldn't take more than a squad, were we free to do as I like. You're right, Buck. I can't order a company. In fact I can't even order in a badge. I can ask a man like yourself if he's willing to go it on his own, and then tell him if he lands in bad trouble I can't come to help. I can't even admit he's a friend of mine, let alone a Texas Ranger."

Buck Duane thought for a moment.

"No jurisdiction," he said then. It wasn't a question. He was stating a considered fact.

MacNelly slapped his open hand on the papers that spread out over the table top.

"Of course. No jurisdiction. Damn it, Buck, we can fight anything that comes into Texas from a Comanche raid to the Mexican Army or the British Navy. Defense is our job, and we can do it. Here's

63

something though that's a worse menace to the people of this state than an army could ever possibly be. I mean that. Officially I can't even admit it's there; let alone go after it. There's times, Buck, when I get so discouraged I begin to wish I'd gone into some other line of work. I swear I do."

"Now, Captain," Duane said. "You don't mean that, and you and I both know you don't. What is this business that's got you riled up? I've ridden myself weary all the way from the Rio Grande, so I think I'm entitled to know."

"You make sense, Buck," the captain said. "I guess that is why you stayed alive all those years on the other side of the law."

MacNelly picked up the whiskey bottle and examined it gravely in the light of the camphene lamp. Then he decided against another drink and put the bottle down again.

"In all that riding you just done," he said, "I take it you passed some cattle creatures on the road?"

"Cattle?" Duane said. "You say cattle, Captain? I came up east of the Chisholm trail and every mile—every yard, you might as well say—the dust of the trail herds stood up like a range of mountains to the west of me. I swear I rode along the edge of a wall of cattle trail dust as long and as high as the wall they say the Chinee built to close their country in. Seems like every critter in Texas has got into column to march itself to a railhead in Kansas."

"You know what that means for Texas, Duane?"

"I know it means butter on the white bread and milk in the baby's mouth," Duane said. "It means money for the ranches and the schools and the towns. It means my salary and the future of men and women yet unborn."

"That's as good a way to put it as I've ever heard," MacNelly said. "I swear it is. When the late dispute with Mr. Lincoln's blue coats ran its course in your father's day, Buck, this state was left with not enough hard money to buy a pot of beans in Boston or a pair of pants in New York. We had land and people and cattle running wild like fleas on a house dog. The cattle bred like rabbits and ate the land clean. They ran wild as coyotes in the mesquite and like to crowded the buffalo off the high plains.

"Lucky for Texas it was, for the people could eat cattle meat. Leastways then as had strong teeth could eat as long as they chew, but that was all a steer was good for—that and making what hides the Britishers and the Prussians and such would send ships to carry away.

"It wasn't till some of the men thought of driving the cattle north to markets where there were mouths to eat beef and money to buy it that we began to come out of the depths of financial disaster that the war had brought to us. Ever since then the herds have flowed north like rivers and beef along the drovers' trails. Ever since then the state has begun to grow and build itself and become strong and great again."

"I know all that," Duane said. "I guess every man woman and child in Texas knows it."

"Then you know too," the captain said, "that one thing we've always had to face was people trying to stop the drives for some reason of their own. When the first herds went up into Missouri it was farmers afraid that their crops would be trampled and grifters wanting to levy a toll on every steer. We met that by shifting the drives West to the Chisholm Trail, the Western through Fort Griffin and Doan's Store and the Goodnight-Loving Trail beyond.

"That took the herds out of farm country, but not into safe traveling by any means. Redskins raided the drives, especially when they crossed the Treaty Nations. Rustlers hit sporadically and scooped in stragglers and stampeded stock. There was always

65

danger and always loss, but somehow the Texas herds went through."

"A big herd with a smart and tough trail boss can fight off most anybody," Buck Duane agreed.

"Sure it can," MacNelly said. "An outfit like that has maybe thirty-forty hands with Winchesters and Colts. Sometimes they've old frontier men for scouts out ahead. Since the rapid fire revolver and the lever action repeating rifle they carry more firepower today than a whole regiment did a few years ago. Mostly the raiders have learned that lesson and act accordingly.

"Raiders don't just quit though. You and me know that. They look for a weak point to attack, and it looks like they've found one. Buck, the big drives are getting through, but the small herds aren't. I don't just mean they're losing steers to hit and run attack or paying an occasional toll to redskin or rustler. That sort of thing will never be entirely stopped.

"This is a lot worse. Small outfits are disappearing. I mean it's like they just ride off the face of the earth. An outfit goes north over the state line and is never heard of again. The men and the horses vanish with the steers."

"That's clear enough," the big ranger nodded. "Somebody waits for the weak outfits and wipes them out. The cattle and horses are rustled and the men killed to remove them as witnesses."

"That's it," MacNelly said, "but how long will it just be the little drives? That's bad enough, but unless this is stopped whoever does the raiding will get strong enough to hit the bigger crews. The whole drive system could be stopped or forced to pay heavy toll. Buck, unless we end this thing before it gets too bad, the whole economy of Texas can be set back twenty years. The trouble is that whoever's back of this operates north of the state line in the Territories, where there's little or no law or in the Indian Nations where there's none at all.

"I can't legally take a ranger company north and wipe him out. All I can do is write letters that maybe nobody ever reads. If they do read them, they haven't the strength to do anything. All I can do is sit down here and watch the Trails cut off and the lifeblood of Texas drained away. It's not right, but it's the law."

Buck Duane reached for the bottle and poured himself another small drink. He tossed it off and followed it with water from the pitcher.

"You don't have to draw the picture out," he said. "You can't go up in force, but one man—me—could go alone and without a badge. With luck I could find the head of this outfit and shoot it off. The trouble is you can't order me to do it, because it can't be official and I can't expect any help from you if things go wrong."

"I knew you'd see it," MacNelly said. "With your old outlaw record you'd be the ideal man to try. Remember, though, I can't order you I can't really even ask you, because it could very easily mean your death. Nobody knows who you'd be going up against or how strong they are. You and I both know there's a limit to what any one man can handle."

"I know that," Duane told him. "I never quite found my own limit yet, but I know it's there. When I come close I'll think about dealing with that. Till then a man can only do his best. I know too that we've got to open the road for the little, family sized herds. Half the beef we need to sell goes north that way. The small ranchers can't be asked to ride to sure and certain death.

"I know too how the sort of owl-hoot crowd that's been hitting them will think. Success breeds success. They won't stop short of going for every beef critter on the trails. Give them time to get strong enough,

67

and it'll take a regular full-scale war to open the Trails again. Wars take time, and Texas hasn't got the time to spare. Of course I'll do it, Captain."

"I knew I could count on you," the ranger officer said. "It's a dirty job and a dangerous one. I'll promise you one thing, Ranger Buck Duane. If you get killed on this assignment I'll come after the man who got you myself, if I have to resign my commission to do it."

"Let's hope there'll be no need for that." Duane spoke gruffly to hide the emotion evoked by the words of his captain and friend.

"I suppose there's no need to ask how you will go about the job?"

"There's only one logical way, seems to me," Duane said. "First off I'll sign on as drover with one of the small outfits that looks weak enough to attract raiders. If they do attack, I'll have a point of contact. I can stay alive and trail them to their headquarters."

"And if they don't attack?"

"Keep trying till they do. Or maybe just go right out to join the gang. A little loose talk in trail-head saloons and fancy dives by the notorious Duane should bring somebody sniffing around to see what I want."

"It ought to work."

"I'll keep trying," Duane said. "I give you my word I'll do the best that's in me."

"That's good enough for me," MacNelly said.

The two men shook hands across the table.

III

When Buck Duane left the captain's office he realized that it was late at night and that he hadn't eaten since a hasty breakfast when he broke camp at dawn. He was, in a word, ravenously hungry.

That didn't present any real problem in a frontier

crossroads town. People were coming and going at all times of night and day. The gambling houses and the fancy women never closed their doors. Food could be bought at any of these places as well as at any of the larger bars and dance halls.

Duane had no trouble finding an all night restaurant, where he had a platter of steak and fried eggs, thick sliced bacon, biscuits and cane syrup, washed down by cups of boiled coffee so black and strong "it would stand the spoon straight up till it dissolved it." The ranger ate with the healthy appetite of a strong and active man.

Only after he'd put away half of a dried apple pie for dessert did he begin to realize how tired he really was from the long day of riding in the open air.

Downtown Fort Worth was still wide open when he started back towards the Alamo Hotel. Bootheels thudded on the board sidewalks that rose like dikes to edge the mud and dust that served for streets. Light flooded out of saloon and gambling house windows. Horses snorted and stamped and switched their tails at the hitching racks.

Ahead of him Duane suddenly spotted a familiar figure. Improbable as it was, that slender back and confident stride had to belong to Jackrabbit Kid. Duane hadn't seen the youngster in a year, and believed him to be still over in East Texas near Galveston, but he still knew he couldn't be mistaken.

Buck Duane's life had depended upon keen vision and instant recognition of friend and foe by a gesture or a half glimpsed silhouette for too many years for him to make mistakes.

He smiled and quickened his stride to catch up with his young friend.

The rider coming up behind Duane wasn't hurrying. The pound of his mount's hooves and the jingle of Mexican silver saddle ornaments sounded

69

no different from those of a dozen others on the busy street.

It was only the built-in instinct of the hunted man—the infallible, intangible "smell" of danger and sudden death that made the ranger turn his head as the rider passed. Because of that he saw the man pull his revolver from its leather holster.

In frontier towns a man doesn't draw until he's about to fire it, and the only person near enough to make a logical target was the unheeding Kid striding along a little way down the block.

Duane didn't wait to see the threat materialize any more definitely. He went for his own right hand gun.

The rider must have had the same almost feral instincts as the big ranger. He caught the flash of movement out of the corner of one eye and realized instantly what was happening. With a movement as swift as a scared sidewinder striking in the dust the man flung himself to the far side of his horse, hanging on by one foot and one hand gripping the pommel of the saddle. At the same moment he loosed off a shot that passed within a foot of Duane's face.

The ranger fired almost at the same instant, but the Indian dodge had caught him by surprise. His bullet passed where the mounted man's body had been just a moment before. Then the horse was pounding off at a dead run up an adjacent alley.

The moment of deadly violence had ended almost before it began.

The shots brought the Jackrabbit Kid whirling in his tracks, gun in hand. It took him only a second to realize what had happened and another to recognize the Ranger.

"Buck!" he yelled. "In the name of all that's holy, what are you doing here?"

"Saving your life, boy," Duane said. "At least

70

that's what I think I just did. Who was that half
Comanche anyway, and why did he want to punch
holes in your back?"

"I wish I knew who he was," the Kid said. "I think
I can guess why, but that's the least important part of
the whole business. This is the second time today I've
had to pull iron."

"Isn't there someplace we can go and talk it over?"
Duane asked. "I've a hotel room down the street a
ways if you'd like."

"Thanks, but not there," the Kid said, putting his
gun back in its leather. "I do want to talk and I thank
God you showed up just now the way you did. I
hadn't realized they thought I was getting that
dangerous. But never mind that. You come along to
my place. I do want to talk, and there's somebody
there I want you to meet."

Duane didn't let his leathery face change expression. He and the Kid had been friends since they'd
ridden together through the wild hills of the Big
Bend country in the rustler band headed by the
mysterious renegade called the Old Man. When the
showdown came, the Kid had elected to stand with
Duane and law, in spite of the risk to his own life that
the decision involved.

Now both of them assumed without questioning
the fact that a threat to one of them was a threat to
both. It was good to have friends like that.

Two blocks further down they turned off the main
stem into a side street that twisted back into the
residential area. It was dark under the shade of
cottonwood and live-oak trees. The wooden walk-
ways ended and a thick layer of dust muffled their
steps. Both men watched and listened for any
possible new attack. Talk would only have diverted
them, and could wait till they had reached their
destination.

The house, when they reached it, was a neat

white-painted clapboard cottage back of a trim, three foot picket fence. The light of a single candle reflected from its tin sconce through the closely drawn blinds at the windows.

When the Kid knocked on the front door, a low voice questioned him from within before they heard the sound of a heavy iron bolt being drawn and a key turning in the lock.

Once through the door they were in a painfully clean, sparsely furnished sitting room. A young woman faced them holding tightly to an old fashioned double barreled cap-and-ball shotgun of ten or maybe even eight gauge. She didn't point the gun at them, and she was smiling at the Jackrabbit Kid.

Even in the dim light of the single candle, Buck Duane was impressed by the young woman's looks. She couldn't have been more than seventeen or eighteen, but her almost classically beautifully face already bore the stamp of early maturity and the hard-learned wisdom of the pioneer.

Her skin was clear and pulsing with life, her eyes a soft and melting brown and her slender figure showing good health and strength. Soft brown hair curled about the oval face and was tied at the base of the neck. She wore a loose-fitting man's shirt and the divided skirt and boots of a frontier horsewoman. She smiled at the Jackrabbit Kid and set the old shotgun down in a corner by the fireplace.

"Eddy," the Kid said. "This is the best luck I could possibly have had. You'll never guess. This is—"

"Mr. Duane," she said and laughed. "Mr. Buck Duane, the man who out-drew a rattler's strike." She put out one soft hand which met the ranger's in a strong and confident handshake. "Welcome to Fort Worth, Mr. Duane."

The Kid was flabbergasted. "Eddy. How? What?"

Duane shook the young woman's hand.

"At a guess I'd say you talk too much," he told the Kid.

The girl laughed again.

"How right you are," she said.

"Mr. Duane, he talks about you all the time. Probably in his sleep too, thought I wouldn't—" She blushed and they all laughed then.

"Honestly I know all about you and the times in the Big Bend Country. You've been described so many times I think I could spot you half a mile away in a racing day crowd."

"I said the Kid talked too much," Duane said. "Mostly at the wrong times and about the wrong things. Suppose you help me out, young lady, and tell me why you carry a man's name and all the other things I need to hear to know what this's all about."

"First come into the kitchen," the girl said, "There's coffee hot on the stove and we can sit and talk at ease."

They went into the big, homey kitchen at the rear of the small house. Duane didn't fail to notice that she carried the shotgun with her and the Kid didn't unbelt his gun as he normally would have done in a private home.

"In the first place," she said, "my real name's Edith. Edith Hayes. I'm called Eddy because I was raised on my father's spread south of here and rode with the hands and learned to do everything they could. I wanted to be called like a man when I was smaller and I guess it just stuck.

"Jack and I have been good friends for almost a year now—"

"Ever since the court in Houston cleared me and I came out here," the Kid interrupted. "Naturally when all the trouble started I offered to help out. I couldn't just leave Eddy alone to look out for things."

"You've been wonderful," Eddy said. "He really

has, Mr. Duane. You'll never know. A good friend and a really perfect gentleman. I'd never have managed even this far without all the help he's given me."

"Of course you would. You're better at managing than any three men I know."

"Hold up," Duane said. "Hold up, now. Why don't you two kids just suspend your mutual admiration society for a minute and tell me what all this trouble's about? I know enough to be sure a nice girl like Miss Eddy here doesn't usually have to carry a shotgun when she goes into the kitchen of her own home."

"It's murder," the Kid said. "Bloody murder and theft and massacre that would've made the Old Man himself proud to have done it."

"How do you know it's murder?"

"Let me answer that, Mr. Duane," Eddy said seriously. "About a year back my father and uncle and our three cowboys started out to drive our herd north on the Chisholm trail to Wichita for market. It wasn't a big herd. We've only a small spread and not more than fifty steers moved out.

"My uncle's old and stiff with the misery in his arms, so he rode the chuck-wagon. One of the hands broke his shoulder when his horse stepped in a prairie dog hole and had to be left behind, but Father and the other two riders were experienced drovers. They should have gotten through easily with that small herd."

"But they didn't?" Buck Duane was more interested than he wanted to show. This was just the sort of thing Captain MacNelly had been talking about earlier in the evening.

"That's right," Eddy told him. "I mean no they didn't. They just vanished instead. I mean they never showed up in Wichita. When I didn't hear from Father and nobody coming back from the drives would admit to seeing him I got worried. I sent a letter up to the marshal there. One of the big outfits carried it for me, and brought back the answer. They'd never got to Wichita or even close. Someplace along the trail they just dropped off the face of the earth like."

"Indians maybe?" Duane asked.

"You know better'n to ask that," the Kid said. "You know how Indians operate. They'd try to drive off the steers and the horse remuda at night. They wouldn't fight any more'n they had to. Besides if they had massacred the men there'd have been scalped bodies and a burned wagon left. Some other outfit would have found the evidence. No. This whole outfit just vanished. Four men and fifty steers don't do that."

"You see," Eddy said. "I agree with Jack that this wasn't accident or Indians. It was white man work. Somebody planned it and organized it. Rustlers, I suppose. There's lots of them in the Oklahoma Territory badlands. Somebody killed my father and uncle and the boys and stole everything we had. I've been looking for that somebody—and Jack's been helping me."

"Looking is one thing," Duane said. "Finding's another."

"We got a lead finally," the Kid said. "We been asking questions all around. I got word today from a man knew what I was looking for. A drifter called Lefty Linkett rode in couple days back. He'd been talking wild like around the bars and fancy houses."

"Not only that," Eddy said eagerly. "He put a watch to pawn that the pawnbroker thought he recognized. He called me to come in and look at it, and I knew it right away. That watch had belonged to my uncle. I'd seen him carry it for as long as I can remember."

"Now you're getting somewhere," Duane said and

75

got to his feet. "Where did you say this Lefty Linkett hung out? I think I'd better have a talk with him."

"You can't," Eddy said. "Sit down again, Mr. Duane. It's too late to see Lefty."

"The time of night makes no difference."

"It ain't the time of night, Buck," the Jackrabbit Kid told him. "I got the same idea earlier today, only Lefty didn't want to talk. He drew on me—twice. The second time I had to kill him or he'd have got me for sure. I'm sorry. I remembered what you used to tell me okay, but he had a forty-four Derringer about five feet from my chest, and there just wasn't no time to argue or do anything else but shoot."

"I'm sorry," Duane said. "There went your case and your only lead. Next time you search a man do it right."

"I didn't search him," the Kid had to admit.

"Do it another time. I suppose the fellow tonight was one of this Lefty's friends?"

"Tonight?" Eddy was genuinely startled.

"Just now on Main Street," the Kid explained, "I was heading back this way and some rannigan rode up behind me. No reason in the world for me to suspect a thing, but Buck here just happened to be on the street and saw him pull his iron—"

"And saved your life," the girl finished for him. "Oh, Mr. Duane, we can never thank you enough."

"Don't try," Duane said dryly. "The thing now is what do we do to pick up the trail again."

"We?" she said. "You're going to help us? Now I know nothing can stop us."

"With Buck Duane riding with us," the Kid said, "nothing and nobody had better try. This fellow's worth a whole army just by himself, and besides that he's a ranger. Why the rangers will—"

"Hold it right there," Duane said. "The rangers won't do one little thing because they can't. Whatever is going on, according to you, is up north

76

of the Texas border. The rangers've got no authority in that country. If I ride with you, it has to be just as a friend. You can't even tell anybody at all I'm a ranger. You'll have to promise me that before I can do even one thing to try and help you out."

"We promise," Eddy said, and the Jackrabbit Kid nodded.

"See to it you don't forget. Now do you have any plan and if so what is it? What were you thinking of doing before this Lefty person hit town?"

"Why the same thing you'd do in our place," Jackrabbit said. "At least I tried to think what you'd advise us if you were here to talk things over with. After a time it came to me that the only sure way to find them killers was to fix it so they'd come find us."

"That's just it," Eddy added. "We figured to make ourselves bait for them to come to, and the easiest way was to join up with an outfit just like my father's. By that I mean travel with a small herd that would look like easy pickings for the rustlers. They must have people who watch the trail for them and send word ahead when the right sort of outfit starts north by itself. That way there'd be a fair chance they'd attack the herd we were with."

"Then what would a couple of kids like you do?" Duane asked. "They'd just gobble you up along with the herd and the rest of the trail crew. What good would that do."

"Don't be too sure they'd gobble," the Kid protested. "I was trained by Buck Duane. I don't gobble that easy. Neither does Eddy. She can use a gun like a man. We figured to at least get away alive and then trail them back to where they operate from. Then we can locate the right authorities."

"You'd be a couple of babes in the woods," Duane said. "I didn't train you so well but you near got yourself killed twice already today. An outfit like you're talking about doesn't make mistakes. When they ambushed your outfit there'd be a surround. For both of you to succeed in breaking out would be a miracle, and if you did and got to the Law what difference would it make? There's no Law up that way but a couple of marshals. For them to ride against a big gang would be just plain suicide."

"But Buck," the Kid said, "we can't just sit here and do nothing. Eddy's father might even be alive and held prisoner someplace."

"I wish I could say I thought so," Duane said gravely. "I don't, Miss Edith. That sort don't take prisoners. I agree though that something ought to be done, but I don't think you two should do it. Let me go see what I can do, and—"

They wouldn't let him finish. They insisted they were going with a trail herd, with him or without. He couldn't lock them up, and that was the only way to stop them.

After a while Buck Duane gave up. They'd go together.

IV

It was less than a week later that Buck Duane and the two youngsters joined up with a small trail herd leaving a ranch just a bit east and south of Fort Worth and headed for the old Chisholm Trail and eventually for the railhead in Kansas.

Though nothing was actually said about it, Duane had a pretty good notion Captain MacNelly had had a hand in smoothing the way for their making the connection. It was just a bit too easy for it to have been purely accidental.

However he didn't want to ask questions. If the captain really had sent the herd owner to him, Duane wasn't the man to insist on looking a gift horse in the mouth.

The rancher who hired them was an oldtimer by the name of Ira Surbey, who'd established his spread in the days before Fort Worth was little more than a crossroads and two saloons. He was thin and tough, bald as an egg under the inevitable broad-brimmed Stetson, and with a short gray beard.

The one drover who rode with Surbey was an ancient vaquero called Juan Gonzalez, who claimed to have been born in Texas while it was still part of Mexico. Nobody knew how old the man really was, but he rode like a centaur and handled the stock as if he could talk to them and make them understand.

Juan's brother Pedro had originally been slated to handle the chuck wagon and remuda, but arthritis had finally caught up with the old fellow and made him a prisoner on the ranch. Edith Hayes stepped into the vacant position. She'd known cattle and the ways of the trail since her toddler years. She insisted on wearing man's clothing and a holstered gun, but it was still plain to anyone who cared to look that this was a woman, and a remarkably pretty one to boot.

Duane and the Jackrabbit Kid rode as drovers.

There were thirty horses in the remuda, mostly the wiry, shaggy coated, wise and incredibly tough plain ponies.

When the herd moved out on the morning of the first day there were a hundred and ten head of cattle. Mostly they were prime stock and the sort to fetch a premium from a Kansas buyer. Old Surbey knew his trade, and he'd been breeding and fattening his stock to improve the yield since before Eddy and Jackrabbit were cradlerocked mites.

It took them two days of easy driving to move west to the fringes of the wide band roughly defining the Chisholm Trail. A cattle trail wasn't anything like a road, of course. It couldn't be narrow or fenced or paved or very well defined. Where possible it spread out to form a band as much as fifty or more miles in width.

Only occasionally did it contract and narrow down to resemble anything that later generations could or would call a road or trail. This was usually at a river crossing or narrow pass through rough country, hills or patches of desert country.

At these places the herds had to cover the same ground and travel in each other's tracks. Wherever possible they avoided doing so, even if it entailed making wide detours that considerably lengthened the mileage of a trip that might already total a thousand or more miles.

The reasons were simple enough. You can't pack lunch for a hundred or a thousand or five thousand hungry steers. It's not possible to feed them from a chuck wagon. At a pinch corn and oats might be freighted for the horse remuda over short and particularly inhospitable parts of the road. For the cattle herd—never.

If the trails had been held to a belt only a mile or so wide, the first few herds to pass each season would have eaten the forage down to the bare ground. Actually that was what did take place at the start of each driving season. Those who came after had to swing wide or starve. The plains grass was deep rooted and grew back quickly as it had done for centuries after the county-carpeting millions of buffalo passed.

By the end of each year the last herds to trail north were walking in the tracks of the season's first comers. In between the outfits kept well clear of each other.

The Chisholm trail was by far the most famous of the cattle roads and ranks with the Santa Fe and Oregon trails as a moving factor in the long and bloody history of the American West. Decades after the last herd had thundered north old timers could still point out traces of its course stretching across the unplowed continental steppes in Indian Territory.

Where the herds had to come together as the uncounted thousands of hard hoofs beat down the ground, it showed as a deep depression sometimes four hundred to a thousand yards wide. Erosion by wind and rain in the years of its use and the starkly bleached bones and skulls of the beasts which had died on the march marked the course.

Low mounds marked the graves of riders who never made it to end of trail, and rotting wagon frames and the traces of circular bedding-grounds could be distinguished for years.

No man living has a count of exactly how many Texas cattle went up that route from first to last. The most educated guesses run from three or five million and up for the Chisholm trail alone.

Other drovers' routes saw great migrations of the horned beasts in their day, and cowboys passing by the thousand. They saw courage and tragedy, hardship and sickness and the dead from flaming guns. The Chisholm trail, winding ever northward from Red River Station to Wichita and on to Abilene, Kansas, was the greatest in history because it first fired the imagination of the nation and gave substance to the tradition and the dream that was to live in all men's minds as the great cattle trail.

Jesse Chisholm, for whom the trail was named, was a half breed Cherokee who cashed in on his Scotch father's canny trading instinct and the friendliness of his mother's painted and feathered relatives to make a name in trading with the Plains tribes. He used the famous route as early as 1865 to bring his wagons of trade goods south from Wichita to Fort Cobb. He found the route that touched the best fords and water holes across the central part of the Indian Territory.

Actually he followed an earlier route first blazed by a Union military force commanded by Lieutenant Colonel William Emory in the early period of the Civil War. In 1861 converging Confederate columns came north from Texas and Arkansas, their objectives Fort Washita, Fort Arbuckle and Fort Cobb in the Indian Territory.

Emory commanded the whole area for the Washington government. He showed decision and energy in collecting the scattered garrisons to go north to his base, guided by an old Delaware Scout named Black Beaver. Chisholm back-tracked Emory's old trail.

Like all herds starting out on the trail old man Surbey's steers were driven hard for the first few days. The rancher insisted on at least thirty miles a day, even though it was hard on both men and beasts. Over the whole route the average day's travel would drop to only about half of that.

The "pop-out" or initial spurt was meant to tire the longhorns so they'd sleep when bedded down and be too tired to think about bolting or going off to seek their home range. It also helped to break the trail herd to the habits of the drive. This breaking in might take a week or ten days to complete, but in the end of the half wild steers learned what was expected of them, what the daily schedule was, and became used to the steady movement and the direction.

On the march the herd moved in regular order. Ira Surbey set direction and pace. He had cattle sense, a nose for water, knowledge of the country, and the ability to handle men and beasts—the basic essentials for a trail boss.

Lacking either watch or compass, the direction for the next day's route, as in many outfits was set each night by pointing the tongue of the chuck wagon at the North Star.

With a big outfit two experienced drovers called

"point riders" formed a point of the leading cattle and kept them headed in the right direction. Similarly there were drag riders at the rear of the column whose job was to keep laggard cattle reasonably well closed up.

Position on the order of march indicated a man's rank as well as the trail boss' opinion of his experience and competency. The point riders were the top hands. Theirs was the heaviest responsibility, particularly at river crossings and times of emergency. Other men graded down as the rear of the herd neared the drag normally being assigned to greenhorns or tenderfeet—in this case the Jackrabbit Kid.

Riding the drag was unpleasant because it meant eating the dust from the herd. In big outfits there was some rotation of duties on the march as a matter of course. On hot days a herd of cattle generated tremendous heat and cowboys riding the windward side were frequently asked to change places with their sweltering and suffering opposite numbers on the heated lee. By the same token drag riders were sometimes given a spell as swing riders for temporary relief.

After the first day or so the cattle gradually worked out among themselves a surprisingly regular order of march. Day after day they appeared in their regular places with the same steers generally appearing in the point. A man who knew the herd could generally tell at what section of it he was by recognizing individual beasts. Day after day they'd be in relatively the same order.

The horse remuda—each man had a number of mounts—was kept either at the side or rear of the main column and tended by a boy or apprentice called the hoss wrangler.

Edith started the chuck wagon each day after the herd had passed, swung wide of the flanks and proceeded ahead of the steers so that camp could be set up and supper cooking by the time the herd caught up at the end of the day.

Buck Duane had a talk with the girl before they started the first day.

"Don't you get far ahead," he told her. "Particularly once we cross the Texas line you stay close to the point. I want to see you and for you to have us in sight all the time."

"I can handle the wagon," she said in protest. "You don't have to think that just because I'm a woman—"

"Your being a woman hasn't got one thing to do with it," the big ranger said. "This is no regular trail herd. Don't forget we're bait and trap all in one. When the rustlers take the bait—if they take it, they won't come to tea. They'll ride in fast with guns blazing. I want you where you can get to the rest of us in a hurry when that time comes."

"Oh," she said. "I forgot."

"That's the one thing none of us can do," Duane said. "We're no good dead. You keep a fast horse tied to that wagon tail. If trouble starts, leave the wagon where it is and set the grass on fire getting back to the rest of us. That's where we need you, not out by yourself where we have to worry if you're alive or dead."

"All right," she said. "I'll promise to be as careful as you want me to be."

Duane had also had a talk with Ira Surbey. This was a good deal more difficult. For one thing, the ranger didn't know how much about the situation Surbey really knew. He'd made an educated guess that the rancher had talked to Captain MacNelly. The way the three of them had been hired on was too smooth and easy to be entirely a coincidence.

On the other hand Surbey himself hadn't tipped his hand by word or expression. He might know only that the captain wanted the three friends to have jobs that would take them to Wichita. Or he might know as much or more of the inside story as Duane himself did.

In any case he'd be sure to notice that the chuck wagon stayed unusually close to the point of the herd.

Duane decided to go ahead.

"I told Eddy to keep right close to the point," he said to the boss one evening. "I hope you don't mind."

"I reckon you got a reason," Surbey answered. It could have been either a statement or a question.

Duane decided to interpret it as the latter.

"Most trail cooks aren't women," he said.

"That's right," the trail boss agreed. "Not many of them's young and pretty women either."

"On the other hand there's always a lot of rough characters riding the trail. Loners going north or south. Men just a hump and a holler ahead of some sheriff. Some would try to rape a young girl with her own father watching, if Daddy didn't pack a gun."

"And some wouldn't go that far would still like to steal my wagon and grub," Surbey said, taking the ranger's lead. "It's okay with me if you want her to stay close where we can watch."

"Thanks," Duane said. "I take that right kindly of you."

The old man snorted. "Long's I have to run a scrub outfit," he said, "I guess I can't insist on big herd rules."

V

Neither Buck Duane nor his friends really expected any trouble south of the Texas line. So far none of the herds that later turned up missing had failed to cross the border into what would later be Oklahoma.

Whoever the rustlers were they seemed to prefer to operate in the lawless badlands then called by the generic name of Indian Territory.

This was land that was truly outside of the reach of law and order as civilized men understood them. Some of the land was nominally ceded by treaty to the Indians who had moved to the land en masse from their original homes in the east.

The tribes couldn't care less what white men did to each other on their lands. They weren't above picking off or raiding a weak herd themselves. As the buffalo thinned out, beef looked better and better as an article of diet.

There were white settlements, usually small and clustered about a trading post or saloon. The people who lived there were on the run themselves. Killings were casual and frequent. Theft and rustling and murder were considered the order of the day and occasioned no special comment. Honest men riding through did well to attach themselves to one of the big trail herds which were strong enough to give a good account of themselves in case of trouble or even to fight a regular pitched battle if the need arose.

Nor was all the danger from human enemies. Coyotes swarmed along the trails, hoping for a sick and straggling cow or a lost calf that could be pulled down and eaten. At night their yips and howls sounded a not-too-distant point and counterpoint to the songs the cowboys on night herd sang to calm the sleeping steers.

More dangerous still were the packs of wolves that drifted south after a hard winter. These fellows could cut out and pull down a full grown horse or steer.

They weren't supposed to be man-eaters, but there were few cowboys who didn't keep a sharp eye peeled when the big lobos were known to be about.

Most feared of all was the occasional grizzly bear who sometimes appeared. As far as the cowboys were concerned old Ursus Horribilis had more than earned his name. Where such a bear was encountered a number of men would gather to be in on the kill. If he could be caught on the open plains, they would try to kill him with long range rifle fire.

The men would ride round and round the enraged beast, trusting to their broncos to carry them out of reach of his wild and terrible rushes. In the end the courage, tenacity of life and almost demonic ferocity of a wounded grizzly was beyond the comprehension of anyone who had not seen him in action. If he ever managed a burst of speed that ran down the pony at short range, bóth horse and man were almost surely doomed.

When Surbey's I-S brand herd crossed the border into the Territory on a blazing hot summer morning there was nothing special to mark the occasion. Indeed there wasn't even a marker to show them where the line actually was.

After that, however, they adopted a different attitude. Nothing changed on the surface, but all five of them, including old Juan Gonzalez, were somehow more alert. They never let their weapons get out of reach of their hands.

It was when they figured they were roughly a hundred miles north of the line—about eight days' travel—that the stranger rode into camp, coming up on their trail from the south.

The man was tall and dark and lean. He wore a black stovepipe hat in the eastern style, long frock coat and pants of worn black broadcloth, and undecorated black boots of first quality leather. Under the coat he wore a shirt of soiled white linen with imitation pearl studs and a black string tie of the sort favored in past decades in the cotton-belt south.

His face, like his shirt, was white and soiled with a blue shadow of whisker stubble. His eyes were black and expressionless as those of a lizard basking on a rock.

He said his name was Wilson Tyler and that he was an ordained minister going up to Kansas to preach. Ira and Juan and the Kid called him Preacher after that. Eddy Hayes never spoke to him directly at all. His black eyes raked her boldly from head to foot. They never met her own glance directly, but she couldn't help shivering whenever he came near her.

Buck Duane found himself disliking the man from the moment he rode in sight. He didn't make the mistake of letting his personal dislike or the role of Preacher cause him to underestimate the man however.

The Preacher didn't wear a belt gun. It would have been out of place. He had a good Winchester carbine in his saddle boot, and the gun looked well cared for and freshly oiled. Duane was also positive the man had a gun of some sort in a shoulder holster under his left arm. With the frock coat buttoned he couldn't be sure just what sort of gun it was, but his trained eyes spotted the tell-tale bulge which gave away its presence.

Ira Surbey saw the direction of the big ranger's glance and grinned at him as they waited for Eddy to dish out supper. Tyler was across the fire talking to the Jackrabbit Kid.

"Hide out gun," Surbey said in a low tone and spat tobacco juice into the dust. "Mebbe just a decoy. I bet that one's got a Derringer in his sleeve or under the top of one of them boots that he really relies on."

"As many fangs as a whole family of rattlers, eh?" Duane said.

"Just about." Surbey seemed amused. "I wouldn't

be surprised if he had the same sweet disposition too."

Tyler camped with them that night. At supper he ate as if his lean legs were hollow right down to the ankle. Eddy's sourdough biscuits were his special liking. He poured cane syrup over them and ate them out of the tin plate, scooped up on the blade of a wickedly shape skinning knife he produced from somewhere under the frock coat.

"You got a hankering for white flour bread?" Ira Surbey asked him.

"I do, brother. Indeed I do. The craving of the flesh is strong."

Duane didn't believe him. He knew from his own experience how an outlaw on the dodge gets to crave the civilized foods that he can't possibly come by when he's on the run. He remembered times when he'd made fireless camp in the hills, perhaps in a cave like coyote or cougar and chewed dry jerky and slept to dream of biscuit and sweet syrup and wake slavering with hunger and bitter with his desperations. There were times he might have been tempted even to kill for a hot meal.

Now he looked at Tyler and thought; *"Preacher or no—that man's been riding with the wild bunch no later than last night."*

Tyler's eyes flicked across the fire to Duane's face almost as if he could sense the big man's thoughts. He stopped shoveling in the food quite so fast.

"Don't I know you from some place, brother?" he asked. "I go up and down this land upon the work of the Lord, and I see many men. 'Pears like to me I've seen you someplace before, or had you pointed out to me."

"Might me," the ranger said, "Might be. One way or another I cover a mighty space of country myself. I don't remember seeing you though."

The man kept looking at him. "Perhaps. What did

89

you say you called yourself, brother?"

Duane kept his eyes on the man's black orbs. "I didn't say." He shifted a little where he sat so that his right hand was a bit closer to the butt of his holstered gun. "You can call me Buck. Just Buck."

Tyler laughed with his mouth, but his eyes didn't laugh at all. "There's plenty men use but one name out here, brother. Plenty good men, I'd say. It's not my way to pry with those who like it so."

He said no more on the subject, but his eyes kept probing Buck Duane. He saw the big man's easy grace, the controlled power back of every move. He saw the two guns in their gunslinger's rig, and the way Duane's hands were never far away from his artillery. He must have drawn his own conclusions.

Along towards dawn Tyler got out of his blankets. For a man of his claimed trade he moved very silently in his booted feet. He went and stood above Eddy where she slept. In the hot summer night she hadn't pulled the blanket over her shoulders and the man's shirt she wore pulled tight across her breasts. Her face was beautiful, at peace, almost childish in the faint starshine that made the night luminous.

The tall, black garbed preacher stood looking down at her. What his intentions were at that moment he probably didn't know himself.

He heard a sound and spun about, his hand flicking involuntarily inside the black brock coat towards the hidden shoulder holster under his left arm. Then he froze.

The tall form of Buck Duane stood just a little way off in the semi-darkness. Tyler saw with some surprise that he had to look up to the rider who was even taller than himself. Duane scuffed at the sand deliberately with his booted toe to show that the noise which had startled Tyler had been made on purpose.

"A beautiful night, brother," Tyler said in a low

voice. "Just up for a breath of fresh air."

Duane spoke very quietly, but Tyler could hear every word.

"Your right hand's under your coat," Duane said. "You think you'll ever look at that girl again? You think that, Preacher—I'd advise you fill that hand before you bring it out. I surely would advise you that."

Tyler was suddenly as full of tension as a snake getting ready to strike. He considered the invitation to a showdown and rejected it. He could feel the butt of his hidden gun, and his draw was fast and deadly, but somehow he knew that this big, quiet spoken man in the darkness was faster and deadlier still. No gunsel would give him such an apparent edge unless he was utterly confident that it was no edge at all. His thoughts that twisted in on themselves were bitter thoughts, but when he spoke his voice showed no trace of this.

"My hand comes open and empty," he said, and drew it out very slowly so that Duane could see. "I'm much afraid that you've misunderstood me, brother. I'm a poor preacher of the Lord's Word. That and nothing more."

In the morning Tyler left the camp right after a hearty breakfast. Whatever he thought of the night's encounter, it had certainly not affected his appetite.

"Life on the dodge," Surbey said to Buck Duane later that day, "would surely be hell for a man who likes to eat like that."

Eddy put out a good breakfast of flapjacks, syrup, bacon, beans, steak, coffee and johnny cake. She seemed to have forgotten her wariness of the night before and fairly sparkled with laughter and good spirits as dawn broke over the plains. Jackrabbit stayed at her side, his mood reflecting hers.

Duane watched the pair of them with approval. He was glad that he, and not the Kid, had been the

91

one to call Tyler's hand the night before. The boy might have let emotion get him killed.

Tyler took his leave civilly enough.

"The Lord's Work makes a man hurry forever," he said drily. "When and where I'm called I must ride fast. Faster than your fine steers can walk, I fear."

"I understand," Surbey said.

"I thank you fine folks for your hospitality," Tyler said from the back of his horse. "I shall not forget you. Not any one of you. Not ever. Someday perhaps we'll meet again and get to know each other a mite better. Till then, may the Lord bless you all."

He rode away at a fast pace and was soon out of sight over the plains to the north.

"I don't like that man," Eddy said as she packed the breakfast things preparatory to starting off the wagon. "I know it isn't right to say of a preacher, but there's that about him that I just don't like."

"Even if he was a preacher," the Jackrabbit Kid said, "and mind you I'm not that sure he is. A fox has worn a sheep's skin before this, but even if he is an ordained man, I don't blame you at all. There's a smell about him of something evil and hidden. At least though, he's gone."

"We're supposed to think he's gone," Duane corrected the boy. "A man may ride fast and straight and still not go far. Today, Miss Edith, you keep that wagon but just ahead of the point. Best not be more than two or three minutes fast riding away from us at any time."

"Oh," she said, "surely you don't think? You can't mean—"

"I don't want to have to think," Duane said. "You can make it easier for me in mind, if you just do as I suggest."

"She will," the Kid said. "We can count on Eddy."

The girl flashed him a smile that made both Surbey and Duane wish they were young again.

Even old Juan Gonzalez beamed under his broad brimmed, sweat stained sombrero.

Surbey, who had been over the route many times before, took his usual place at point when they moved out that morning. Before riding out he asked Duane to check with him in about an hour when the herd was settled into its marching order for the day.

When the ranger rode up he found Surbey in a serious mood.

"I didn't like that skinny preacher feller last night," he said. "You reckon he's what I reckon he is?"

Duane decided not to either ask Surbey what he knew or hold back anything he knew himself.

"I think he's the scout for the gang that's been swallowing up small outfits," he said openly. "Maybe there's more than one of them, but I think he rides the trail to see which crews are weak and what herds are worth running off."

Surbey nodded. "'Pears reasonable to me. I reckon too the look he got at Miss Edith sure makes this outfit of ours a prime target. Might be you should have gunned him down last night."

"I know," Duane said, "but he's not the one we want. It's a risk, but we'll just have to handle it when it comes."

"When it comes," Surbey agreed.

VI

They made an early camp that night. There was a river to be crossed in the morning. It wasn't much of a river as Eastern rivers go, but on these continental plains it rated the name. Near the crossing it was probably not more than fifteen or twenty yards wide at any point. Only in the central channel was the water over six feet deep and the channel was a narrow one. Nor were there large boulders in the bed

93

of the stream or sandbars and quicksands.

The danger in the crossing was that the banks were heavily wooded with cottonwood, pin oak and scrub. The tree roots held the soil right up to the edge, where it dropped steeply down to the water level. A steer running blind into the scrub could tumble over a six or eight foot drop into the water. A herd could pile up on itself and kill or maim half its number in five minutes.

The trail crossing for which they were headed was actually not so much a ford where the stream shallowed as it was a place where the steep banks had been broken down to a gentle slope. The herd could be walked into the water on one side and walked out on the other. Even the wagon could be gotten over without any great fuss or bother.

In the beginning it had probably begun as a buffalo crossing, when the immense herds made their annual migrations following the grass. The cattle drovers had long since adopted it as their own.

Surbey wanted the herd held far enough back so the cattle wouldn't be made restless at night by the smell or sound of the water. If they were too close, there'd be no sleep for man or beast. As it was, they could be bedded down as usual, then watered at the crossing about midday and moved clear away from the river before the next night's camp.

The weather for the week just past had been hot and oppressive with a brassy sun that seemed determined to bake the whole plains into a sort of gigantic slab of toast.

Day and night the wind blew up from Texas and the far south bringing a breath that was somehow hotter even than the still air. The grass was dry and rattled under the pushing of the wind. The snakes kept deep in their holes all day. A few minutes under that sun would have set their blood quite literally to boiling and "cooked the rattlers in their own juice."

Even at night the dry ground did not lose all its daytime heat. When the crew slept it was the blankets under, not over, their bodies.

On this evening the sunset blazed red in the west along the far horizon ominous, towering cloud banks could be seen. The men thought they could make out the far sound of rolling thunder. Supper was eaten hurriedly and the men got into their saddles instead of their blankets immediately afterwards. It was "stampede breeding weather" and they all knew it.

Nothing in the Old West exceeded the feelings of fear and expectation that accompanied the buildup to a real stampede. The herd of cattle were bedded down as usual, but the cowboys circling and chanting their cattle lullabies would notice that they did not lie fully relaxed. They kept their heads up and sniffed the wind and were constantly snorting and lowing like a tide of sound.

Some of the steers crouched with their legs drawn up as if readying themselves for a sudden spring into action. Sometimes one would rise and stand spread legged and quivering with tension as it sniffed the air. The night was pitch black except where lightning played about the distant sky and the distant rumble of thunder sounded a warning.

All about the bedding ground the men knew there were crooked gulches and gully washes, slashing across the ground which was also full of a running horse by night or day.

The air became saturated with static electricity. Off in the direction of the river Duane observed the terrible, dancing blue globes of St. Elmo's Fire. At sea this is observed as luminous bulbs of light at the ends of spars and masts on similar nights. As the electric charge built up, something like it appeared within the herd.

Small lights danced on the tips of the broad horns

like devil's candles and cast a frightening glow about the increasingly restless steers.

Duane became more and more certain that they were in for real trouble. He was all the more restless and spooked because he was no real cowboy. From the time he'd killed his first man at an early age his life had been spent on the secret outlaw trails out beyond the fringe of frontier civilization. The horse and the gun were his tools rather than the reata and branding iron. He knew about stampedes of course, but had never actually been involved in one.

Both Jackrabbit and Edith had accompanied trail herds before. Ira Surbey and Juan Gonzalez were veterans of this sort of night.

Suddenly the whole dark world blazed in the white light of a blinding flash, accompanied by a terrific crash of thunder which echoed and re-echoed, dying down at last in earth shaking reverberations. The rain came down in sheets, as if man and mount had suddenly stepped under a waterfall. Then more thunder and still more.

But the final crash and rumble was not heard. It was drowned out instead in a new tumultuous rumble and thunder of hoofs all drumming at once, and bawling cattle, clattering hocks and clashing horns as the herd came up to its feet with one wild, surging motion and bounded off into the darkness of the new downpouring rain.

Luckily for Duane and the rest the first rush missed the camp. Everything there would have been trampled into a shattered and rain soaked mess. Edith would probably have been safe in the wagon, but that was all.

Instead the herd went straight north towards the waiting river and the death trap posed by its precipitous banks.

At the beginning there was no use at all in trying to head off the fear-maddened creatures. They would run down and trample underfoot anything at all which came in the way of that blind, terrible rush. In daylight and unafraid cattle will run past or leap over anything in the path. On the night of a stampede not even the terrible grizzly could turn them or survive the terrible rush.

The only hope of a rider when the stampede began was to follow the herd at the top speed of his horse. Duane rode full speed over prairie dog holes where a misstep into a burrow would have broken Bullet's leg and hurled his master to sure death under the thundering hooves of the steers. He skirted yawning gulches or plunged directly down into them, trusting as he must the sure footedness of his horse.

In the blackness no man could see hand before face, let alone well enough to guide a mount. The cattle, once in motion, had lost their levin lights and could be followed only by the tumultuous sound of their pounding hooves.

Gradually the herd strung itself out as the fastest and strongest beasts forged to the front and out-distanced their weaker brothers. The herd which had started in a compact mass thinned and elongated until it more nearly resembled an arrow in flight.

Buck Duane knew that this was taking place but he could not have told you himself how it was that he knew. He couldn't see in the dark. His ears were deafened by a tumult that kept him from isolating any one specific sound. Rain still came down upon him in sheets.

Still he knew, by the heritage of his cattle raising ancestors, what was going on.

There was a last frightful bolt of lightning which struck somewhere over to his right on the other side of the running steers. By its light he could see that he was right, that the compact mass of cattle had stretched out to an uneven, snake-like column.

At the same time the rainfall diminished to a major extent as the storm continued to move across the plains.

Although real visibility did not return there was a general lightening of the almost pitch darkness. Duane could dimly make out the mass of the cattle, though even his night trained eyes couldn't distinguish individual beasts.

As far as trying to spot any others of the men was concerned, that was absolutely hopeless. He might have been the only human being left alive in an infinity of confusion.

The ranger urged Bullet to his ultimate efforts of speed and slowly began to outrun the steers as their first panic stampede ate up their strength.

The herd had bolted due north. Within a very few minutes—it was impossible for him to tell how far they'd come—the cattle would charge headlong to the line of the river, well to the west of the regular crossing. They'd go over the banks like redskin driven buffalo herded over a cliff and pile up in a bloody tangle of dead and crippled beasts in the stream bed. All of Ira Surbey's years of toil could be destroyed in less time than it takes to tell.

Duane's only hope was to reach the head of the column and somehow manage to change the direction in which the steers of the point were going. The rest would follow their leaders, and in time a circle could be formed and the herd forced in upon itself to mill about, exhausted. The danger would be over.

The speed and endurance that had been bred into the magnificent horse, Bullet, told now. By some miracle he avoided the hazards underfoot and gained ground steadily.

Duane realized at the last moment that he was not alone. Another rider was already at the point; yelling, lashing with his quirt and charging at the

98

leaders. They were beginning to turn. Buck Duane's arrival would certainly have swung the point.

Then, without warning, the shadowy pony lost its footing and fell, with an almost human scream, full in the path of the rushing herd. The rider was hurled over his bronc's head to roll on the wet ground. He scrambled to his feet, but it was obvious that he'd never succeed in clearing the path of the charging beasts, which bore down on him with tossing horns and thundering, knife sharp hooves.

As if he realized the danger, Bullet produced a last burst of speed of which even Duane hadn't realized he was capable, and bolted across the path of the stampede. There was a moment when the big Texas Ranger reached down to the standing man on the horse's back behind him, and Bullet was clear of the rush.

Not only that but the herd had swerved to avoid the fallen bronco, thrashing about on the ground. The beast was trampled anyway, but the cattle had swung from the line they'd been following. Other riders appeared out of the darkness, and the job of turning the herd to get them circling in each other's tracks could begin.

There was still an hour of hard riding ahead in the wet and windy dark, but at least the crisis had been passed. The riders knew their business and the steers were beginning to really tire from the heedless rush which had worn down their strength.

As the rain ceased and the night began to clear the job began to get a great deal easier.

It was only then that Buck Duane noticed that the man he and Bullet had snatched from the jaws of death was the herd owner, Ira Surbey himself.

VII

When dawn broke wetly over the plains and the herd was bunched and exhausted, the Jackrabbit Kid rode back to bring up Eddy and the horse herd. The other men waited glumly without wood for a fire and with only two horses between three of them.

Old Juan rode off presently to recover Surbey's saddle and bridle from the fallen and trampled bronco and the ranger and trail boss were left alone together.

"You're quite a rider," Surbey said. It was the only direct reference he was to make to his rescue of the night before, but it told Duane more than another man could have expressed in hundreds of words.

"*De nada,*" Duane said, using one of Juan's favorite expressions.

"I wouldn't say that," Surbey said. "Anyway I think this's as good a time as any for us to have a little talk. I suppose you realize by now that I know what you're doing riding drover on this trail." He paused and spat tobacco juice into the mud.

"I kind of got the impression you knew more than I remember having told you myself," the ranger said. "How much or where you got it is something else again."

"The thought didn't cross your mind that I could be working for the other side?" Ira Surbey asked. "That Kid shot his mouth off so much around Fort Worth that they know for sure what he's looking for. Feller you stopped from gunning him on the street proves that. Could they get him in a herd run by their friends, they'd like that for sure."

"You're not that kind," Duane said. "A man has lived as I have gets to know the judging of people."

"Why thankee, son," Old Surbey said drily. "The captain told me some of your story. Wouldn't be here at all I guess, less'n you could judge men."

"The captain?" Duane tried to keep surprise or any other emotion out of his voice.

The old man laughed. "T'ain't widely known even around Fort Worth, boy. For reasons of keeping my

100

health mostly, but I was one of the first company of rangers mustered into the service of Texas. Not the old Lone Star Republic—my daddy rode with them—but the state. Had a recruit once that I trained. Name of MacNelly. Best I ever had, bar none, bar none at all."

Buck Duane squatted on his heels and looked the wiry old man up and down.

"That explains a lot," he said. "I reckon that explains a lot of things."

Surbey nodded and spat again. His keen old eyes swept the horizon with the caution bred of a lifetime of danger and adventure.

"Now that we both know who we are, son," he said, "I figure this as good a time as any to sit by the council fire. Not that we got a fire of course."

"It's time to talk," Duane said. "I think our time is running out."

"So do I. That preacher feller had to be a scout for the folks we're looking for. He saw the Jackrabbit Kid and the girl, so by now his bosses know they have to take this herd. Fat beef to sell and a chance to wipe out the two who've gotten too nosey. That's too good to pass up. Trouble is they'll take extra care for this one. The raid will be mostly for a wipe out of the crew and only second to rustle the steers."

"I know," Duane said. "I know. I don't think they know who you and I are, though. Might make them just a shade careless, if they think things'll be easy."

"Don't count on it, boy. That preacher ain't no fool. He knows you for a gun fighter for sure, even if he cain't put a name to you. They also know the Kid was fast enough to put down their man Lefty and that he's all riled up prodding for trouble. I don't think they know my ranger connection any more than they do yours.

"But even at that my local reputation around Fort Worth ain't exactly that of a harmless, soft headed

101

old coot that has trouble gumming his milk-toast. No, boy. When they come they'll come fast and deadly and hard. They'll ride in to kill, and they'll take no chances when they do."

"I fear you're right," Duane said. "That kind just don't believe in taking chance anyway. They rather take a shotgun to kill a mouse than run the danger of a bit thumb any day."

"What would you suggest?" Ira Surbey said. "Oh, I got ideas of my own. Don't worry about that. Just like to hear what the new style ranger thinks of first."

"You know this country and I don't," Duane said. "Where do you think the hit will be?"

"I think soon, real soon," the old man said. "We'll get the steer critters cross the river today. 'Bout ten miles to the other side we'll hit a stretch of rough going. Brush and scrub and little hills and gully wash draws running every whichway. Hard for men to keep the cattle and themselves in sight. Lots of nice hidy holes for an ambush to wait. It's my guess that they'll try to hit us in there—and if they do, the advantage is all theirs."

"Yeah," Duane said, "and with the deck all stacked to favor an attack. We better not do as they want us to about that. Any way we can go round and keep in open country?"

"Good," old Ira Surbey said. "That's exactly what we do. East the rough hills come down to the river, so we go upstream to the west as soon as we get on the north bank. About twenty miles of that and the badlands peter out. We can turn north again on open plain until it's time to turn east again and hit the trail. It's longer, but at least we can see anything coming at us in time to get set before we're hit."

"Just what I wanted to know," Duane told him. "I think for that stretch also we should bed down by day and move the herd at night. It'll be harder for them to come on a moving herd at night, and in the

102

daytime one sentry can see all around while the rest sleep. Shorthanded as we are, it'll be to our advantage and their disadvantage."

Surbey smiled and nodded. "Couldn't have figured it better myself. You'll make a ranger yet, you will."

"We'll keep close together at all times and rally on the wagon in case of being cut off. Otherwise we'll have a picked line of retreat selected in advance. If they corner us, then sooner or later they'll wipe us out. So what we have to do is get clear of the attack and then follow them till we find their base. Of course it means not defending the cattle."

"MacNelly said that was just what you'd suggest," Ira Surbey said. "I guess he knows his men as well as I used to know mine. Don't worry about the value of the cattle. In case of loss they've already been bought by the state of Texas under the captain's special procurement powers. There's always a way to handle the paperwork on a deal like that."

"How much do we tell the others?" Duane asked.

"Tell 'em the whole story now," Ira said. "Old Juan I trust and the kids are your responsibility. Reckon you wouldn't have let them come along if you hadn't thought they could be depended on. I figure people always fight better if they know what the fight's about."

It was noon before they got the herd moving, and the river crossing was completed just after dusk. The steers were weary from the night of stampede and easy to bed down.

A big outfit, driving at least three thousand head, was coming up behind them, ready to cross in the morning. So Ira and Duane agreed it'd be safe for all hands to relax that night. "Nobody'll attack with that big outfit within hearing of gunfire. They'll wait till we're off by ourselves again."

When not on watch themselves Ira Surbey, Buck Duane and old Juan Gonzalez slept easily. They knew they needed every possible moment of rest to recover from the night before and get ready to fight for their lives in the near future.

Only Edith and the Jackrabbit Kid were restless that night, after the manner of young people in general and most particularly of young people facing what they believe to be a crisis of High Adventure.

They had both been told what Surbey and the ranger believed the situation to be and briefed on the parts they were expected to play when the attack finally came. After that they saw lurking rustlers in every shadow and the distant clouds along the night horizon loomed like the dust of charging hordes of merciless raiders.

About two in the morning they both found themselves awake and sitting on the grass near the rear of the chuck wagon. The waning moon hung low in the sky and gave a vaguely luminous and romantic shine to the late night.

"They really are coming," Edith said. It was more question than statement. "They really are going to attack us."

"Buck seems to think so," the Kid said, "and there's nobody in the world knows more about these things than he does. With him along it's the other fellows had better do the watching out."

"I know," she said, "and now we know Mr. Surbey used to be a ranger too. Still I can't help but wonder. What will it be like when the shooting starts? What will I do and feel? Will I be able to do my part?"

"Will you be afraid the first time?" the Kid asked. "Of course you will, Eddy. But it's nothing to be ashamed of. All the fellows are. Why I am myself, even now, just for a second when I have to pull a gun.

104

Most everyone gets scared. Not a real giant like Buck of course, but all the rest of us. You'll be all right though. You'll fight instead of run."

"I hope so. I do. These are the men who killed Father."

Her voice broke just for an instant. "I must remember that. Not only Father. All those other men who've vanished on this trail and the women and children who waited for them in Texas as I've waited."

"Don't forget any of it," he said. "This is what you've wanted, and worked and planned for—the chance to set things right for your father. It's what I've waited and planned for too."

"Oh, Jack—"

"Oh what?" he said. He reached out and put his arm around her shoulder. She instinctively pressed against him.

"I mean," her voice was low, "if it wasn't for me you wouldn't be here. Waiting for them. You might be killed, Jack, and then I'd know it was all my fault. You doing this all for me. I'd—why I'd be responsible."

He didn't belittle her words. When he spoke his tone was very serious and steady and full of the high dreams of youth.

"Not you," he said. "Of course from the minute I knew what you were doing I wanted to be a part of it, because I love you. There's more to it though. Buck isn't here because of you. There's something big at stake. Big and important to Texas—"

"Oh, Jack . . ." she interrupted him.

"What now?"

"Jack. You said you loved me—"

There was no more talk.

VIII

They made an early start in the morning. Ira Surbey wanted to be well clear of the crossing place before the big outfit waiting to cross came up at their heels.

Their drive went west, staying parallel to the river banks, which they could see as a low fence of cottonwood and pin oak off to their left. They stayed far enough away so that the trees were dwarfed by distance. The steers wouldn't smell the water so keenly that way and be tempted to bolt back to the stream.

They kept the herd moving at a good clip all that day and completely ignored the usual late afternoon stop to camp. Instead the surprised cattle were driven on into the night despite their bellows of protest. Surbey didn't call a halt till almost dawn. By then the cattle and horses alike were weary and dragging their feet. There was no trouble bedding down the herd.

"Will it be tonight?" the Kid asked Buck Duane.

The ranger smiled. The boy had been riding and walking all day with a swagger and exaggerated bravado and manliness which let the others guess that he and Edith had come to some sort of understanding during the previous night. When a boy like Jackrabbit suddenly starts walking ten feet tall there's only one conclusion that older and wiser heads can draw.

"Not tonight," Duane said. "Maybe tomorrow or the day after some time, but not tonight."

"Why not?" the Kid asked. He hefted both the big guns hanging from his belt to see that they were loose and easy in the holsters. "Why not tonight? If they're coming anyway, I wish they'd get it over with."

"That's a boy talking," Duane said. "A grown man never says hurry up to a killing time. Kill or be killed is all one. Something to be avoided. It isn't good to take life, even the life of an evil man."

"These men don't deserve to live," the boy blurted out.

"No, they don't. I grant you that, but killing is still no game."

The Kid said, still impatient, "But why not tonight?"

"They lay off a ways last night," Duane said, "so the drovers behind us wouldn't see them. Today they went back in the badlands to wait for us. We didn't come up, but the big outfit did. They had to wait to let that pass. It would take most of the day. I doubt our killers got back to the river to cut our trail much before sunset last night.

"Just about now they'll spot our trail going West and figure we turned off to keep to the plains. If they ride hard, and I think they will, they'll come in from the north tonight at just about this spot. That is, the place we'd be if we had stopped last night the way a regular drive would have. As soon as they read the sign, they'll know what we've been up to, and of course they'll be able to tell just about where we turn north again.

"Remember, they know this country better than we do. They know just where a herd this size will have to go to circle the badlands and get back on the Chisholm Trail.

"By that time they may have figured out that we know they're coming. That'll make them all the madder. They can cut cross country easy enough with no cow cirtters to slow them and set up an ambush. My guess is we hit them sometime tomorrow while we're still on the move, tired from a night drive, and hampered by need to guard a moving herd. If I was them, that's the way I'd figure to do it."

"You aren't them, Buck," the Kid said. "You always told me a smart man thinks himself an edge before any fight. What edge do we have in this one? We'll be all the things you just said, plus outnumbered five or six to one, won't we?"

"No," Duane said. "Not exactly we won't."

"I don't follow you, Buck."

"Then think it over till you do. One of the things I said they'd count on just ain't so. Now you figure out which one it is and why it is, and you'll know the edge I got planned for us."

"I still don't see. You always think one long one ahead of the rest of us."

"If I didn't try the coyotes would have eaten me before I was the age you are now. One more thing, boy—"

"What's that?"

"You make yourself bodyguard for Miss Eddy. Oh, I know you think you would anyway, but I'm telling you just so it's an order. Getting her out of this safe is more important than you getting to be a hero. This is Texas business we're riding on, Kid, and I command for Texas here."

They rested through the heat of the day without incident. Along towards sunset Eddy cooked them all a hearty dinner.

"Don't worry about the smoke of the cook-fire giving away our position," the ranger said. "By now they've got it figured where we are within a half mile one way or the other anyhow."

Old Surbey nodded, "That's the way I got it figured too, young feller."

On this night the men slung their bed rolls back of their saddles. They carried extra ammunition and oilcloth wrapped packages of cooked beef and biscuit, canned tomatoes and peaches, and an extra canteen of water apiece. Hand picked spare mounts from the remuda were cut out and tethered to the tailgate of the wagon so they'd be at hand even if the rest of the horses bolted.

108

Eddy had a big cap-and-ball revolver that had belonged to her father strapped around her waist and the ten gauge shotgun loaded with number one buck beside her on the wagon seat. For added safety Buck Duane had told her to put the wagon in the drag position tonight and eat cattle dust for a change.

Old Surbey chose their route carefully. At this point the river they had crossed the morning after the stampede made a big loop so that for miles it ran almost due north and south instead of east and west. They kept this wooded line on their left hand. On their right the edge of the badlands they had been circling extended almost to the river itself. The low hills were gullied and eroded, crowned with clumps of brush and low trees. They made good cover from which the outlaws could spring their surprise attack.

By the same token they also ensured nearby cover to which Duane and his friends could retreat when attacked. At all costs they had to avoid being surrounded and pinned down on the open grasslands. If that happened, they'd be as good as dead.

The cattle herd was kept just about midway of the halfmile corridor of level plain between hills and river, and driven steadily north.

Because of the smallness of the party—only five guns including the girl—they dared not split up and send out a scout ahead. They had to rely instead on being able to spot hostile riders crossing the grass while they were still some way off. The half moon and starshine gave light enough for this.

The outlaws were smarter than Buck Duane and Ira Surbey had figured on. Instead of relying on a charge out of the cover of the hills to run down the little party, they'd managed to set a rather effective ambush in spite of the openness of the country.

When Surbey's people were first spotted coming north along the corridor about a dozen of the rustlers had walked out from the hills about a third of the way to the river and concealed themselves in a slight depression in the ground. It wasn't really a gully, more like a shallow saucer, but the grass was tall enough to give them cover when they sat or lay there.

They deliberately picked a place close to the hills, figuring that when they opened fire the drovers would seek cover along the river. The main body of outlaws were at the river bank to cut them down when they did so. Only three or four men were in the hills. Their job was to bring out mounts to the men hidden in the grass as soon as the shooting started.

The Texas party came on through the grass, pushing the cattle at a good pace and watching for mounted men to come out of hiding on the right or left.

Actually it was the half dozen steers on the point, and not the men, who first detected the ambush. The smell of men and guns and sweat-soaked clothing came to them on the gentle, fitful night wind. The animals had no cause to panic of course, but they snorted a little and tossed their horns and tried to swing a bit wide of where the ambushed outlaws waited.

Ira Surbey noticed the change in behavior of the steers even before Buck Duane. After all the old man had lived with cattle for years. He realized instantly what their uneasiness meant, drew one of his guns and fired it into the air, at the same time letting out a wild, cowboy yell at the top of his voice. He swung his horse in a tight curve to come in behind the steers.

The cattle, always spooky on a night march, lowered their horns and bunched up behind the leaders. Old Juan and Duane rode in behind them with Surbey.

The men in ambush were jumpy too. Although the herd was still five or six hundred yards off and well out of effective aimed fire range for their Winchesters, some of them fired their guns anyway.

All hell broke loose on the prairie.

Surbey, Duane and Juan Gonzalez rode in behind the cattle, shooting and yelling. The beasts stampeded straight at the men hidden in the grass. Once launched, the herd had the speed and irresistible force of a racing locomotive as they thundered down upon the outlaws. The fact that the men were dismounted in the face of that racing herd panicked some of them. They jumped to their feet and ran towards where their friends were leading the horses out of cover from the hills. The steers ran those men down and trampled or lanced them with the needle-sharp long horns.

The men who kept their heads shot down the leading steers and forced the herd to split around their bodies. Most of those men survived.

Way off to the left, the men along the river burst out of ambush, shooting and riding to the rescue of their comrades.

Inside of sixty seconds the whole plan of the ambush was perfectly clear to such seasoned fighting men as Surbey and Duane. Together with the old vaquero they turned their mounts away from the river and rode for the cover of the badlands.

Duane looked over his shoulder and noted that Edith and the Jackrabbit Kid had abandoned the chuck wagon and were riding on the same course, leading or driving the preselected spare mounts with them.

So far so good. All five of them had about a quarter mile of open grass to cross before reaching broken country where they could hide or make a stand.

The outlaws rallied quickly from their first confusion. The survivors of the party which had been run over by the stampeded herd were the closest. They got the horses brought up by the horse-holders and followed at a roughly parallel course. There were eight men in all, including the horse-holders, and they didn't feel themselves strong enough to close in for the final showdown.

A dark mass of at least twenty more riders was coming up at a pounding run from the river-ambush party. These posed the real danger.

Duane knew his people had to get under cover before the two groups of riders united into one striking force of overwhelming power. In the open his party would kill some of the outlaws but still be ridden down by shere force of numbers. He bent over Bullet's neck and let the big horse carry him.

They barely made it.

The riders from the river bank had twice as much ground to cover, but their horses were perfectly fresh and rested. They hadn't been driving cattle for the past seven hours, but only taking their ease in the cool shade by the water. They came fast with a burst of speed that cut down the distance between the two parties.

They just made it to the first substantial rise of land, a low hill standing some thirty feet above the mean level of the plain and crested with a cock's comb of thick brush. As fast as they got under cover they swung off their horses, grabbed Winchesters from the saddle boots, and settled to a firing position in the brush.

The men riding in from the river were either faster or more reckless than the others. They came on fast and bunched together, trusting either to darkness to make aimed fire difficult or to panic to keep the fugitives from making a stand.

When they were still a good hundred yards away the Jackrabbit Kid opened up. He was firing

112

downhill in very tricky light and hit nobody. The shots did alert the outlaws though, and they began to spread out.

At the last possible moment before the charging men fanned out Duane, Surbey and Juan fired together. These were old hands. Three shots were fired and three outlaw saddles emptied. The charge broke away, as the outlaws circled back to a safe range. Such deadly fire wasn't to their taste in the least.

"Get going," Duane yelled. "Mount and ride."

"We stopped them," the Kid said defensively.

"All we did was spread them," Duane said. "Quick as they get out of range they'll fan out both ways and work around behind us unless we get out of here fast."

Edith ran up, holding the big shotgun in both hands. "Buck—Mister Duane—one of those men is riding my father's horse. I'm sure of it. I'd know the markings of that black and white pinto anywhere."

Duane didn't question the excited girl. "Mount and ride, Miss Edith. If we take that horse later, he'll be evidence. Right now we have to move."

"I don't want the horse," she said with a terrible intensity. "The man who rides him must be the one who killed Father. That's who I want."

"Move out," Duane said to the others. "Kid, you get her on a horse and out of here. Get a move on now."

He forced his own horse through the brush and down the far side of the little hill into a draw angling back through the badlands. He heard brush pop and horses hooves thud as his friends followed.

Buck Duane didn't look back. He needed every bit of alertness and riding ability the years had taught him to find a viable path through the thick brush at night and in perfectly strange country. He trusted to Bullet to find footing and kept picking his

113

route by instinct as much as anything else.

To flee straight back would only have meant being swept up eventually in the loose net of riders being spread out behind him. What Duane wanted to do was angle off, get past the flank of the pursuit, and let it sweep on past them to wear itself out in the brush and gullies. To manage this at all they had to go at breakneck speed and avoid any possible delay. They rode for about ten minutes.

Suddenly and without warning Duane heard a booming crash a long way back in the brush. It couldn't be anything but Eddy firing both barrels of the old shotgun at once. Right on the heels of the explosion came yelling and the whang-whang of Winchester fire. Then silence.

By the time Duane got Bullet pulled up to a halt he realized that there were only two riders with him, and knew without telling they'd be Surbey and Juan.

Edith and the Jackrabbit Kid were missing.

"That was the girl's gun," Surbey said to the suddenly quiet night. "It didn't fire more than once."

"It's my fault," Duane said bitterly. "She thought she recognized her father's horse in the charge back there. Wanted to kill the owlhoot riding it.

"I should have brought her out myself. Like a fool I told the Rabbit to do it."

"Then it's his fault," Surbey said.

"No, mine. I forgot he was in love with her, and a boy in love can't say no to his true love. I should have kept them with me. Well, you two ride ahead. The outlaws will rally to that firing. You should get clear easy enough."

"What about yourself?"

"I told you it was my fault," Buck Duane said. "I think a man should pay for his own mistakes. I'm going back in there and bring them both out if they're still alive."

"If they aren't?" Surbey asked.

114

"You know better'n to ask that, old man. I'll go to find the men who got them."

"You'll go to find your grave," the implacable old voice said.

"So be it then. It was my fault, not yours. That makes it my responsibility, and so I'll go. Texas needs you alive to finish this."

"Don't be a fool, Buck," Ira Surbey said. Duane knew that nothing could stop them from riding with him.

IX

Curiously there had been no more shooting after the single burst. The three men sat their horses, but they heard no yelling and no shots.

Somewhere up ahead a party of riders went crashing through the brush. Buck Duane thought wrily that he might have met these men head on if the firing hadn't made him stop.

He realized suddenly that the visibility was getting better as dawn broke far away in the east.

"Might as well get on with it," he said. "All we can do is go back over our own tracks and try and find where the fight was or where those two young fools branched out on their own."

"Old Juan's a tracker," Surbey said. "I've seen him work many a time. He can find the place a bird's shadow crossed hard rock. You wait and see. You and me just follow along now."

Old Juan gave a noncommittal grunt and started back over the way they'd come. This was such a clear trail that he didn't even seem to be looking at the ground.

A long way back he turned off the direct track. Eddy and Jackrabbit must have left the path there. Duane could probably have followed the track from there on by himself, particularly as day was now

115

breaking, but he certainly couldn't have done it as easily and quickly as Juan Gonzalez. The old vaquero rode as if following a well-traveled road even in thick brush and broken country.

It wasn't long before they came to the place where the fight had happened. With gestures Juan indicated where Eddy and Jackrabbit had concealed themselves in a thick clump of mesquite overlooking the floor of the draw down which Duane and the others had ridden.

The outlaws had ridden right under their guns. The first group of three of four riders had been allowed to pass unchallenged. Apparently Eddy was waiting for the man on the horse she felt had been her father's.

He must have been in the next group of outlaws. She'd fired both barrels of the old shotgun at a range of only about twenty feet and literally blown the man's head off. His body still lay where it had fallen.

There was another dead outlaw a few feet away. This one had fallen to the Kid's Winchester.

There had been no chance at all of the two young people getting away. The outlaws had done the only possible thing, wheeled their mounts and charged the mesquite with guns blazing. They'd ride over the kids in a matter of seconds, and that's just what the sign showed. The horses of the two young people were down and dead. There were no other bodies.

Old Juan got off his horse and circled the area. Then he said something in Spanish and waved to the other two men to follow him.

A hundred yards back in the brush they found the Jackrabbit Kid, unconscious in a pool of his own blood. He must have been left for dead and then tried to crawl away to safety as soon as the outlaws had ridden off.

The boy had been wounded three times. Two of the wounds were superficial. One bullet had just grazed his left cheek. It would leave a scar but nothing more. A second had ripped a gouge in the flesh of the left thigh. The blood had already clotted here. The third would at first appeared to be a good deal more serious. The whole right side of his shirt was soaked with blood.

However, when the three rescuers ripped away the shirt and examined the wound they breathed a collective sigh of relief. The Kid had been hit while turning, and the impact had been a glancing one. A couple of ribs had been smashed, but, because of its angle of entry, the slug hadn't driven on through the rib cage into the lung. Such a wound would have almost surely been fatal. Instead the bullet had sliced along the rib line and come out of the body near the right arm.

All three of the men possessed some elementary skill in treating wounds by the rough methods of "frontier medicine." They knew what to do and did it. Within minutes the Kid's wounds were cleaned with whiskey and bandaged. Strips torn from Duane's blanket bound the rib cage tightly.

By this time the boy was beginning to recover his senses, partly from his natural recuperative powers and partly from the shock of the pain of dressing the wounds.

His first word was a question: "Eddy?"

"We was hoping you could tell us," Surbey said. "There ain't no body back where the fight was, if that's what you mean."

The white-faced boy spoke with effort. "They've got her then. Her horse was down, but she was on her feet last I seen."

At this moment there were sounds in the brush. They whirled, reaching for their guns, but it was only a saddled horse which must have belonged to one of the dead outlaws. The beast was used to the company of men and readily allowed itself to be caught.

"Something for me to ride," the Kid said from where he lay.

All of them knew what he meant. With Edith Hayes in the hands of the outlaws, they had no choice but to follow and attempt to rescue her. Somehow the Kid had to go along, even as weak and wounded as he was. They know he'd never consent to stay behind even if it had been safe to leave him.

For any one but frontier-wise and battle-hardened veterans such as Duane, Surbey and Juan Gonzalez the mission would have been doomed from the start.

The outlaws must have been complete idiots—which they most certainly weren't—not to realize that possession of Eddy as a prisoner guaranteed that her companions would follow and attempt a rescue.

They must be aware that Buck Duane and his companions were looking for them anyway. They'd known enough to try to kill Jackrabbit after Lefty Linkett's death in Fort Worth. The way they'd scouted and then ambushed this particular herd was further proof they were alerted to their own danger.

Add to that the failure of the ambush that night and the mauling they'd taken from a much smaller band of men, which would make them all the more dangerous and vengeful. Duane and Surbey were going up against very long odds, and they knew it perfectly well.

"Best get started," Duane said. "Kid, we'll put you on this horse and help all we can, but it's up to you to keep up. I think you know that."

"I know it," the Kid said. "I was a damn fool to let Eddy talk me around to her fool notion of waiting for that guy. Now I'm going to have to pay for it.

Don't worry about me. And don't worry about Eddy telling them about us either. I know that girl. She won't talk."

"It's not her talking that bothers me," Duane said as kindly as he could. "They'll have guessed most all she could tell them by now anyhow. It's what they'll likely do to her whether or not she talks that hurries me now."

"Let's ride," Ira Surbey said.

X

They rode hard all that day without coming up to the outlaws. Indeed the condition of the trail indicated they were drópping behind. The wounded Kid slowed them down somewhat, but they wouldn't and couldn't either leave him or push him to the point of collapse.

Actually they might not have done much better without him. The outlaws had all the advantage of knowing the route. Even more to the point; they had relays of fresh horses and could transfer to new mounts whenever those being ridden grew tired.

Duane's party had lost their horse remuda along with the cattle, the chuck wagon and all their reserve supplies at the time of the night fight. They had to husband the strength of their own mounts at any cost.

"No use to come up to them varmints with horses too wore out to run," Surbey said. "Once we locate the rattler's den, it'll be in and out fast or not at all."

The Kid gave them a white-faced smile. He was riding between the two older men, and at times when pain or weakness made him falter in the saddle one or the other of them would put out a hand and support him briefly.

"What will we do when we catch up, Buck?" he asked.

119

"Only two things we need to do," Duane said, "and there's just a chance we can carry it off. We go in fast and get Miss Eddy out. While we're there we kill the snake."

"What do you mean by that?"

"Just one way to be sure of killing a snake, boy. Make sure you kill the head, smash the head. That's all. When the head stops living the longest snake dies inch by inch."

"We don't even know who the leaders are," the Jackrabbit Kid objected.

"We'll find out when we get there," Surbey said. "You don't fret your head about that. Now save your strength for riding."

That night they moved about a mile off the outlaws trail before camping. While it was still barely light, Surbey made a fire of buffalo chips, dried splinters of bone and twists of dead grass. It wasn't much of a fire but the heat boiled a soup of shredded jerky and a few beans for the kid, and the thin smoke was invisible in the dusk. After full dark they put the fire out and rolled in their blankets.

In the morning the Kid was stiff and very sore, but the natural vitality of youth was working to bring him back to better condition. He drank what was left of the evening's soup and they gave him coffee laced with whiskey.

When they picked up the outlaw trail they saw where a body of men had back-tracked along their own trail during the night, and then returned to the main body.

"They come back to bushwack us," Surbey said succinctly. "Had we camped right on the trail, we'd be dead right now."

"They got to learn," Duane nodded, "it can be a mite hard to bushwack rangers. I reckon we're getting close to their base."

"So do I," Ira Surbey agreed. "Not likely they'd

120

hole up more than a couple of days' ride from the Chisholm trail. That kind of varmint is bone lazy anyway. Won't even ride any further than absolutely necessary."

Ahead of them they saw a range of wild and broken hills; a sort of magnified version of the badlands on the edge of which Edith had been captured. None of the hills were really high, but it was a fearsome country.

"Right in there," Buck Duane said, and the others nodded agreement. "First nice sheltered valley with water for the rustled cattle will hold them. First nice easy pass will hold the ambush they'll have waiting for us too. I think it's time we got off their track and swung wide to come in on them from behind, where they won't be looking for us."

It was the tactic he and the old ranger had decided upon in advance. Instead of continuing to track the band ahead, and so leaving themselves wide open to being spotted and ambushed, they made a wide circle designed to bring them around behind the outlaw hideout.

It was rough going in the absolutely unknown badlands, but these were not eastern tenderfeet or even cowboys. These were men whose whole lives had been spent in scouting through hitherto trackless wilderness with their lives always at stake should they make the slightest error.

They were as close to the skill of Indians as it was possible for white men to be. The sights and sounds and smells of the country were as easily read by them as street signs to a city dweller.

They could and did plunge into country that would kill any other men, and ride it as easily as if it was the broadest and most comfortable highway. In addition they had the help of old Juan, who was not only a master tracker but a man whose instinctive "feel" for the country and knowledge of the probable

121

behavior of the outlaws provided what was almost a sixth sense.

The old fellow could judge the country ahead and what they were likely to find there almost as easily and accurately as one of the hawks or buzzards circling high above on tireless wings.

It wasn't long before they crossed a trail over which cattle running into the thousands of head had been driven west over a long period of time.

Buck Duane allowed himself one of his rare, wintry smiles when he saw the hard beaten trace.

"Just like I hoped," he said. "This is the way they drive the stolen herds out to market. The other end of this trail likely connects with one of the Great Western Trails, maybe even the Goodnight-Loving. That don't concern us now. What does is that here's the back door to the rustler's hideout we're looking for. All we have to do is follow it on in."

It was late in the afternoon so they got off the trail to rest, let the horses graze, and take a frugal meal of cold dried jerky, cold coffee—with a shot of whiskey for the Kid—and for each a can of the treasured peaches; rare luxury of the dry plains. All of them knew they must be at their best for the night to come.

Duane and Surbey changed the bandages of the Kid's chest wound. In spite of the riding and lack of formal medical care the wound was closed and beginning to show signs of healing. The Kid's right side was very sore, and he had to swing his gun holster over to the left side, but otherwise he was able to get about.

Because he was a right hand shooter with the right hand out of action for fast work, the Kid had taken Eddy's shotgun. The outlaws hadn't bothered to pick it up back at the scene of the fight, and there had been shells in the saddlebags of the girl's dead horse. Even supported mainly by the left arm, the big gun still made a formidable weapon.

The other three had their sixguns and Winchesters, and Surbey, surprisingly, produced two sticks of dynamite from his blanket roll. He adjusted fuses to each and gave one to Duane.

"Mighty powerful stuff," he said. "It can sure help even things up when a man's outnumbered."

"I've heard of this," Duane said, "but never had any before. What do I do with it?"

"What you don't do is drop it," Surbey said. "Might go off, might not. If things get tight you light the fuse and throw it as far as you can into the other fellers. Don't hand it—throw it. Then burrow like a old badger or get behind something big. This stuff got power. Man throws it through a window—the whole house won't be there any more."

"Here," Duane said. "You take this back. I know my guns. Man should stick to what he knows." He stuck to his statement, and made Surbey take back the explosive.

They mounted and rode back along the wide cattle trial. It was impossible to miss even at night. Within three miles the trial went into a narrow pass. At this point it was fenced off.

"There'll be a valley in there with both ends fenced and full of stolen beef critters," Duane said. "Likely that's where they keep the horse herd too. Their town or whatever will be at the other end since it ain't at this one."

They rode along the rim of the valley for another mile. The sounds of resting cattle told them this was indeed the holding point for the stolen beasts. The valley lay like a shallow saucer in the hills. It was about a mile across and rimmed with wooded hills. Only at the two ends was it necessary to fence.

Apparently there was also a spring inside, for a small stream, hardly even a brook, ran out the lower end of the valley.

123

The lights of the little settlement were clearly visible from the valley mouth and the nearby rim. Actually it wasn't big enough to call a town, even by frontier standards. The little stream ran down the center of another valley, this one long and narrow. There were trees and good grass, a fenced horse corral, and then a straggle of shacks along the stream. At the end of the shacks was what might be dignified as a town square. There was at least one general store and a couple of false fronted buildings that were probably saloons. These would be run by merchants willing to supply the outlaws with basic necessities for a high price.

On the far side of the square they could dimly make out the loom of a much larger building with lights shining through at least two levels of windows.

"There she is, boys," Surbey said. "Outlaw heaven."

He and Duane conferred briefly in low tones. Then the big Texas Ranger turned to the others.

"I'm going in and scout the place," he said. "If possible, I'll try to bring Eddy out. If I don't come back or if you hear gunfire, Ira knows what to do."

"Let me go, Buck," the Kid said. "At least let me go with you. Eddy's my girl. It's my fault she's in there."

"You stay here and do like Ira tells you," Duane said sternly. "No fancy notions of your own, boy. You try in there alone with your bad arm and you're dead."

"Can you do so much better? It's my girl." Jackrabbit was almost defiant.

"I was riding into hostile towns while you were busy with your mother's milk," Duane said. "If you do as you're told and the Good Lord loves us we got one chance in a hundred to make this. So don't you stretch the odds out any longer. You just do like you're told."

124

Buck Duane rode along the rim of the narrow valley until he had passed the first of the row of shacks where the outlaws bunked. He left Bullet just inside the shadows of the scrub that crowned the gentle slope.

He didn't have to tie the big horse. Bullet and Duane had lived together in the marvelous symbiosis of the horse nomad and his mount for years. The beautiful animal understood and obeyed an oral command. He would stay within a few feet of where his master left him until Duane either returned or signaled to him.

The big man walked easily across the bare couple of hundred yards of open grass to the edge of the settlement's one "street."

He wasn't worried about being recognized, even if he should be seen. Men were continually moving about, especially in the central square, and one more dark figure would occasion no comment. If there was any watch being kept, it would be on down the trail in the direction from which the rustlers would expect him to be following on their trail. He had no doubt that direction was well guarded.

Besides, he doubted if most of the men would take alarm or spot him as a stranger even if they got a close look at him. In a camp such as this one, men must be coming and going all the time. New drifters would join up and others move on with their loot. The composition of the band would not likely be the same from one week to the next.

Only a hard-core group of the leaders and their immediate associates would be permanent party in this place. It was these men Duane wanted to find. The logical place to look would be the large building he'd seen from the edge of the brush. He headed in that direction.

When he reached the town square he skirted it rapidly, taking care to keep out of the lights spilling from the fronts of the more public buildings. These included a store selling groceries and general foods and another that apparently specialized in saddlery and horse furniture. A couple were openly drinking and gaming rooms.

Duane was getting his old familiar bout of tension that always gripped the big man when a gunfight was impending. His stomach was tied in a hard, cold knot. His nostrils dilated like those of a panther questing for the scent of an enemy. His eyes grew keen so as to miss no possible sign of danger. Unlike many famous gunmen of the old West, Buck Duane did not like to kill another man.

He never drew and fired until it was absolutely necessary. Perhaps it was because of this that he was all the more deadly when the moment of action finally arrived. Then nothing could stand against him.

Now he moved swiftly to the main building, the town hall for this nest of murderers, thieves and ruffians. He could hear the sounds of drunken revelry from the drinking dens. His ears blocked them out, leaving a sort of selective hearing range to pick up any footstep coming close.

The building was built like a fort of heavy logs that must have been cut elsewhere and hauled into the valley. It was certain the ragged badlands scrub could not have supplied such massive timbers. The windows were small and framed by heavy plank shutters that could be swung to and barred to leave only slits for riflemen to fire through. When Duane circled the building he found the shutters already secured there and the one rear door securely fastened.

If he got in at all, it had to be by the front, and gain access he must. This had to be the headquarters for the brains who ruled and manipulated these wild and bloody men. It was the fort that held their records, their loot, their leaders and all the elements of their strength. It was also the only possible place where a prisoner like Edith Hayes could or would be held.

Duane saw at once that the responsibility was his and his alone. No four men could force their way into such a fort. By boldness and daring a single man might anticipate the first alarm. That was what Buck Duane knew that he had to do.

He went round to the front of the building again and up on the broad verandah running the whole length of the building. Through one of the small windows he could see the front room inside held a bar and gaming tables. Several handsome women were mingling with the dozen men inside. There was no yelling or drunken brawling going on, but instead an atmosphere of nervous tension and watchful waiting.

These were the elite of the murderous band. They would know that some sort of attack impended, and be waiting for the storm to break. They'd be ten times more dangerous than the rabble in the drinking dens across the square.

Duane moved with confident, unhurried stride. There were a couple of men with rifles near the single entrance, but they'd both been drinking and never thought to question a man who moved with such assurance. Before they really looked at him he was past them and inside the room.

He'd already made up his mind that, if Eddy was being held prisoner in this building, it would be on the second floor, where most of the sleeping rooms would be located. His eyes spotted the stairs off to the left as he came in the front door, and he headed for them.

No one in the big room gave him more than a casual glance. They were busy with their own affairs.

He went up the stairs slowly and easily, keeping both hands close to the holstered guns at his sides. At the second floor landing he came face to face with a woman just about to start down. She was tall and dark with black hair and eyes and she wore a tight fitting black silk dress. Around her neck was a string of garnet and amethyst and another of pearls.

"See here," she said with an air of command, "you know you men aren't allowed up here." Then—with eyes suddenly widening—"Oh—"

"That's right," Duane said quietly. "I'm new here. I came to bargain for the woman prisoner."

In spite of herself her eyes flicked off to her right down the hall.

"You lie," she said. "I can scream and you're dead."

"You never saw me move," Duane said. "I can break your neck with my hands before a scream gets started. Besides, if you meant to scream you wouldn't talk about it."

"You lie," she said, watching his hands.

Duane took a long chance. "I think you're the preacher man's woman. At least I think you were till he brought the girl in. Help me take her out of here, and you'll be his woman again."

There must have been Indian blood in the woman. Her dark eyes smoldered hatred and jealousy.

"You need me," Duane said. "If you kill her yourself, Preacher won't forgive you. Has he forced her yet?"

"No," she said. "I stop him. Big Mack wants her too. I say they better cut cards for her. Big Mack is out now waiting to kill you and your friends. How did you get past him?"

"I can get by anybody," the ranger said. "I have big medicine, strong medicine. You show me the girl. I'll take her and you can't be blamed. Then we go away."

He hoped she'd believe the last statement, though he was sure neither Preacher nor this Big Mack would have. The woman wasn't likely to sit in their counsels—or at least so he hoped.

He watched emotion flicker back of the black eyes. She wasn't young any more, and she was afraid of losing Preacher. He knew when she made up her mind and guessed what the decision was. She'd take him to Edith, let them try to escape, and then give the alarm so both of them would be killed. He didn't for a moment trust her.

"Here we stand," he thought to himself. "Each of us lying to each other. I wonder which of us lies best? There'll be killing soon. The cold in me says so."

"Come on," she said. "I help you. Then you go quick."

She led him down the hall to the right. The third door was padlocked, but the key was on a nail. She took it and opened the door. Inside the room Eddy was lying on a cot with her hands and ankles bound with rawhide. She was gagged with a dirty bandana.

Duane made her a sign to keep quiet and then cut her loose. The dark woman lit a single candle to give him light.

"Can you walk?" Duane asked.

Eddy got up and almost fell. She sat down and began to rub circulation back into her legs and ankles.

Duane turned to the woman. "Is there a back way out of here?"

"No," she said, "only the front door. I go with you. After you get out, you're on your own."

"You go with us to our horses," the big man said. "Yell or warn anybody, and I'll kill you."

Eddy looked up at Duane. All she said was, "The Kid, Mr. Duane?"

"Only wounded," Buck Duane told her. "He's waiting for me to bring you out."

"That preacher man is the leader here," she said, getting to her feet. "He and a big one they call Mack."

"No time to talk," Duane said. "Come on."

They went down the hall to the top of the stairs without meeting anyone, and started down to the floor below. Eddy and the woman were a step behind Duane and walking arm in arm. A couple of men at the bar looked up, but when they saw the woman looked away again. Buck Duane began to think that they might make it through the front door. Once in the darkness outside, he was confident he could get Eddy out of town safely.

Then Preacher Tyler came in through the front door. He saw the three of them facing him, took in the situation at a glance, and went for his gun.

Buck Duane drew with a movement so swift and smooth that the eye couldn't follow it. The big forty-five in his right hand boomed like a cannon in the enclosed room.

The Preacher died on his feet. He got off one blind, instinctive shot, unaimed, fired by dying reflex. The black haired woman who had loved him took the bullet in the heart. Her body crumpled where she stood.

Given any chance at all, Duane would have made a break for the door, but the two guards on the porch blocked exit. One of them looked into the room, and Duane shot him through the head. The other stayed outside in the dark, ready to kill anyone coming through the door.

Inside the big room men swung away from the bar and jumped up from the poker tables. All of them were pulling guns. Women screamed. There was a thud of running feet from outside.

Duane and Eddy did the only possible thing. They ran back up the stairs. At that only the confusion of the people in the big room saved them. Bullets splintered the steps where they had just stood.

In the upstairs hall a drunken woman and a man clothed only in long red underwear and gripping a gun belt in his left hand, had come out of one of the rooms. The ranger pistol whipped the man and tossed his gun and belt to Eddy. Then he grabbed the unconscious rustler by one arm and the seat of his underwear and pitched him bodily down the stairs. The woman ran after him, and immediately repaid Duane's mercy in not shooting her by shouting: "There's only two of them!"

Some of the men below made the mistake of rushing the stairway.

Duane stood at the far side of the hall where he couldn't be seen from below and waited with a loaded forty-five in each hand.

The three leading men came to the head of the stairs side by side, and a scythe of lead from the ranger's guns cut them down. None lived long enough to fire a shot.

The men behind them ran for their lives. Some got out of sight from the stairs. Others ducked behind the bar. Several ran out into the street. Shouts and yells told the waiting pair that the rest of the outlaws from the square and shacks were running to the scene of the fight. Some of them were firing drunkenly into the air as they came.

A moment later there was a wild clamor. Someone was pounding an iron triangle with a metal bar. In that empty country the sound would carry for miles.

"What do we do?" Eddy said. "What do we do, Buck?"

"Mostly we wait," the big Texas Ranger said with deceptive calmness. "All that ruckus will tell Ira we're in trouble. He'll come get us."

She looked ready for anything, Duane thought. For a moment he envied the Kid.

131

"How can he help us?" she asked. "It sounds like there's a hundred of them."

"We made a plan," Duane said. "Right now you stay here and shoot if anything comes near the stairs."

He checked the other rooms to see that the outside shutters were barred and closed. One room, the office where the leaders kept money and records, was closed. Duane shot the lock off the door. There were papers here to expose and smash the whole operation of the gang.

When he was sure the windows were fast and there were no outlaws on the floor, Duane went back to Eddy.

"Nobody came near," she said.

"I didn't figure they would," he said. "Only way they can get at us is up the stairs, and they know that's suicide. So we're safe for now. I don't think they'll want to burn their own fort. Leastways not right off, they won't. They figure we're trapped anyway."

They waited for ten minutes.

"What's that?" Eddy asked. In the distance there was a sound like thunder rumbling.

"That's Ira," Duane said and smiled. "He's using the same tactic we did at the ambush. Only this time it's their own herd he's driving over the outlaws."

It was true. Surbey, the Kid and Juan had opened the gates to the fenced valley where the stolen stock was kept when they heard the shooting and alarm. It was simple enough to get behind the main herd and stampede it down the valley along the line of the stream.

A tide of between five and six thousand half wild steers roared into the little outlaw settlement. The creatures were fear maddened and smashing down everything in their way.

The outlaws ran for the hills or cowered in their

132

shacks. Some of the latter were pushed down on their heads. A few saved themselves by ducking into the fort.

The herd went on along the stream. Down at the lower pass Big Mack and his men, riding back from ambush at the sound of the alarm, heard them coming. The outlaw leader realized what had happened. He and his men turned tail and rode for their lives. The game was up and Mack knew it.

Behind the herd rode Surbey, Juan and the Kid. They saw the fort still standing and men with rifles at the windows. Shots were fired into the dark and the three circled back behind the shelter offered by other buildings.

There was a moment of quiet. Then the voice of Surbey called out of the dark. "Are you in there, Buck?"

Someone answered from the lower floor. "He's here. He and the girl. They can't get out and you can't get in. We want a deal."

There was a wild whoop out in the darkness and the sound of a pony running. It was the Jackrabbit Kid, riding like a Comanche brave. His pony was fast and shifty on its feet. Rifle fire sounded but he came on along the front of the big building.

He swung his arm and something trailing sparks thudded onto the verandah in front of the closed and barred door.

Buck Duane guessed what it was and hurled himself and Eddy down on the floor of the second floor hall.

There was a crash and a roar like the end of the world.

The stick of Surbey's dynamite blew out the door and a section of front wall a wagon and team could have driven through.

The outlaws didn't know what had happened. Those who still lived threw down their guns.

133

RUSTLERS
OF THE CATTLE TRAILS

The man in the greasy buckskin shirt sat quietly on
the crest of the knoll and watched the small spark of
fire that glimmered in the night, a good half mile
away across the West Texas high plains.

His dark eyes watched the little fire in the
distance, but his senses were alert to the sights and
sounds and the familiar, hidden life of the tall grass
in which he rested. He knew equally when a distant
coyote called its mate and when a small rodent
shifted in the grass to avoid the hoofs of his grazing
horse.

The man was lean and dark and tough as
whipcord. His teeth were yellowed and stubbed and
his body stank of bear grease and sweat. There were
lice in his long hair. He was alert and feral as a lobo
wolf—but more dangerous, for alone among the big
carnivores of the Western plains this man preyed
upon his own kind. He had a Winchester low-wall
carbine and a Smith & Wesson forty-four revolver
and his favorite weapon—the silent deadly fang that
was a hand forged, horn hilted foot-long Mexican
bowie knife.

He called himself Comanche George, and he was
waiting to kill whoever might have lit the fire he
watched. It made no difference who sat by the fire, or
even whether he had any personal goods worth
stealing. It was this man's nature to kill.

He waited without movement and almost without
thought while the stars blazed and shifted above him
in a moonless sky and the evening breeze died away
into the still of deep night. The small feeding
creatures in the grass gave him a wide berth as if they

sensed the deadly nature latent in his silent, dark bulk.

After a long time he got up and moved off in the direction of his prey, disturbing the grass no more than the shadow of a wind-drifted cloud. The fire was out by now, only an ash-buried coal or two remaining at best, but George's sense of direction was infallible. He homed on his prey like a magnet-drawn filing of iron.

When he neared the site of the fire he circled it carefully. He was so good at the deadly stalk that he did not even disturb the hobbled mount that grazed a little way from the impromptu camp.

George opened his nostrils to savor the almost imperceptible drift of air from the little camp. Someone had boiled coffee and fried bacon and heated cold beans in the bacon grease. He had not smoked at all. The horse grazed and dozed nearby. The master showed as a long, blanket wrapped bulk stretching away from the saddle used as a pillow.

The deadly stalker moved in the grass as silent as a snake. There was nothing to betray his approach. At the last moment he rose to a feral crouch with razor sharp knife in hand ready to dart the last step or two between himself and his sleeping victim.

There he froze suddenly like a statue. There was a wrongness that the beast in George sensed even before his senses could pin it down.

Comanche George held still like the shadow of death itself.

"That's right," said a soft Texas drawl behind the killer. "Just don't move. I've got a cocked gun pointed at your kidneys now. Right now."

Fear washed over Comanche George like a chill. Fear and surprise and then a killing rage that turned him to stone.

"Don't do it," said the voice. "Don't even think about it. I can kill you before you even blink."

135

There was a moment of silent deadlock, a clash of unspoken wills. All about them the night was silent.

Comanche George said at last, "Why don't you go on and kill me?" It was what he would have done in the other man's place and he was expecting the shock of knife or bullet in his back at any second. "Get it over with. You got me under the gun."

"I've had you under the gun for half an hour," the calm voice said. "I been expecting you ever since I spotted you trailing me yesterday noon. I picked you up before you started to make your circle of this camp, and been following you ever since. I could have killed you ten times over."

"No," Comanche George said then. "There ain't anybody living is that good. Not even no Injun!"

The other gave a low laugh. "Right back of that little rise to the west you stopped maybe half a minute and scratched under your left armpit. Right?"

"Who in God's name are you?"

"Just a man who learned to stalk the same way you did," the voice said. "Living with every man's hand against me and death in every shadow. You and I shouldn't be killing each other. We belong on the same side. I bet we're even heading for the same place."

Comanche George relaxed a little. "We should smoke the peace pipe then. That is if we both heading for Harpetown."

"You named it," said the voice. "You willing to ride together with the peace pipe? No killing and no treachery?"

"I will," George said. "What could I try against a man can stalk like you. I ain't planning no suicide. Besides the road to Harpetown is a road of peace for all of us."

"Go in and stir the fire up then."

George did as he was told, blowing on the embers

136

and then adding dry grass and a few bits of root and wood. Only then did he turn to the shadows.

"Now show yourself."

The man who stepped out of the shadows was tall and lean and moved with the lithe, fluid grace of *el tigre*, the dreaded jaguar of the Yucatan jungles. His grey eyes were steel-hard and his tanned face as expressionless as any Indian's. He wore the heavy woolen shirt and vest, the pants tucked into high heeled tooled leather boots that were the uniform of the Texas frontier.

A Winchester forty-four caliber carbine was cradled in one arm, and two big Colt's revolvers of the same caliber were tied down on his legs. For the moment he wore no hat—his Stetson making the "head" of the dummy Comanche George had stalked.

The killer studied that face. Then: "I know you. You're Buck Duane."

"If I didn't know you were the best friend that Buck Duane has in the world," the Ranger captain said, "and if this wasn't a time when Buck's going to need a friend, I wouldn't even think of letting you make a guess where he's at right now."

The little Ranger captain was stretched out fully dressed on the bed in a room in the second best hotel in Austin. His hat was on the bedpost and he was smoking a long, dark cigar imported from Havana, Cuba by way of Brownsville, at the mouth of the Rio Grande, and brought up by ox-wagon freight from there. It was an expensive cigar, but the captain had few vices of any sort and could afford the price.

The young fellow standing by the none-too-clean window and looking out into the street turned then to face the bed. He was young, not more than twenty

137

at the most, and tawny bronzed by sun and Texas wind.

Underneath the gangly youth however there was a curious and deceptive maturity. It revealed itself in the ease and familiarity with which he wore the big revolver at his belt, in the constantly alert eyes, the confident set of the handsome head on his broad shoulders.

"You're telling me Buck's on another one of your missions then." He made it a statement and not a question.

"That's right, Kid," the captain said. The young man had a name of course, but his friend, the former outlaw Duane, had long since christened him "Jackrabbit Kid" and now no one called him by any other handle.

"Why didn't he tell me then? He knows I'd want to go along with him?"

"You know Buck," McNelly said "He's an independent cuss. Besides he doesn't like to ask a friend into a real tight spot where that friend might happen to get himself hurt before it was over."

The Kid gave the older man a steady look. "I suppose that's just your way of tipping me that this is a real rough one."

"It's a rough one all right. Maybe the roughest Buck's ever been up against. That's why I'm telling you, even though I'm pretty sure he'd ask me not to."

"Well?"

"You ever hear of a place called Harpeville, Kid?"

"Not that I can call to mind just now. Sounds like it ought to have to do with either Angels or Irish colleens though."

"You're way off the track," the already legendary Captain MacNelly said. He took the cigar out of his mouth to emphasize his words. "Harpeville, if it exists at all will have more to do with devils than angels, I'm afraid. For one thing the name's spelled

H-a-r-p-e, not H-a-r-p. Named for the old Harpe brothers, who headed up the "Hole-in-the-Wall Gang" on the Natchez Trace. Bandits they were, and murderers—Cannibals to boot, some say. The worst sort ever lived. You can imagine the type of man would name a town for them?"

"I begin to remember now," the Kid said. "There've been rumors, but I thought they were just that and no more. Something about a Wild Bunch capitol up near the Indian Territory border. A place where all the outlaws and rustlers and men on the run could live outside the law and run things their own style. I didn't credit it for truth though."

"I'm afraid none of us did," the little Texas Ranger told him. "Now it looks like that was our mistake. The wild bunch are gathering up there in strength. Whether they really have a town or not we don't know for sure. That's one of the things Duane's to find out. Only one. There's more serious things than that afoot."

The Kid sat down in the one straight backed, rush bottomed chair and put his booted feet up on the edge of the bed.

"Now we're getting to the point you wanted to see me about, aren't we? Go ahead and spill it, Cap. I'm all ears."

"There's times when I think it's all mouth you are." MacNelly told him. "All right then. Listen closely. I can't tell you exactly where I got this, for reasons you'll understand. A source close to the Governor, let's say.

"The word is that this time the Wild Bunch want more than a badlands hide-out. They want a place where they can really be safe, where nobody can come at them at all."

He paused.

"There's no place in Texas where law don't run," the Kid said. "They must be plumb loco this time."

"Oh, no," MacNelly said. "Not loco. They know they can't be safe in Texas, so they mean to make a State of their own. A State where they're the law and no Ranger can come in. From what we hear, they may do it too."

"I don't believe it," said the Kid.

"Neither did I till I was told something else. Back when Texas stopped being the Lone Star Republic and came into the Union it was with the condition that it could, at any time the people wanted it that way, be split up to make three States instead of one. A petition and a vote is what it'd take.

"Now somebody in the Wild Bunch has got hold of that idea. Found a town way out beyond where the settlers are now. Fill up the area with a population of rustlers and owlhoots and riff-raff. Then split that area off by a vote of its "people" and make it a new State.

"That's what's in the wind, Kid. Or at least we think so. The State of New Texas or whatever name. A State where decent Law don't run. A State where the Wild Bunch make their own law and not a thing any decent man can do about it all."

"Good God on the Mountain!" the Kid said. "Wouldn't that just set the sagebrush afire though!"

"It could do an awful lot more than that," MacNelly said seriously. "Otherwise we might let them get away with it. Think how easy it would be for us to have all those thieves and crazy gun hands gone out of this State. Why a Ranger could grow fat and sassy with them gone."

The Kid laughed. "Why don't you?"

"Because I told you where this new State would be. The whole of the northwest part of the State. Like a roof over Texas and the cattle country. Why, man, every cattle drive to the railheads and the market would have to go through that state. It cuts across every one of the big drive trails.

140

"Whoever holds that land could levy tribute on every head of cattle that Texas sends to market. It could ruin the State if it's true and they get away with it. That's what I sent Buck Duane up to find out."

The Jackrabbit Kid swung his booted feet to the floor of the room.

"I can see that I'd better go look for Buck," he said.

On the rare occasions when he visited Harpetown he wore a mask. It was no little domino designed for a costume ball in New Orleans or Memphis, but a long, loose black cloth mask that extended from the lower brim of his black Stetson Hat down below the chin. There were eye holes in the mask and a square black bushy beard below, but that was all anyone could see. The rest of his visible clothing was black also and covered by an ankle length cloak with gold buttons.

The people of Harpetown couldn't be sure if he was old or young, fat or lean. They never saw enough of him to tell. They called him Mask or Hood or—to his face—just Boss.

He came and went in a black traveling coach with relays of good horses led behind. His driver and shotgun guard and the four outriders who were always with the coach were killers who rode armed to the teeth.

The citizenry respected his privacy.

Harpetown was not a place where personal questions were either asked or answered. One just a shade too personal could mean sudden death for the asker.

The town itself was a huddle of log and frame structures, sod shanties and floored tents straggling along both sides of a single muddy street.

141

The location was good, in a sheltered valley with grass and clean water from a meandering creek. There were cottonwood and pin oak trees to make a windbreak and good, high prairie grass to nurture horse or cattle creature. On occasion buffalo and antelope grazed only a mile or two from the saloons.

In the winter the cold winds blew all the way down from the Arctic tundra without hindrance, and in summer their hot cousins came back up from Mexico.

Only the town itself was a blot upon an otherwise beautiful landscape. Only the town and the people of the town befouled and shamed clean air and sweeping miles of grass.

On the day following Captain MacNelly's talk with the Jackrabbit Kid, the Mask came into Harpetown from the East and summoned a council of the leading citizens in the luxurious second floor quarters maintained for his use in the same building which housed the Golconda Bar and Gambling Hell.

Lady Nell was there, the statuesque, red headed, ivory bosomed owner and manager of the Golconda, in an expensive silk afternoon dress imported from Paris by way of New Orleans. She had a derringer in the silk sash at her waist and was smoking a miniature Mexican *cigarro* and drinking Jamaica rum.

"Judge" Lorimer sat across the table from her in his rusty black coat and soiled white linen shirt. The judge was drunk as usual, but not sloppy drunk or talking drunk. The liquor served only to still his nerves and keen the feral mind under his shock of white hair. His degree, they said, was from Harvard, and he had come West thirty years back after the sudden suicide of his best friend's wife in some Eastern city.

The man on his left called himself Skiddy DaVinci. He had been a riverboat gambler, first on the Big Muddy and then on Old Man River itself, and a legend even in his youth. When the War Between the States had called a halt to his profession, he had turned his hand to darker things.

They said he had gone into a locked room once in Natchez-Under-The-Hill with four men who had sworn to take his life, and come out alone leaving the others dead on the floor.

In Harpetown he was Sheriff DaVinci appointed by the Mask himself, and wore a solid gold badge of his own designed in the shape of a five-pointed star centered by a death's head with diamond eyes.

Even the murder-calloused and ferocious men who prowled the streets of Harpetown stood in deadly fear of Sheriff Skiddy and his guns and knife.

Only one member of the ruling camarilla of this capital city of the Wild Bunch was missing. That was banker Joseph Bacon, whose place of business stood across the rutted main street from the Golconda itself. He had left town a couple of weeks back for a business trip East to Kansas City and St. Louis on matters of import to the whole community.

The Mask opened the meeting. Even in this company of the select and intimate he kept his face covered.

"Gentlemen," he said to the others, "I believe our plans are going to succeed, and sooner than we have dared to hope. I've come direct from the Capitol, and things there have been arranged so that the bill to create a New Texas, Texas North, whatever we choose to call it, should pass Congress without opposition."

"By arranged," the judge said, "I suppose you mean the necessary votes have been paid for."

The others laughed.

"Nothing quite so crude as all that," the Mask said. "Most of the Congressmen and Senators have no real interest in this affair at all. It is only necessary

143

to influence a few key figures who can pass the word at the right time and in the right places. Most of those who vote our new State into being probably won't even have read the bill itself. It will be all over before they know what they've done."

"Suppose the Texas delegation to Congress objects?" the judge asked. "That might throw a real hitch into things. Can we buy all those men?"

"Of course we can't," the Mask assured him. "When it comes to Texas some of them are fools enough to be honest patriots, and as long they're in the Congress, they can't be killed.

"However there are other ways. One particular member of the House of Representatives is currently consoling himself for his wife's lack of charm in the arms of a young woman who answers to our good Lady Nell here. For that and other reasons this Texan will introduce the bill for us at a time when the members of his delegation who might object are absent or otherwise occupied."

"But can we be sure that such an opportunity will present itself?" DaVinci asked. "The success of the whole plan depends on getting that bill through both houses of Congress without its becoming a major issue. We can't stand investigation."

"Leave it to me," the Mask assured them. "I've handled the Washington part of this without a hitch so far, and I'll continue to do so in the future. I've a plan that can't fail. Meanwhile it's up to you to do your part out here.

"When the bill is passed it'll be put to a vote of the citizens of the area affected. You have to attract people into this part of Texas who will vote our way and—uh, discourage any settlers who won't."

"You leave that discourage part to me," Sheriff Skiddy said, "Any of these nesters or small ranchers who might vote a 'no' are going to find mighty good reasons to get out or at least stay clear of the polls."

Lady Nell laughed. "You and your boys can supply those reasons okay. You're just the ones to do it."

The sheriff of Harpetown laughed with her. "Right you are, my beauty. I never saw a dead man yet could mark a ballot. That's a fact."

"So that's settled," the judge said then, and reached for the bottle. "Everybody does his part as planned, and we can't fail." He raised his glass. "Here's to the State of North Texia, gentlemen."

"We had better succeed," the Mask said. "Don't forget there's a great deal of money already been invested in this project."

"That's been your part. Yours and Joe Bacon's," the sheriff said. "You ain't going to run out when things are ready for a showdown, are you?"

"Of course not. I picked backers of ample means to begin with. The point now is that those people are going to expect results.

"One way or another they're putting millions into the creation of this new State because they expect to get back even more millions from the activities we'll permit here. This will be a national center for all sorts of illegal activities. The profits they expect will be enormous.

"By the same token they won't show any mercy to you at all if they're disappointed. These are powerful and totally ruthless men in the Eastern States, even a couple of them from Europe. These aren't people to be taken lightly. It won't go easy with us if anything should go wrong."

"What could go wrong?" the judge asked over his half empty glass. "You handle getting the bill passed and we handle things out here. What can go wrong?"

"Texas," the Mask told them. "If the Governor and the honest authorities in Austin could ever get proof of what we're planning and present it to Washington authority we could never on God's green earth get that bill through Congress. It isn't likely that they could, because they'd have to have real, honest, indisputable proof.

"They can get that only here, you know. That's what you have to prevent—because God help us if you don't."

Buck Duane and Comanche George got definite word of Harpetown at a self-styled tavern on the rim of the Llano Estocado—the fabled Staked Plains, out beyond the edge of the really settled parts of the Texas cattle country.

It wasn't much of a tavern, just a soddy that started with a cellar dug four feet down through the roots of the high country prairie grass. Squares of the dirt were then used to build up walls another four feet above ground, sapling trunks were stretched across for roof beams and the roof itself made of sods and turf and bundles of tied grass.

There was a hearth on the dirt floor and a hole in the roof in lieu of chimney to let out the smoke. No windows. A door of iron hard dried steer hide stretched on poles. The owner was part Mexican and part German and part tumbleweed, with a touch of breed Comanche to hold it all together. He and George spoke a mixed patois that Duane could barely make out at all.

The two of them proceeded to get howling drunk on a concoction of raw trade alcohol that had been strained a vaguely whiskey brown by having plugs of rough cut chewing tobacco shaved into the cask to soak for a month or two.

When they got to squalling at each other too loudly, Duane took his blankets a quarter mile out in the grass, where he could sleep through the balance of the night in peace.

In the morning he found George and his distant cousin sleeping side by side on the hearth. One of the proprietor's feet had gotten in the fire far enough for the moccasin leather to singe. It hadn't awakened him.

When Duane and George finally rode out of camp, they steered a course of slightly more west than north from that point on.

"It's only about a four-day ride from here," George assured his companion. "Then we hit a post, maybe what you call a check point. Men watch the trail. They think we belong in Harpetown, then they pass us in."

He spat tobacco juice into the grass. "If they don't like us, they kill us or we try to kill them. I think they like us though. Why not?"

"Why not, indeed?" Duane echoed in his mind. If these men had heard of him at all, it would be as Comanche George had. Buck Duane, the lone outlaw rider whom the law had hunted for ten long years over the length and the breadth of the wild border country. Buck Duane, who had run with the coyote and the lean, lone lobo wolf and slept in the rocks and in caves where only the bat and the night flitting owl had eyes to see. That was the man the outlaws would remember.

The new Duane who rode as agent and under-cover man for the Texas Rangers and who had long since made his peace with the law for services tendered above and beyond the call of duty was not known to them. Except for some unforseeable accident his cover would be safe.

The border guard of Harpetown were waiting where the trail came out of a narrow canyon splitting through a range of low hills.

There were six of them, and they were camped around a spring that seeped out of the ground to make a muddy buffalo wallow there. There was a clump of cottonwood and some smaller brush of willow and sapling for cover and the two riders were out of the draw and under the gun without warning, or at least without warning that a lesser man could have detected. Both Duane and George had heard and sensed the camp well in advance.

The men there questioned them briefly and then passed them on with only a brief word of warning. "When you get to town report to Sheriff DaVinci. He won't care what you done or who you're running from, but he talks to every man rides into the town."

Buck Duane knew Skiddy DaVinci by name and by the grapevine that took all news of the Wild Bunch through the camps and small towns of the far frontier. He'd never met the man and as far as he knew, DaVinci hadn't seen him either, certainly not in his new role as Ranger.

Despite himself the big man felt a chill of warning touch his spine. DaVinci was a fabled gun. If it came to a showdown he would be tested to the utmost by such a duel.

Duane wasn't a bloodthirsty man. He killed only to save his own life, and then reluctantly. He knew perfectly well though that on a mission such as his present one he might have to kill at any time. It was one of the hazzards of his profession, a part of the deal that he had made with civilized society in the person of Captain MacNelly.

So he accepted it as such, without soul-searching.

The two riders smelled the smoke of Harpetown well before they sighted the place. They came up wind and the smoke of cooking and heating fires blew down to them. After that they heard the sounds of a town, of voices and the stamp and snort of tethered mounts and the bang and scrape of metal on metal, the pound of a hammer, and the piano in a saloon.

When they rode into the one long street, they

knew what to expect.

In many ways this was a typical frontier town, yet there were subtle differences which Buck Duane noted instantly.

For one thing there was a conspicuous absence at the hitching racks and the commercial stables of the big utility wagons used by homesteaders and small ranchers come to town for supplies. There wasn't a buckboard or surrey in sight, not to speak of a jump-seat wagon, a six passenger rockaway or a family wagonette. Most of all the work horse vehicles—platform spring wagons—were missing.

Most of the horses waiting more or less patiently at the hitching rails were saddled and cinched with the Spanish single rig, much favored by the riders of the Texas badlands.

The men walking the narrow board sidewalks that fought an endless losing fight with dust and mud were not townsmen or rancher types, but the familiar swaggering bravos Duane had expected to find.

The few stores sold rider's gear, guns and bowie knives and cartridges, clothing and horse gear. There was only one general dry goods store. The rest were drinking places, barrel houses, fancy houses or gambling hells.

The only really substantial building in the place was the Golconda saloon itself. That one had heavy log and adobe walls, solid doors and iron grilles over the windows. A few men could fort up there and hold the place against an army.

Right across the way was another building, also substantial but smaller and of only one story. This place had two doors. On one was a brass plate that said: *The Harpetown Bank—J. Bacon Esq.* On the other someone had painted in bold letters: *Sheriff—Jail.*

Inside they found two deputies seated by a desk in

front of the usual wall rack of assorted rifles and shotguns. Both were lantern jawed, mean faced fellows in bright red and blue checked flannel shirts to which they'd pinned oversized brass lawman stars.

The faces and the professionally tied down guns didn't match the stars.

"You fellers checking in?" one of them asked idly as the two riders came in the door.

The other one looked up then and suddenly snapped to attention as he studied the tall, grim featured Ranger.

"I know you from someplace," he said to Duane. "I seen you use a gun like it growed to your hand."

Comanche puffed up with pleasure at being the friend of a well-known desperado.

"You should ought to know him if you ever seen him shoot. He's Buck Duane. This here's the man out-drew the striking rattler down in the Big Bend country. You sure heard of that."

"We heard," the deputy said. "Are you that man?"

"I am," Duane admitted.

The man, who seemed to be the more intelligent of the two deputies, looked him over carefully. This fellow was of medium height and so thin as to be almost emaciated. He had a knife scar on his left cheek and walked with a pronounced limp in his left leg. He could neither read nor write but his knowledge of men and their motives could have given lessons to a psychologist of seventy years in the future. His name was Sam. Just Sam. At least he never used any other name in Harpetown. He was the sheriff's number one deputy.

He looked Duane over with a cool, professional eye.

"I guess you're him all right," he said then, "Sheriff Skiddy will want to talk to you personal, Duane. You rannies go find yourself a place to bunk down and come back late this afternoon. That's a good time to see him."

Once outside the office Comanche George ran into an old friend he'd ridden with in a rustler gang in the past and the two of them went happily off to drink together.

Buck Duane didn't mind. He wanted a clean, quiet place to sleep if he could locate one and George would be no asset with the sort of landlord the Ranger was looking for.

The town was crowded. In the "hotels" and boarding houses unwashed men were packed in three to a bed and sometimes even sleeping in shifts. Most of them were very rough characters indeed who would cut a roommate's throat for his gun or boots or "just to see him bleed"—if they were drunk enough.

Duane finally found what he wanted. The town blacksmith and his wife agreed to rent him a shed out back of the smithy. It was clean and there was a floor of sawdust and woodchips on which he could spread his bedroll.

The bugs running the board walls were roaches and not body lice. There was no window through which anyone could spy. Ventilation came through cracks in the walls and under the overhanging roof. Best of all there was a door that could be padlocked from the inside against intruders.

The blacksmith was an honest German by the name of Schwartz, up from the old German colonies near Houston, and his wife was a clean, motherly soul. They had preferred not to rent to the riff-raff and because Schwartz stood six foot three in his socks with shoulders and biceps that let him swing a six-pound sledge the way another man could a carpenter's claw hammer, they'd managed to survive.

Schwartz was a privileged character anyway by

virtue of his trade. The only blacksmith in a border town was far too valuable a citizen to be shot out of hand. He stood under the unspoken protection of sheriff and town fathers as long as he minded his business and plied his trade efficiently.

It was a perfect place for Duane to camp and he in turn a perfect boarder for the honest German couple.

Back in the sheriff's office Duane and George were hardly out of earshot before Sam had turned to his assistant.

"I think the tall one likely is Buck Duane," he said. "You mosey over to the Golconda and tell old Skiddy who's in town. Then you go on down to them lousy barrel houses at the end of the street until you find Three-Finger Miles."

"What you want with old Three-Finger?" the other asked.

"I don't want nothing with him," Sam said and spat in the general direction of the brass spittoon on the floor. His aim was poor.

"I don't want nothing with him," he repeated, "but I want you should tell him Buck Duane is here."

"What does he care about that, Sam?"

"What kind of deputy are you anyway?" Sam asked him. "Don't you know nothing goes on in this town? Even a fancy house loafer like you should know Three Finger Miles hates the guts of Buck Duane. He says Buck shot his brother years ago in San Antone. Every time he gets real drunk he talks about how he's gonna kill Duane."

"You think he can do it?"

"Not in a standup-and-draw he can't, you dumb fool. I just don't want no bushwacking before Skiddy decides can he use Duane. You tell Three Finger this—anything happens, to Duane, me or Skiddy will hang him on the big oak tree right quick.

Make sure he ain't too drunk to hear. You mark me now."

Buck Duane stowed his gear in the shanty and stabled his big horse, Bullet, with the blacksmith's own two horses. Then he stretched out on his blanket roll for a couple of hours sleep.

He got up about five in the afternoon and prepared to go look for Sheriff DaVinci. He had a pretty good idea what the talk was going to be about, but he still made sure his two big revolvers were loose and ready in the holsters.

If any word had reached Harpetown of Duane's association with the dreaded Texas Rangers, he could expect short shrift and no mercy at all. There probably weren't three men in the town's floating population who hadn't lost friend or relative to the Rangers' guns, and those three were likely enough on *Wanted* posters themselves. It was an occupational hazzard that Buck Duane had to face every day of his life.

At the sheriff's office he found DaVinci back of the big desk this time and the deputy, Sam, in a chair by a table over near the window. It wasn't right in front of the window. Sam liked to be able to see out but not to be seen himself from the street.

Sheriff DaVinci's black frock coat and white linen shirt were impeccably clean. There was a diamond and ruby pin in his neatly tied black stock and jewelled rings on the fingers of both hands. The butts of his two Schofield model forty-five revolvers were of elephant ivory and silver. His black hair was neatly combed.

The cynical black eyes were tired and there were bags beneath them from a round of nightly dissipation. He looked Duane up and down carefully when the tall Ranger entered and then motioned to a chair by the desk.

"You're Duane all right, or his double," he said easily, producing a bottle of good whiskey and a couple of glasses from one of the desk drawers and motioning the tall man to help himself. "I've heard you described. Besides you and I both know the look of a top gun hand. Make yourself comfortable."

The two men took each other's measure over the glasses of whiskey.

"I suppose you came to Harpetown for the usual reasons," the sheriff said then. It wasn't a question.

"The usual reasons are close enough," Duane said without any particular emphasis.

"I'm glad to hear it. That case you're welcome here. I talk to all new men coming in, as you may have heard. Just like to be sure they know the rules."

"I'm not looking for trouble," Duane said.

"That's the spirit," DaVinci said. "We allow no personal feuds here. No stealing from each other. No cheating at cards—at least we hang the cheats we catch. No killing except in self defense. If the people who come here are to live at all, it's got to be in peace with each other. On the other hand the town feeds and sleeps any one of us who's temporarily short of cash."

He stopped talking and looked keenly at his guest.

"I can pay my way," Duane said.

"I thought you could," Skiddy DaVinci said. "With you it wouldn't be a question of that. The people who run this town are going to need gun hands—top guns. You may have heard?"

"Rumors," Duane said. "Just rumors."

"Now you're hearing the fact. Fast guns are needed, and there's money to buy. I can offer you board and room, all you can drink, and two hundred dollars a month in cash while you wait for action.

After that, for a man of your reputation, the price can go up. All you do now is stay in town and be ready to take orders when you get them. Orders from me and nobody else, that is. So what do you say?"

"Does that offer include cartridges?" Duane said.

Then both men laughed and tossed off their drinks.

"Go across to the Golconda and get the best steak in the house," DaVinci told him. "Anything you want. Just sign for it. The town picks up the tab."

Duane left the office a few minutes later and started across the street to get his dinner. It was early evening and the wide street was unlighted except for lamps lit behind a few of the building windows. The rising night wind blew dust and trash in quick vortex and gust and the few men and horses on the move cast kaleidoscopic shadows in the night.

He never knew which shadow moved in a way that was somehow terribly wrong and raised the hairs along his spine. It was instinct that woke him with a touch as sure as it was indefinable—instinct that dropped his right hand to gun butt even as he jumped to one side and whirled around with lightning speed.

He pointed as a startled wolf will point, without knowing whether it was eyes or ears or nose or some sixth sense out of the dawning of man's hunting past that showed him where the danger lay.

The man in the dark alley next to the sheriff's office was ready for murder but not quite prepared for the big man's lightning fast reaction.

He swore and pulled the trigger of his gun, but even as the hammer fell he took Buck Duane's heavy slug in the hand-sized triangle over his own heart.

He died with the hammer half down and his own shot geysered up dust from the street near the big Ranger's feet. His body twisted and hit the wall of the building. Then his knees unlocked and he sprawled flat with his face out on the board sidewalk and his mouth open with surprise and with the shock of sudden death.

Sheriff Skiddy DaVinci was out of his own office with gun in hand almost before the echoes of the two shots had died away. He saw the body at his feet and he watched Buck Duane drop his own gun back into its holster.

"I thought you said bushwackin' was against the rules," the tall, steely-eyed man said quietly. His right hand almost touched the holstered gun.

The story of how Buck Duane had killed the bushwacker was all over Harpetown within half an hour after the shooting.

"He's got to have eyes in the back of his head," they said at the bar of the Golconda.

"No warning," they said. "At night like that and he couldn't have seen or heard anything."

"He just turned and fired into the dark and he killed his man."

"Now we know what they mean when they say he can outdraw a striking snake. Now I believe that he could do just that."

It made him a celebrity in Harpetown.

He was a hero in the saloons and the fancy houses and the gambling dens.

After that men stepped out of his path on the narrow board sidewalks even if it meant putting their own boots ankle deep into dust and mud.

"Was it really like they said, Skiddy?" Lady Nell asked the sheriff later that night in the privacy of her own personal quarters back of the Golconda.

"He's faster than the lightning," the dark man told her. "I was watching him go through the office window without really expecting to see anything.

156

Then he was round and his gun smoking, all before I knew he'd started to turn. That man's one of the fastest guns who ever lived."

"Who was the man he killed?"

"Just a saddle tramp named Three-Finger something-or-other who thought he had an old grudge against Duane. Sam says he sent the man word to stay out of trouble, but I guess Three-Finger didn't believe him. Maybe he was just drunk. Anyway it was plumb suicide to go up against Duane even from the back and in the dark of night."

"Just suicide," Lady Nell agreed.

Sam the deputy was thinking much the same thing as he ate his dinner of steak and beans and sourdough bread on the desk top in the office and washed it down with a pitcher of beer.

"I sent that fool Three-Finger Miles warning to leave Duane alone," he mused with his mouth full of beans. "Them saddle tramps don't have brains enough to save their own lives. Had to go and try it anyway. I wish I'd got to talk to him though, before he went and got himself killed. I meant to ask about something he said one time when he was cursing Duane. Seems like it was important, but I can't remember now what it was."

Sam poured himself another tall mug of beer and drank it down.

"Well, no matter. I sure can't ask him now."

Across the street in the main room of the Golconda business was booming. Drifters and outlaws stood three deep along the front of the long pine bar and occupied every seat at the gaming tables. Scantily clad ladies of the evening moved among them. Unlike the ordinary border town there were neither merchants nor ranch hands anywhere in evidence.

Buck Duane, as fitted his new notoriety in this place, sat alone at a table with his back to the wall,

157

where he could watch both the entrance from the street and the crowd which milled about the long bar.

He was eating steak and eggs and hot biscuits straight from the cook's sheet iron oven. As befitted his status here he had also side dishes of canned tomatoes and peaches and a half of a dried apple pie with a big slab of soft yellow cheese on the table before him. These were luxuries reserved for the elite of this city of the gun and knife. They had been brought to him without his even asking.

Duane ate with a hearty appetite after the austerities of a week's long trail diet of bacon and beans. It was a measure of the big Ranger's way of life though that he washed down the hearty meal only with frequent cups of strong hot coffee sweetened with brown sugar in the pot. The watchers understood. Many of the lone men who lived by their guns preferred to go very lightly on the drinking of alcohol. A slowed reaction might mean sudden death.

He seemed casual and relaxed as he ate but his eyes never ceased their scanning of the room. Unlikely as it might be there could be another Three-Finger Miles in any pair of boots which stamped through the door. A top gun lived in constant danger, not only from old enemies but from the young and reckless men who hoped to become famous in their turn by bringing down a giant.

He was halfway through the pie and cheese and beginning to feel the warm comfort of being well fed for the first time in days when he saw the door behind the bar swing open and got his first look at the woman who stood there.

The beautiful, redhaired, ivory skinned Lady Nell was a figure to stop the eyes and race the pulse of more sophisticated men than the big rider. In a crimson dress cut low in sweeping decolletage over her magnificent breasts, with diamonds on her fingers and a necklace of three long strands of pearls and with her eyes flashing in the light of the flaring lamps above the bar mirror, she brought a sudden stop to the loud talk and laughter that had filled the room.

Everyone watched as she crossed the room and paused before the table where Buck Duane sat.

The big man pushed back his chair and started to rise with a gesture of instinctive courtesy that was alien to this wild setting. She put out her hand to stop him.

"Don't get up, Buck," she said in a voice low enough to be heard only by him. "Let me sit down with you while you eat instead."

She took the chair opposite him. Her back was to the crowd in the bar, and none of them could make out what she said.

"It's been a long time, Buck Duane," she said in her beautifully modulated voice, and laughed. "You don't recognize me, do you?"

She was right, Duane thought. He didn't recognize her for a fact. Though he'd seen and known most of the famous beauties of the wild outer fringe of settlement, none that he had ever looked at could rival this beauty.

Then he looked again. He'd not known Lady Nell, that much was certain, but there was something about the line of cheek and jaw that was somehow familiar even though strange and new. He tried to think how the mouth would look without makeup. Younger perhaps?

He said: "I have to tell you the truth. No. I don't recognize Lady Nell."

"I should be disappointed," she said, "but I can't really blame you. Look again."

He did, but recognition still eluded him.

"I said a long time," she said gravely then. "Try

almost twenty years back, Buck Duane. Try a dark night at a hidden crossing of the Rio Grande. Try riding out of the dust and wind of a norther to find two men taking a girl into the water. Think hard."

He looked and the face before him softened and grew young in memory. The face had been tear streaked but firmed with a terrible rage as the girl had struggled to free herself. He felt once more the impulse that had made an outlawed youngster pull his gun against two brutal men.

"Helen," he said.

He could see her eyes light up and a smile curve those beautiful lips.

"That's right. Helen, Little Helen Rudd, who ran away from her father's ten-cow spread over by Brazos to look for adventure and found it in a way she hadn't expected and didn't want. Helen who was being kidnaped over the border by a man she thought she loved and would have been sold into a house in Tampico if big Buck Duane hadn't come along."

"I remember now," he said.

"I've never forgotten. You were the man who listened to me out there in the middle of a stormy night. When they drew on you, you killed them both. Even then you were the fastest draw I had ever imagined. Then, instead of taking me for yourself like I half expected, you gave me money and one of their horses and told me to go on home."

"You didn't go."

"Of course I didn't," she said, not laughing now. "I told you I was a silly girl. I thought I couldn't go back and face my mother. She's dead now, I hear. So I took the road that finally led to this place instead. I own the Golconda, Buck, and a share of everything this town is going to be. Not bad, is it, for the little girl you watched ride off into the rain that night so very, very long ago?"

"Not bad at all," he said because it was what she wanted to hear from his lips.

She gave him a quizzical look.

"We've both come a long way," she said. "A long, long way, big Buck. They tell me you're the fastest gun in the West today that nobody can stand against you because you've got eyes in the back of your head and are fast enough to dodge lightning out of a summer thunderhead."

"A man learns," he said and ate the last of the pie. "It's good to see you, Helen. Very good."

"They tell me too that Skiddy's hired your gun," she said. "And don't call me Helen here. Nell. The only name they know me by is Lady Nell. Are you really with us, Buck."

"I hired on today," he said, "though I'm not really sure what for. I only heard rumors of this place, Nell. I came looking for a quiet spot, and that's the whole of it."

"It'll be quiet as far as the law goes," she said. "No posse and no hangman's noose will follow you in here. I promise it. For the rest there may be shooting before we're done. We play for high stakes, Buck, maybe the highest you've seen yet."

"I'd like to know," he said.

"Sometime I'll tell you, but not now." She reached out a hand and touched his briefly. It was a warm and vibrant touch. "For now you live easy and watch your own back. When the time comes, Skiddy will give your orders. For now there's only two rules. No fighting amongst ourselves. That's the first. The second is to guard the bank. When the alarm bell sounds, if it ever does sound, all our guns rally to the bank. It must not be robbed or broken into on any count. We have that in the bank that all our lives hang on and—"

She didn't get to finish. A man had come in through the swinging doors from the street and was walking over to the table where the two of them sat.

At first there was nothing really extraordinary about him, nothing to account for the way the wild and violent men who crowded the floor of the Golconda moved aside and made an aisle to let him through. He was of medium height and medium weight, neither thin nor unduly fat. His hair, under the expensive broad brimmed Stetson hat he wore, was a medium pepper-and-salt gray brown. He wore the black frock coat, and unpressed tailor-made trousers, the white shirt with a black string tie, the flowered vest and hand made boots that were a uniform with well-to-do townsmen in this time and place.

Nothing out of the way here. From the confident way he moved Duane assumed he was well-known locally; probably the Banker, Joseph Bacon, he'd heard mentioned.

It was only when the man was almost up to the table and raised his glance to meet Duane's that the tall rider had a shock.

The eyes were the most powerful he had ever seen with an absolutely level stare, unblinking. The pupils were gray, shot through with yellow like those of lobo wolf. They sent a cold chill down the Ranger's spine. If he lived to be a hundred, he knew that he'd never forget those eyes. They were the stuff of nightmare.

For a long moment the two men locked their gaze, and despite himself Duane felt the cold killing knot form in his gut—the strange, icy nexus that had always warmed him when the moment of decision came close. His every nerve and muscle sprang to full alert. Would he have, once more, to kill or be killed.

The two men faced each other unblinking. A circle of the wild bunch formed to watch in fascination as the terrible, unspoken duel of wills began to mount.

"Stop it, you two." It was Lady Nell who broke the spell by rising and stepping between them so that her face blocked the gaze of both and the tension suddenly broke.

"Joe, this is Buck Duane," she said. "You probably heard he came into town today and Skiddy signed him up. He's one of us, and I'm glad, because he's an old friend of mine.

"Buck, this here's our banker, Joe Bacon. Along with the sheriff and me and the judge he's one of your bosses."

The two men relaxed and nodded, but neither made any effort to shake hands. They were like two coiled and alerted serpents, each waiting for the other to strike.

"I've heard of Buck Duane," Joe Bacon said. "I've heard a lot of things about him. Some of them I'm not sure I remember very well. You say he's a friend of yours, Nell?"

"An old friend, Joe. I can speak for Buck."

"That's good," Bacon said. "but I'd like to hear it from Buck Duane himself. I'd like to hear him speak it with his own mouth. Are you one of us, Duane?"

"I signed up with your sheriff today," Buck Duane said. That at least was truth. "It was him said I was in with you. Is that enough?"

The banker stood and studied him with those strange yellow wolf eyes.

"It had better be good, Duane," he said at last, "for once you enlist with us there's no turning back." He skinned his lips in a bitter smile. Like the preacher men say, Duane, it's till death do us part. Now come on, Nell. We've business to settle in private. Leave Mr. Duane to his pleasures."

They turned away.

Duane thought: "Till death do us part." It was a sobering thought.

163

Buck Duane slept late the next morning. It was almost seven o'clock and the sun was well up before he left the shed in back of the Smithy and let Mrs. Schwartz give him a breakfast of biscuit and fried eggs and German sausage in her warm and spotless kitchen. From the way she looked at him he could tell that the good woman had heard about the killing of Three-Finger Miles. She said nothing about it to him however, nor did he expect her to do so.

After finishing a hearty breakfast Duane decided to walk up the length of Harpetown's single street. It was still early enough so that most of the wild bunch would be asleep and the streets fairly empty. He wanted to case the town, particularly the bank which he was supposed to defend at all cost. After seeing the banker he wondered even more what it might contain.

He hadn't gotten far up towards the center of town when he saw that a noisy knot of rough characters had gathered in front of one of the larger hotels up near the Golconda and the bank.

The center of attraction seemed to be a gaily painted wagon which had just driven into town, pulled by a pair of mules. This vehicle, which had obviously begun life as an Army four wheeled ambulance wagon, had been taken over by a traveling medicine show pitchman. The wagon body and wheels had been painted in vivid stripes of vermillion and yellow. The canvas sides and top were decorated with vivid depictions of howling Indians, ferocious wild beasts and oversize bottles of Indian Snake Oil.

The proprietor himself—Doctor Healzall according to his advertising signs—had tied up his mules and was standing near his wagon facing the loafers.

His slight figure was clothed in a frock coat, but

164

this one was not the usual rusty black wool. The whole left side and sleeve was of brilliant scarlet cloth and the right side of an equally shocking Prussian blue. He wore a buckskin vest sewn over with silver conchos and brass and silver coins which jingled when he moved. His trousers were white cotton and tucked into boots of bright yellow morocco leather sporting giant, jangling, Mexican style spurs.

Instead of a revolver this figure was armed with an ancient sawed off cap-and-ball shotgun of around eight gauge which was slung around his neck and one shoulder by a braided rawhide lanyard.

On his head he wore an equally old fashioned white beaver top hat with a braided rawhide band into which had been stuck the ends of three rather bedraggled peacock tail feathers.

His back was to Duane and he was apparently saying something in a low voice to the crowd of jeering loafers who had gathered to greet him.

The tall Ranger could see that the mood of the crowd was an ugly one. These were the rag tag and bobtail of the wild bunch, the saddle bums too poverty stricken to have gotten properly drunk the night before. They were dirty, hungry and hungover in the morning and considered the traveling medicine pitchman fair game for ridicule, abuse and robbery.

There was something familiar about the slight figure in the ridiculous, parti-colored frock coat. Duane lengthened his stride as he approached the group and let his hands drop near the butts of his holstered Colt's.

The action boiled up before he could get there however in a burst of yells and violence.

First one of the drunken loafers pointed at the showman and started to shout: "Hey you. I know you. You ain't no doctor but a—"

The drunken saddle bum never got to finish what he wanted to say.

The doctor's right hand and wrist twisted and flipped in a lightning fast movement which Buck Duane recognized even from the rear and at a distance of thirty of forty feet. A forty-one caliber derringer dropped out of the sleeve into the man's right hand. With the same fluid movement he flipped back the hammer and pulled trigger only a few feet from the yelling man's face.

The heavy round ball which the derringer fired went in and up through the roof of the outlaw's mouth to blow out his brains.

Almost before the others knew what had happened the doctor had pocketed his fired pistol and swung the heavy sawed-off shotgun free of his neck to cover the crowd.

At such close range the gun was as terrible a weapon as a small cannon might have been.

There were at least twenty of the wild bunch though and the gun couldn't possibly cover them all. They were drunk and mean and rousing to a killing pitch from the sight and the smell of their friend's blood.

In another second they would go for their guns with the deadly ferocity of a killing pack.

It was then that big Buck Duane appeared at the side of the slender medicine oil pitchman. The Ranger didn't even draw his guns, just let his hands swing near the butts. His voice was soft and even but the eyes he swept their faces with were like two bits of chilled blue steel.

His gaze swept over the men, chilling each one as his eyes touched theirs. This was no stranger in an outlandish rig, but one of the famous gunfighters of all time, a figure to start fear in the boldest heart. Insensibly the mob that was forming fell apart into its component units. No one of those units dared to face the big rider down.

"Let's all hold it now," the Ranger said in his calm even drawl. "This here feller fired in self defense. The man he shot badmouthed him and was reaching for a gun. We all saw that."

His cold eyes dared any man of them to deny that they had seen it as he said. There was no one bold enough to accept the challenge.

"We all know the sheriff's rules," Buck Duane went on in that same easy tone. "In this town we draw on each other only in self defense. Your friend broke that rule and when he did he risked everything that makes it a safe town for all of us. The medicine man here had the law to draw. The only thing we can do now is to forget the whole thing."

Nobody said a word in answer.

"You've heard what I said," Duane told them implacably. "I'd take it personal if anything happens to this man for the shooting."

They turned away then. The protection of the tall man's terrible guns had been given to the gaudily dressed stranger. In ones and twos the erstwile mob drifted back to their favorite bars.

Only one man remained nearby. Never part of the mob, he had watched the whole incident from where he leaned against a store front about thirty feet up the street. It was the sheriff's deputy, Sam.

Buck Duane himself turned to continue his walk up the street.

"I'm mighty grateful to you, mister," the medicine man said. He took off the outlandish tophat and mopped his brow with a blue bandanna handkerchief.

"Why that's all right," Duane said carelessly. "It's just that I'm partial to fair play."

"I'd like to give you a couple of bottles of my medicine for thanks," the other said. "Just for a token, say. It's good for anything that ails a man from foot corns to bad blood."

"Not now," Duane said. "I eat at the Golconda if you look for me later and I live at the Smith's. It's not needed though."

Then he walked on up the street, nodding a greeting as he passed the watching Sam. He wondered how much Sam had noticed.

The little medicine pitchman was the Jackrabbit Kid.

In spite of his surprise at seeing his friend the Kid in Harpetown, Buck Duane went on to finish his original purpose of looking over the bank building.

To his disappointment he found it a veritable fort. The walls of log and adobe were by at least four feet thick, to judge by the window embrasures. The windows themselves were small and heavily barred with iron. There was a small room built on the second floor, with windows from which the roof could be defended and water poured on any firebrands thrown up by attackers.

The place was a fort, and the adjoining office of Sheriff DaVinci, which was staffed at all times at least a couple of his death's head deputies, provided a ready made garrison of hardened and professional gunfighters in case of attack.

If the proof of conspiracy that Captain MacNelly and the Governor needed really was stored in that building, Duane began to wonder if he would ever manage to get it out.

While he was out on the street he pretty well covered the rest of the town. Without appearing to be particularly interested, his trained eyes nevertheless etched an indelible map of the town and its features on his brain for future reference.

He noted the alleys and rear exits of buildings, the approach and escape routes he might need by day or night.

The rear of the Golconda he found to be a real

strong point, like the bank across the street. As he came out of the alley running along the side of the saloon and gambling hall he encountered Sam the deputy on the board sidewalk.

"Morning, Buck," the deputy said aimiably, "You seem to be getting a mite of exercise today."

Duane said only: "Morning, Sam," and kept on walking down the street.

That afternoon he saddled Bullet and rode out to look over the country around the town just as he had inspected the streets and buildings during the morning. It was a precaution learned during the outlaw days and never since neglected by the tall Ranger. He made a wide sweep that completely circled the town. As far as he could tell nobody followed or showed any interest in his activities.

In the evening Buck Duane went back to the Golconda to eat his dinner. It was the center of all the really important activity in the town in any case. Whatever he wanted to learn would be known to someone there.

He took the same table he had used the night before, hoping that Lady Nell might once more join him. She didn't. This time it was Sheriff Skiddy DaVinci who came in the swinging doors, spotted Duane where he sat, and came over.

"Mind if I eat with you?" the darkly handsome sheriff said. It wasn't really a question. The man moved about this room with an air of easy command that would have allowed for no refusal. The diamond stickpin in his black syock flashed back the lamplight as did the sinister gold star with its grinning death's head design.

Duane merely nodded and waited while the sheriff got his dinner, hot and steaming, on a tray from the kitchen. They must have known when he'd be in and been waiting, for a girl brought out the food as soon as he had sat down. Along with it came a full bottle of good imported Scotch whiskey.

The sheriff pitched into his meal.

After a while he wiped his mouth with a fresh linen napkin which looked strangely out of place in those surroundings and condescended to address the man across the table.

"I hear you had a bit of trouble this morning."

"No trouble at all," said the laconic Ranger.

"Something about a medicine show man had got himself into some sort of trouble?"

"No trouble at all," Duane repeated. "Some loafers spotted this feller when he drove into town I guess and figured to have some fun ragging him. When the man stood up for himself they were just drunk and rough enough to get dangerous. He had to shoot one in self defense."

"Any particular reason for you to stand up for the medicine doc?"

The question sounded casual enough, but Duane wasn't quite sure if it was. He kept his own manner unruffled when he answered.

"Just law and order," he said and then had to laugh at using those words in this place. "You said keep the lid on and I figured if the word got round we let peddlers and such get shot up, none of them would come to town. We going to live here, we'll need the notions and truck that sort bring in their wagons. I did right, didn't I?"

"Oh, you did right enough, I guess. No need to let a bunch of drunks scare off legitimate trading men. It's just that something about this doc sort of stuck in the craw of one of my boys. Wonder if you have any idea why that might be."

"None at all," Duane said. "I never saw nor heard tell of this one before. You tell Sam he's jumping at

170

shadows this time."

"I didn't say it was Sam."

"You didn't have to," Buck Duane said. "I saw him watching. Wondered why he didn't step down to help me, him and me both working for the same boss, so to speak."

That seemed to take the sheriff aback. He drank some more of the whiskey and wiped his mouth again. It was a habit he had.

"I didn't think of that, but I guess you got a point there, Buck. Probably thought you didn't need no help."

"Why don't you ask him?" Duane said. "He's been over there at the bar watching us for five minutes running now."

The sheriff grinned at that. He lifted a hand and beckoned without even turning his head. Sam saw the gesture and started to walk over to the table. He wore two guns and had a shotgun cradled in his left arm. He said: "Yes, Skiddy?" to the sheriff.

"Buck here wants to know how come you didn't help him break up that ruckus this morning," the sheriff said.

"Because I didn't like that there little rat in the fancy duds," Sam said. "Maybe he got shot it'd been okay with me. Does that satisfy you, Buck?"

"No," Duane said. "It doesn't."

"Then how about this?" Sam said. "I don't like you neither. Something smells wrong about you ever since you come into this town. Someways that medicine doc is mixed up with it. I don't trust neither of you."

He had swung the muzzle of the shotgun to cover Duane, and his hand was creeping back towards the trigger.

"Just hold everything right there," Buck Duane said quietly in his deep Texas drawl. "My hands are under the table, gents. One of them has a cocked

171

Colt's pointed straight at Sam's belly. I'll pull the trigger if he gets anywheres near the trigger on that shotgun. The other is aimed for your mid-section, Sheriff, just in case you got any notion of taking a hand in this game."

Duane's voice was low and serious, but his eyes and the set of the lean jaw were deadly. Men in the big room began to notice, by the sure instinct of the hunted, that a crisis was born and insensibly, without any word being spoken, a clear lane opened behind Sam as they moved out of Duane's line of fire. They weren't sure yet what was up, but they played safe.

"See here, Buck," Sheriff DaVinci said, and his voice too was steady. "I don't know what this's all about and that's a fact, but I'm taking no part in it." He put both hands flat down on the table top in front of him. "See?"

Duane ignored him. "I don't know what's troubling you, friend," he said to Sam, "but if you got a play to make, this is the time. Otherwise put that gun away and we'll forget it."

"No," Sam almost shouted. His face was contorted. "There's something phony about you, Duane. If I could just remember what I know. You ain't what you say. I'm calling your hand right now."

"I think you're crazy," the sheriff said. Nobody paid any attention to him.

Sam started to back away from the table.

"Stand up," he said to Duane. "Stand up like a man. I'll let you get on your feet."

He moved a quick step to the side to place the seated DaVinci's body between himself and the guns Buck Duane held under the table.

As soon as he thought he was shielded, Sam's hand shot back to the trigger guard of the shotgun.

There must have been a hundred men and women in the big barroom at the Golconda. A dead silence

172

had fallen and every eye was fixed on the two gunfighters, yet afterwards no two could ever agree on just exactly what had happened.

Duane was out from behind the table and on his feet with a movement almost too fast for the eye to follow. His guns were held waist high in steady hands.

Sam had the shotgun levelled and fired instantly, but he fired where Duane had been only a split second before. The charge of buckshot splintered the back of the chair where the Ranger had been sitting, and buried itself in the wall behind.

He never had a chance to fire the second barrel.

The heavy slug from Duane's right hand Colt's took Sam squarely in the heart. He was dead before his twisted and broken body hit the floor.

Buck Duane pushed an unbroken chair into place at the table and sat down facing Sheriff DaVinci. The movement with which he holstered his guns was so swift and sure that none of the watchers could be certain when he did it.

"Well, Sheriff," he said then in the same calm drawl he'd used moments before, "if you don't mind, I think I could use a glass of that whiskey of yours."

DaVinci relaxed visibly and then shoved the bottle across the table top to the big Ranger.

"Take the whole bottle if you want, Buck," he said. "You need a drink anyway to celebrate. Take all you want."

Duane poured two fingers of the imported whiskey into a tumbler and tossed it off easily. Only then did he ask: "Celebrate?"

"Your new job," the sheriff told him. "Sam was my number one deputy here because he could outdraw and outshoot any other gun in town except me. You beat him and he's down. That means his job is yours. The badge he was wearing belongs on your shirt from this point on."

173

Buck Duane sat at the table with his face an impassive mask, but behind that mask his mind was racing. When he had shot Sam it was in self defense and without the slightest idea it would mean that he'd inherit the deptuy's job. Duane had never in his life killed a man to gain a personal advantage for himself.

Undoubtedly Sam had remembered or started to remember something about Duane's working for the Rangers. There was a suspicion in his mind which might well have led to the exposure of the Ranger and disaster for his mission. Fortunately for Buck Duane, Sam hadn't waited for his memory to clear, but had forced the issue on suspicion alone.

That had been his fatal mistake. He had paid the price in full. The only question remaining in the Ranger's mind was as to how much of his suspicion the dead deputy had managed to confide or convey to the sheriff. He didn't think he had done that though. DaVinci had taken no part in the fight.

As it was Duane had suddenly found himself in the best possible position to carry out his instructions from Captain MacNelly. As chief deputy he'd be able to move about freely and get into places that would otherwise be barred to him.

"If you've finished out here," DaVinci said with a wry glance from the dinner plates to the floor where his erstwhile ramrod still lay in a pool of blood, "we'd better go into the back and talk to the rest of your new bosses."

Duane got up without a word and followed him. On the way to the door behind the bar the sheriff stooped down and took the badge off Sam's shirt and tossed it to Duane.

"Get rid of that body," he said to the crowd. "Buck here is taking over Sam's job."

That made it official.

They didn't go upstairs to Lady Nell's quarters this time. Even a chief deputy didn't quite rate that. The big inner office, furnished in part like a sitting room was luxurious enough however. Lady Nell and Judge Lorimer were waiting for them there.

"Where's Joe Bacon?" DaVinci asked.

"He rode out of town a couple of hours ago," the judge told them. "Said he had to meet the Boss in Kansas City for a council of war. Independence Day for Free Texas is getting close."

"Great news, eh Buck," the sheriff said.

Duane nodded. "Couldn't be better. Now that I'm here though, shouldn't I know who this boss is?"

They all three looked at him as if he'd opened a box and let out a rattlesnake on the floor of the room. Finally the judge said forcefully, "that's the one thing you don't ask about, Duane. The boss wears a mask when he rides into town, and as far as you're concerned that mask stays on. All you got to know is he's the Boss and we give you his orders."

Duane reached up his hand to the coin silver Death Head badge so newly pinned to his shirt. "If you don't trust me, maybe I hadn't ought to be wearing this."

"It's not that we don't trust you, Buck," Lady Nell said. "It ain't like that at all. The boss is an Easterner, I think. He works out in the open most of the time. If it were known who he was, he couldn't do the things he does. He even wears the mask when he talks to us, Buck. I wouldn't lie to you."

Duane sat quietly and appeared to be thinking. Then: "I guess that's fair enough."

"It has got to be fair enough," Skiddy DaVinci said then, and his voice was as cold and even as Duane's own. "You work for us, Duane. That means we give the orders. To be exact, as far as you're concerned, I give the orders . You don't ask any questions. Matter of fact you don't even think any questions. Any time you get any different notions you just turn in that badge and get out of town. Otherwise you'd have to be killed, and if I say you get killed, you're gonna see every gun in town on you all at once. Not even you'd last a minute. Understand?"

"Don't get me wrong," Duane said. "I just asked. If that's the way it is, why should I try to be different?"

"That's the way it is," DaVinci said in the same icy tones. "The Boss does the thinking, and I give the orders. That's the way it is and the way it's going to be."

"I understand. No argument now that I know."

The sheriff relaxed. "Okay. Now you know. So now while you're here we better tell you just what your job will be from now on out."

The Ranger sat back and listened.

Two hours later as Buck Duane stretched out on his bedroll in the shack back of Schwartz's blacksmith shop he heard a very gentle tapping on the door. When he opened it, very carefully, his friend the Jackrabbit Kid slipped in. The Kid had shed his elaborate medicine man costume and wore the usual Levis, vest and heavy wool shirt. He also wore his guns.

There were no chairs in the shack, so the two of them squatted on their heels, cowboy fashion, to talk.

"You shouldn't have risked coming to town," Duane said.

"I had a talk with your friend, Cap MacNelly. He seemed to think you could use all the help you could find up here." Then the Kid laughed. "Besides I always wanted to try the medicine doc pitch. I like it. I've been making a fortune selling tonic and Kickapoo Snake Oil Liniment all the way up here. But never mind that, Mister Chief Deputy. Do you

176

think you can get what Cap sent you up here after?"

"Enough of it," Duane said, "but it's not going to be easy. At least I found out most of what I need to know tonight. After the sheriff gave me the new badge he and the others briefed me on what goes on here. They pretty much had to."

"DaVinci's the boss then?" Jackrabbit asked.

"No he isn't. He and Nell and the judge and Banker Bacon run things here all right but there seems to be somebody else over them. He lives someplace in the East and is always masked when he comes here, which isn't often. We may not be able to get to him from here, unless he happens to be in town when we make our play, and that ain't likely."

"Why not wait till he does show up?"

"For two good reasons, Kid. In the first place we got to move fast. This Boss is about ready to put his Independence Bill through Congress. We got to spoil his play before he gets the chance to do that. Every day we wait from now on is a danger to Texas, so we got to move fast. Second, I'm sure we can spoil their play from right here, even if we never do see that Boss. Let the Government nail him after we draw his fangs, or the Governor down in Austin. It makes no difference once we've beat the pat hand he thinks he holds."

"I guess that's right."

"It has to be right, Kid. Like I say we can't afford to wait. What we want won't be easy to get though. It's in the bank here, in the strongest vault between New Orleans and San Francisco."

"Money?"

"No not money. Oh, they got some of course, but they don't need much money in a place like this. The real war chest is on deposit in Eastern banks. The thing they're guarding here is a tin box of papers. It's the names and stories of the men they control in Congress. The names of the the financiers who are really backing this play. It's the evidence they use to blackmail people in high places, proof of the bribes this Boss has paid and what he expects to get for it. If we can get that box out and to the Governor, the whole plot's finished."

They sat in silence for a time. The Kid rolled himself a Bull Durham cigarette and lit it with a sulphur match scratched on the heel of his boot.

Finally he said: "You got a plan?"

"I been trying hard to think of one," Buck Duane admitted. "The nut of the whole thing is how to bust that vault. It's not a steel vault like they say the New York banks have of course, but it's locked and double locked and padlocked. Take at least five keys to get through that door, and I don't even know who holds those keys."

"I do," the Kid said, and grinned at the expression on his big friend's face. "One reason I picked the medicine doc act was so I could use the wagon to pack along some doodads Cap and I figured you could maybe use but couldn't pack in on a horse. I got blasting powder enough to take that whole building down. Trouble is after that we still got to face the sheriff and every gun in town."

"Don't worry about that," Duane said. "With that powder for a key, I got a plan."

The following day Buck Duane went looking for Lady Nell in the Golconda. He had to wait until late in the afternoon before she would be up and about, but when he sent in his name he was admitted to the back office without any trouble.

"I'm glad you came, Buck," she said with a smile as soon as he sat down. "I been hoping that what with the new job and all you and me could get to be friends."

"I never been anything but your friend," he said.

"Oh I know that, but it wasn't what I meant. I mean to get to see each other more and really get to know each other. I been hearing a lot about you all these years, Buck, and it's all been things I liked."

Duane smiled at her. "I hope so too, Nell. So far this here town has sure been good to me. No reason it shouldn't go right on being that way. Which brings me to what I come over to talk about. It seems like all I've done in this town so far is use my guns, which is all right so far as it goes, but I don't want to start off being nothing but hated. Folks have got to be some afraid of a man in my job. I grant that, but why be any more unpopular than I have to be."

She threw back her beautiful head and laughed. "I do declare, Mister Duane, you got the makings of a politician inside you some place. So what do you want to do about it?"

"Why," Buck Duane said, "I been thinking about that this morning. What I want to do is throw a party for this town, that's what. Feed the boys and liquor them up good to celebrate my new job. How does that strike you."

"It strikes me as a real good idea," she said seriously. "Just what do you have in mind."

"Saturday's only two days off," he said. "Must be somebody in this town can barbecue good meat. I buy a steer and a couple hogs and pay to have a pit dug out back of your place down towards the creek. Then I'll buy all the beer and whiskey the boys and girls can drink. Start in the afternoon and by dark they should be drunk enough to come up here and let your dealers take their money at faro and poker. How does that strike you?"

"It strikes me fine," she said. "It surely does."

By Saturday the news of the party Buck Duane was throwing had reached every man and woman in Harpetown, and everyone was planning to take full

179

advantage of the opportunities it would offer for a riotous drunk.

The sky was heavily overcast that morning as a solid wall of cloud blew up all the way from Mexico and the Gulf and there was promise of rain later in the day, but that failed to dampen the spirits of the celebrants. The barbecue cooks had dug their pits and began heating rocks the day before and were up and hard at work long before dawn so that savory odors blew on the winds.

Kegs of beer had been broached and also the smaller kegs of the fiery potion most of the drifters and gunmen dignified with the name of whiskey. By nine in the morning the bars overflowed and revelers staggered and reeled through the streets.

Duane himself and one other deputy were on guard inside the bank. That institution stayed open till noon on Saturdays to accommodate the saloon and brothel keepers, merchants and gamblers who wanted to withdraw or deposit funds.

Just before closing time there were at least eight or ten men transacting business in the front room of the place as well as a single teller behind the partition. The single front door stood wide open to the street. The rear door to the alleyway behind was closed and locked as was the heavily barred oak door to the walled-off cubicle called the vault.

The men in the front room were fully occupied with their own affairs and payed no attention as the Jackrabbit Kid, again wearing his normal rider's clothing instead of the medicine doc rig, came in from the street. He walked quietly and easily and there was nothing unusual about him except for the small round keg he carried under one arm. Nobody noticed that.

The vault itself occupied a space about ten feet by six in the left rear of the ground floor as one came in the door. Its wall, facing the street, was blank and formed a rear wall to the space railed off for the teller. The massive vault door opened parallel to the rear wall of the building. It faced a desk where the bank president sat to transact business. On this morning Joe Bacon was still out of town and the desk was unoccupied.

The Kid walked to the rear of the room and set the small keg directly in front of the vault door. About a foot of slow burning blasting fuse stuck out of the bung hole of the keg. The Kid leaned over and lit the end of the fuse from the glowing coal of the cigar he was smoking. Then he ran out the front door into the street.

The men in the bank heard the fuse start to sputter and hiss and looked to see what was causing the noise.

Just in case any one of them might have missed the point Duane yelled: "My God! That's a powder keg with a lit fuse."

The men bolted for the door, yelling and jostling.

The bank teller was an elderly man who suffered from arthritis and a bad conscience concerning certain embezzlements back in Arkansas, but he reacted like a youngster. Instead of running around the partition behind which he stood, he vaulted the counter with one bound and beat a couple of the customers to the door.

Buck Duane went the other way, getting behind the counter and flattening himself against the blind wall of the vault. He had hoped the other deputy would run for the street, but the man followed Buck's example instead.

The fuse was slow burning and the last of the terrified bank customers was out on the street before the little keg of powder exploded.

When it did it blew out the lower half of the vault door and filled the room with suffocating smoke.

"It's a robbery," Duane yelled to his half stunned

deputy. "Shoot anybody tries to come through that front door."

He himself went round the corner of the vault wall fast, stooped over and slipped through the shattered lower half of the door into the vault itself.

The little room was nearly pitch dark and half full of smoke from the explosion, but Duane had been shown the location of the small, iron dispatch box he was supposed to defend at all costs. He hefted the box, looked to make sure he had the right one, and then waited there in the choking half dark.

Just outside he heard the crash of a fired Colt's as his deputy obeyed orders and fired at someone trying to get into the bank. Yells and shouts told him that drunken men and women, coming from the street and the barbecue pits behind the Golconda, were converging to form a confused and angry mob in the street.

Buck Duane waited and smiled to himself.

The crash of the second explosion jolted the tall Ranger even through the shelter of the thick vault walls against which he crouched.

After lighting the fuse inside the bank the Jackrabbit Kid had gone out the front door and slipped back through the alley alongside the building before the powder exploded and attracted the crowd. Then, while everyone was congregating in front of the bank, he'd touched off a second powder charge to blow the rear door off its hinges.

Duane slipped out of the vault and through the broken rear door with the speed and agility of a coyote slipping through a rock pile. Not even his own deputy, who was still preparing to defend the front entrance, really saw him go.

The Kid had horses, his own and Duane's magnificent Bullet, tethered a bare two hundred yards away, and the two of them were mounted and riding off at a gallop within minutes after the second explosion and long before anyone in the town could possibly have realized what had actually taken place.

Only when they were over the first rise of land and safely out of sight of Harpetown, did the Kid slow his horse's headlong pace and pull up close to his big friend.

"Went off just like clockwork like you said it would, Buck," he said then. "Pretty as a picture, and I figure that little box you're totting there spells the finish of New Texas."

"Only if we get it back to Cap MacNelly's hands," Duane said. "There's a Ranger patrol waiting for it down the line, but because of the way this country's watched from Harpetown, they had to stay at least a couple of day's ride away."

"We can dodge those patrols easy, you and me."

"I'm not worried about the patrols," Duane said. "That DaVinci's no fool. He'll have this deal figured and be after us before we know it. He's a real fighting man, and he'll have trackers like Comanche George to make sure he finds us. This ain't over yet, Kid."

"I guess it isn't," the Kid said then. "Here comes the first of them now, and a lot faster than we figured."

A single rider on a beautiful dun mare had topped the rise behind them and was coming up from the direction of the town at a hard gallop. The Kid slid his Winchester carbine from his saddle boot.

"Put that thing away," Duane said, watching the rider's approach. "There's no need for shooting here."

He was right, and the Kid realized it as the speeding dun mare grew closer. The rider was a woman wearing a man's shirt and pants and bent low over the pomel of her saddle.

"It's the gambling house woman," the Kid said in surprise.

It was in fact Lady Nell. She rode swiftly up to

183

them and then reined in her mount.

"You didn't think you could fool me, did you, Buck Duane?" she said and brushed the long hair back from her face with one hand. "I figured what you were up to as soon as you were gone and came after you as fast as I could get mounted."

"Where's the posse?" the Kid asked her.

"I don't know and I don't care," she said. "Still running around in circles waiting for Skiddy to get them organized I suppose. They'll be along."

"Then why are you here?" This time it was the tall Ranger who spoke.

"Because I've got sense enough to know it's all up and done with back in Harpetown now. You blew the Bank to get the evidence that would end the whole plan. I know that, and I also know it'll take more than the riff-raff DaVinci can bring after you to get it back. There's nothing for me to stay there for now."

"I'm not so sure," Duane said.

"I am," she told him. "Take me with you, Buck. Maybe it's not too late for me to get back on that trail you pointed me to that night so many years ago. At least give me the chance."

The tall man sat his horse for a long moment before he answered. "I can't, Helen," he said then, using her real name. "I'm a Ranger. You must have guessed that by now. If I took you with me, I'd have to turn you in to the law for your part in the Harpetown plot. I don't want to do that. We're old friends and you've helped me a lot here.

"Better that you go back to Harpetown now. Get your money together and move on. If you aren't with me I can forget to tell the law about you. They'll be after the really big game.

"Perhaps we can meet again, if you're serious in what you just said. Then I think I can help you. You understand?"

184

They sat and faced each other while the Kid drew his mount a little way off. When she finally spoke her voice was steady though he could have sworn her eyes were moist.

"I understand. Later on I hope—I honestly do hope, Buck Duane. Oh, believe me, I do hope it's not too late."

She turned and rode away.

Harpetown was situated in rough country on the northern rim of the famous Staked Plains. Though not actually in that wild tangle of rock and mesa and blind canyon it was still a broken land that surrounded the town.

The two friends rode hard for a couple of hours and then pulled up behind a pile of boulders just over the brow of a hill, where they could watch a couple of miles of their own back trail. Duane wanted to rest the horses and hold a final conference with the Kid.

"Some sort of posse will be hot on our trail by now," he said. "You sure you planted that wagon of yours exactly the way I told you?"

"You can bet I'm sure, Buck," Jackrabbit answered. "I spent all yesterday and most of the day before setting up exactly what you wanted. Those boys from town gonna get the surprise of their dumb lives. I still don't see why we don't just out run them though."

"Because they'll have relays of horses and they're real tough boys to start with," Duane said. "Sooner or later DaVinci will catch up with us, and I'd rather he did it when I want him to and when I'm ready for him. That way we got the edge, and that's what makes all the difference."

They sat for a moment, smoking and watching the back trail.

"I still wish we could have got the boss of this whole shebang," the Kid said reflectively. "You don't think there's a chance Sheriff DaVinci is him?"

"No, I don't," Duane said. "Not any chance at all. This Boss operates mostly in the East and the sheriff hasn't left Harpetown since it started. Anyway I'm pretty sure they'll find enough evidence inside this strong box we're carrying to spot the man for sure, that is once they cut it open and get to study the papers. This Boss is fixed right now as sure as if we had him under our guns."

"Suppose they don't?"

"Then his fangs are drawn anyhow. His scheme is ruined. Let him run. Besides I think I know who he is right now."

"Who?"

"It's easy enough to figure," the Ranger said. "He has to keep his identity hid in Harpetown and his Harpetown connection hid in Washington. At the same time he has to go back and forth between the two places and he can't be in both at once. Who is it that's always gone from Harpetown when the masked Boss rides in? Who's in Harpetown when the Boss isn't in Washington? Who's the only man out here with the education and the connections to operate in the East? Comes and goes all the time like this Boss would have to? Who's the toughest and slickest man in this whole snake pit? Think, boy."

"The banker," Jackrabbit said.

"That's it. For my money when they open this box it'll be Banker Joe Bacon the papers point to. You bet on it."

Far off on the back trail there was a flicker of motion. No eye less keen than that of the owlhoot trained master tracker Buck Duane would have made it out, but he did and got to his feet.

"Here come the boys," he said to the Kid. "Let's

186

go and start the party so they'll be ready when they get here."

The two men rode on together for another mile, not trying to hurry. There, in a small wooded draw, they found Jackrabbit's Medicine Wagon with the two hobbled mules grazing peacefully nearby.

It was the work of minutes to get the mules hitched and the wagon rolling out across country. Just a half mile ahead a line of flat-topped table buttes reared itself like a solid wall pierced by one narrow but clearly defined pass which offered the only road for a wagon to get through. The Kid, on the driver's seat, headed straight for this pass. Duane rode near the wagon, leading the Kid's mount.

The two friends were still a good way from the pass when a dark knot of riders came boiling up over the lip of the last rise of land some way behind. A chorus of yells coming down the wind signaled that the posse had sighted them.

The Kid had the mules at a run, but it was clear that the vengeful riders behind were coming up fast. In spite of that the two fugitives stayed with the wildly careening, gaudily painted wagon until they were outside of the narrow cleft of the pass, and their foes were less than an eighth of a mile behind.

Then the Kid suddenly pulled the wagon to a halt and he and Duane uncoupled the mules and sent them galloping at the pass. The two riders then swung back onto their horses and set off at a run after the mules.

In the dust and confusion, and the whooping excitement of the chase, none of the posse noticed the Kid duck under the wagon canvas for a moment just before riding away.

In that instant he managed to light the fuse, carefully measured in advance, to his last small keg of blasting powder. The smoke of its burning was masked by the wagon top.

Duane and the Kid galloped into the pass, only three hundred yards from where they had left the wagon with its lethal charge and quickly got their mounts around the first slight bend.

Behind them the posse, stretched out on their galloping ponies and whooping with excitement, came on. Reaching the stranded wagon the group split to pass it on both sides.

Duane and the Kid had timed the powder fuse as carefully as they could, but it was impossible to know exactly how long it would burn, or even when the posse would reach the danger zone.

As it was the spearhead of pursuit had passed the wagon before the powder keg blew, sending showers of jagged splinters into men and horses. Beasts were stunned or killed by the shock. Men rolled bleeding and screaming in the wiry, knee high High Plains grass. The very ground shook from the force of the explosion.

Riders at the tail of the posse who had not come up close enough to be hurt turned tail and fled in terror. A tall pillar of black powder smoke shot up into the blue and at its foot wounded men and beasts scrambled and shrieked out in terror.

Sheriff DaVinci and three others, better mounted than the rest, had gotten far enough past the wagon to escape the force of the explosion. They pulled their terrified beasts to a halt.

Behind them the posse fled or bled and died in utter ruin. Ahead was the mouth of the narrow pass between the two largest of the table-top mesas.

Out of that pass onto the level ground the Jackrabbit Kid and Buck Duane came riding side by side.

The men with Sheriff DaVinci, half stunned with shock and terror, had no stomach to face the terrible, grim tall rider and his friend. They turned

188

their ponies' heads and ran.

The sheriff was made of sterner stuff. He knew that for him there was no choice, no running and no escape. If he ran from Buck Duane he would forever be a haunted man whom no one feared. His personal prestige would be blackened and ruined forever. The loss of the iron box would destroy all that Harpetown stood for.

He could only stand and fight. If he could kill the tall rider everything would be won back again. It was his only choice.

He got down from his horse, slapped the beast away, and stood stiff-legged and braced in the grass to wait his enemy.

At the sight Duane got down from his own big Bullet, let the Kid take the rein, and walked forward towards the sheriff.

Above their heads the gray curtain of clouds blown up from the Gulf so far away shut out the sun. A pair of buzzards circled below the clouds as if they sensed a kill or waited for the bodies still warm around the blasted wagon.

Duane came on at an even pace. He saw the sheriff's ice cold eyes under dark brows, the muscles tensed like those of a coiled and deadly serpent as he waited to draw.

A slight wind blew the grass so that it rustled and tugged against the Ranger's boots as he advanced.

Deep in the pit of his stomach he felt the forming of that icy killer knot that the big Ranger knew so well. His own muscles were tensed and ready, his whole attention focussed on the man who waited there for him.

DaVinci held his breath. He knew just when he'd make his play. He was fast with a gun, so fast that he'd never yet been beaten in fair fight. Now desperation steeled his nerves. Perhaps he could take even the legendary Buck Duane: He had to.

The Ranger came abreast of the clump of bluebonnet flower in the grass that DaVinci had chosen for a marker and the sheriff went for his guns.

He was lightning fast. He got both guns clear of the leather, which no other living man could have managed against Buck Duane.

And then he died with his guns still unfired. The big Ranger had been faster still, The sheriff died and with him Harpetown and the hopes and plans of the men who had made Harpetown.

When Buck Duane was still on his way to report to Captain MacNelly in Austin a family was making preparations for a funeral far away in New Orleans. But this was no ordinary family and the dead man wasn't just another corpse. The family name was DaVinci and its many members, even cousins to the eighth removal, had journeyed long distances, by train, riverboat, stagecoach, carriage and on horseback, to pay their last respects to the man known on the frontier as "Skiddy." Such was not his given name, of course, and while the man who wore it had brought them sorrow in life, now they were gathered to honor him in death. In the city across the river from New Orleans known as Algiers the dead outlaw sheriff was known of only as Benito. In his time he had come far from his respectable Italian origins. First, he had Americanized his name to Ben, much to his family's disapproval, for they were proud above all, and then for some reason no one knew or could remember, he had become "Skiddy." A few thought the name had come from his dexterity with cards; the way a crooked dealer can "skid" cards off the bottom, or any other way he likes. Anyway, whatever its origin, the name stuck—and he had died with it.

All the DaVincis were there: old Michele, dark

and hot-eyed, who had grown fat and prosperous as a tobacco importer in Tampa. Federico, his brother, a few years younger and rail-thin where Michele was fat, had left his successful shipping business in Savannah. Antonio, another uncle, for years a power in Philadelphia politics, had arrived by train. Then there were all the cousins, some so Americanized that they spoke Italian haltingly, had come when the word spread from New Orleans, family center of the DaVincis.

Pietro DaVinci's father had been dead for many years. A proud man, the leading Italian importer in New Orleans, Angelo DaVinci had died of shame, so it was said. He had tried to reason with the boy, and when that failed he beat him. Nothing did any good. The boy, later to become notorious as Skiddy DaVinci, wanted no part of his father's business. A life of office routine, bills of lading, wayward creditors, meetings for prominent merchants, had no interest for him. There was a whole world outside the confines of his business-minded family; and he wanted to see it, to be a part of it. The quarreling had gone on between father and son; it didn't end until the War Between the States, as it was known in New Orleans, broke out—and so did the boy. Though he wasn't more than fifteen when Fort Sumpter was fired on, Benito DaVinci enlisted in the colorful and soon-to-be-famous New Orleans Zouaves; he had served under General Beauregard in several major battles. Now and then he wrote to his mother, never to his father, and said he was helping to win the war for the South. In time his father became proud of him, especially when he was decorated for bravery at Shiloh. When the flag bearer was mortally wounded, Benito DaVinci, now Ben, picked up the Stars and Bars before it touched the ground and ran forward in a rain of bullets.

Back in New Orleans his father bragged that

Benito was made of the right stuff. Blood would tell, the father said. Terrible though it was, the war would make a man out of young Benito, and he would come home older and wiser, ready to take up the responsibilities of a man, of a DaVinci, for the family had grown richer even while the Confederacy plunged toward ruin. Wisely, they had divested themselves of their land holdings and concentrated their business enterprises in the cities. There was a great future waiting for Benito DaVinci, everybody said.

But Benito didn't want the future they had planned for him. Bad or good, he wanted to make his own life. There was a restlessness about him that seemed almost to vibrate. In some way he was a throwback to some wild bandit ancestor roaming the craggy mountains of Sicily, living only to plunder, laughing at the soldiers and police, finally dying as defiantly as he had lived. If Benito had any such thoughts he kept them to himself. The darkly handsome boy grew into a reckless, arrogant man who fascinated women and evoked fear and respect in men. So, seeking adventure, he turned his face to the West, to the Mississippi and the great rolling plains beyond. On the great steamboats, in the glittering, mirrored salons where tens of thousands of dollars were gambled away day and night, he became a legend. Here he got the name he bore for the rest of his life. Skiddy was hardly a flattering name, but in his perverse way he liked it, because he knew its taint of the cardsharp and the trickster would annoy his very proper father. He became as fast with a gun as he was with a deck of cards, and one hand suited him as well as the other. Yet despite his name as a fast gun, or because of it, perhaps, men challenged against him. Some were fast and some were just pretty good. It made no difference. He killed them, as they came. In his twisted way he prized honor above all. Whatever else they said about him, and they said many things, in truth no one could call him a coward. In Natchez, wildest of the brawling river towns, he went into a dark, locked room with four men, and when the shooting and stabbing was over, Skiddy DaVinci was the only one who came out alive. Wounded badly, hardly able to stand, but still alive.

Tired of life on the river, where there were no more challenges, he went to Texas, where there was much use for his iron nerve and fast gun. Notoriety grew as the bodies piled up. He was in Mexico for a while, fighting in some well financed but hopeless revolution. News of his exploits drifted back from Central America. But always he returned to Texas because this was the most wide-open country of all, an empire within an empire. Texas had been part of the United States for years, but its bond with the Union was still loose. Once it had been a republic coveted by the British and the French. Today it was American but there were greedy, ambitious men who saw it as a prize to be taken by connivance or force. Part of it, anyway. And that was how Skiddy DaVinci finally came, after all his wanderings, to the place called Harpetown. There, far from the centers of law, Skiddy DaVinci hoped to become a power, a founding father of an outlaw state, a dictatorship of criminals ruled by a few criminals smarter and more ruthless than all the others. It was an idea far ahead of its time, and it almost succeeded. It was an idea born of a master criminal's mind and only by the Grace of God... and a tall, tough, laconic under-cover Texas Ranger named Buck Duane...

And now Skiddy DaVinci was dead.

People often remarked that Captain MacNelly, known through Texas as "Mister Law and Order," should have rated a better office. He should have, but the short, wiry man who bossed the Rangers, just didn't give a damn. The office he had suited him fine. It was a dusty, cluttered room full of papers, saddles and guns, and he liked it the way it was. Everytime a new Governor was elected he paid a call on the grizzled Irishman. In many ways, MacNelly wasn't just the state's top lawdog. He was a power in his own right, an institution. So they all came for their own reasons and they all tried to get him to move to better quarters. They tempted him with hardwood floors polished to a shine, new furniture, a view of the Capitol building, even a private lavatory, one the other Rangers didn't mess up when they used it. The answer from MacNelly was always a polite but firm no. To MacNelly his shabby office, his battered table that served as a desk, were like an old and comfortable pair of boots.

"I got it broke in just right," MacNelly always said. "Why mess around when you got a good thing going for you."

One and all, no matter how many orders they dished out to other men, they learned not to bother MacNelly. If they did, his faded blue eyes grew hard and his voice took on an edge that warned them to leave him be. Captain MacNelly, it must be said, had little use for politicians of any kind. They were part of the system he was sworn to protect, and he did so with the tenacity of an old wildcat, and there were times when he was ready to agree that it wasn't such a bad system, at that. But when it came down to the wire, he was most at ease with his own men, his Rangers, his boys, as he thought of them, though he never called them that to their faces. To the old lawman, a boy stopped being a boy when he buckled on a gunbelt. If he didn't measure up MacNelly got rid of him. Or he got killed.

The crease-faced Ranger captain respected few

men more than the tall man named Buck Duane. There were two reasons. He liked Duane as a man, and every time he left to handle some difficult assignment, and Duane got most of the bad ones because he was the best, MacNelly wondered if he would ever see him again. That was how it worked in the law business, and there was no time for sentiment. A man who didn't expect to get killed had no business joining up. It was too bad Texas wasn't more peaceful, more settled, for like all good lawmen, MacNelly wanted no part of killing, but Texas wasn't settled, wasn't peaceful, and there was no arguing with the facts. Besides, as MacNelly said drily, that would throw him out of a job. That was just a joke, as he knew all too well. Always there would be guns and killing.

Now, on this bright spring morning, he looked up as Buck Duane came in. His leathery face creased in a smile and he held out his hand and waved Duane into a chair. Duane returned the smile, then grimaced as the wire-mended chair creaked under his lanky body.

Captain MacNelly smoked better cigars than the Governor, the best Havanas money could buy. Good cigars were the Captain's only luxury, as law enforcement was his only interest. He took a rich dark cigar from a japaned box and bit off the end and struck a sulphurhead match on the top of his desk. The match scorings were just part of the many gouges on the desk.

Puffing clouds of fragrant blue smoke, MacNelly fixed Buck Duane with a steely, humorous eye. "Took your time getting back, didn't you. I was beginning to think you were coming back by way of Denver."

Duane grinned back at his old friend, the man who had given him a fresh start in life when the rest of the world, and especially the sovereign State of

Texas, had branded him an outlaw. To the rest of the world, he was still a notorious outlaw, and only MacNelly and a few friends knew that he worked undercover on the side of the law. There were times when he longed to shake his past forever, to come out in the open, wear a badge like any other Ranger, but for now that was out of the question. He was too valuable the way he was.

"You're a fine one to talk," he told MacNelly. "Loafing here in luxury while I was making cold camp, eating beans out of the can, risking my precious neck for God and country."

This was their way of easing the tension they both felt. Then the banter was over. "You got what you wanted?" MacNelly asked, placing his hand on the leather bag Duane had put on his desk.

"It's all in there waiting for you to look at it," Duane said. "Names, dates, letters. It's going to raise your eyebrows when you see some of the names. Some you won't be surprised at, knowing the men they belong to. Others will throw you for a loop, Captain. It was even bigger than you thought, all worked out. They came within an ace of pulling it off. I'll say one thing for them, they did their homework, as the saying goes. It's going to be hard for them to start up again."

"Don't think they won't try," MacNelly growled, knowing that the smell of money and power always made men do anything.

While Duane waited, the Captain opened the leather bag and began to pile papers and envelopes on his already cluttered desk. The stack grew higher and finally MacNelly began to read with the concentration he was famous for. His frown deepened as he plowed through the evidence of the most sinister plot against Texas since it became a state.

The old wooden wall clock ticked on, and it was

silent except for the rustle of papers read and placed to one side. Now and then the Captain grunted in outrage or surprise. Watching, Buck Duane knew how the older man felt. He had been surprised too. In that stack of papers were the names of men who were national figures; men given to lofty speeches and fine sentiments. But there was no getting away from it—they were in there with all the other crooks and highbinders.

Somebody knocked on the door and MacNelly told whoever it was to go to blazes. The footsteps went away and MacNelly read on until he reached the end of the pile. He pushed the papers together and slammed his fist down on top of them. Duane didn't know when he had seen the "old man" looking so mad.

MacNelly looked at Duane. "By God, I don't know what to think. In all my born... It's like a nest of vipers, as the Bible says. I don't know whether to laugh or cry, so I'll do neither. You know what would happen in some other country. They'd take these fellers, these weasels, and stand them against a wall. What beats me is there ain't a one of them that ain't already well fixed. Got money, position, more power than any sane man needs or wants. Tell me something, Buck. Maybe you can tell me so I'll understand. What made them do it? Sell out their own country to a pack of outlaws?"

"More money and more power," Duane said. "For some men there's never enough. You know that, Captain."

MacNelly had chewed his cigar to shreds in his restrained anger. He threw it in an empty bean can and lit another. Blue smoke billowed up to the ceiling of the shabby little room he called an office. Duane waited for his boss to simmer down.

He did. "The hell of it is we can't do much about it," the Captain said at last, still angry but in control of his feelings. Once again he was the professional mancatcher, the nerveless lawman. "Shootings too good for them, so is jail, and the pity is they won't face a rifle or a prison breakfast. If I thought they could be shot I'd lead the firing party myself. Honest to God, I would."

Duane knew a little about politics, but even he was surprised. He thought of the Alamo, of all the men famous and unknown, who had made Texas the greatest State in the Union. Politics or no politics, it didn't seem right that traitors should go unpunished. "You mean they just walk away from this?" he asked in quiet anger.

MacNelly lay back in his chair and blew smoke furiously. It was a good cigar, but he wasn't enjoying it. "Not walk away from it," he said. "They'll be warned and some of them will want to resign. By God, they better resign. Some of them will brazen it out, and we'll have to let it go at that. There can't be a trial. Bad for the state, bad for the country, bad for everybody, if there was a trial. I know what you're thinking and don't think I'm not as mad as you are. Maybe I'm madder because I've had to deal with more of this than you have. Here and there I have. But I'll be hanged if this doesn't take the everlasting biscuit!"

For a man not given to swearing, "everlasting biscuit" was pretty strong language. Duane felt sorry for his die-straight boss. Here was the straightest man who ever lived caught up in dirty politics.

"You know what has to be done better than I do," Duane said evenly. There wasn't much else he could say.

Maybe it was the wrong thing to say. Maybe anything he said would be wrong. MacNelly's anger flared again, and Duane just happened to be there. Any man who was there would have caught some kind of hell.

"What're you gaping at, you damn fool!" the Captain growled. "Go on, tell me to shuck my badge and tell the people everything I know. And if the people, if the windbags over there in the Capitol, don't listen, then take it to the newspapers. Blast this whole rotten thing wide open, and let the chips fall any damn place they like. Go on, *Mister* Buck Duane, tell me that's what I ought to do."

Duane grinned at the sawed-off Irishman. "You were talking to me, Captain?"

MacNelly found it hard not to grin back. They had been friends too long. "Thanks for not snapping back at me, Buck. I would've had it coming if you did. Lordy, but it sticks in my craw. You know, old friend, I could do all the things I just said. I don't know that I could change things a whole lot. If I thought I could I'd quit the job right this minute. And that's saying something, damned if it isn't. I sort of like the work I do."

"No man does it better," Duane said, knowing that any kind of praise would get a sharp reaction from his peppery boss.

The reaction came quick and sour. "Let's not get carried away," he growled. Growled and grinned at the same time. "What happened up there in Harpetown? You want to tell me, or are you too busy trying to get on the good side of me."

For Duane it was a relief to get back to the business of making his report. One name he mentioned was Skiddy DaVinci.

The body of Skiddy DaVinci, packed in ice from head to foot, lay in an ornate casket in the parlor of the great stone mansion on Villiers Street. Outside, straw had been strewn in the street for two blocks to muffle the rattle of traffic. Now and then an ancient, white-headed Negro manservant in black and purple

199

livery, went out to warn the street boys to be quiet, to show some respect for the dead. In front of the DaVinci mansion carriages were drawn up at the curb, their drivers waiting. The blinds were drawn and a huge funeral wreath hung on the massive front door.

Behind the door, in this house of sorrow, Elena DaVinci, slim and erect at seventy, stood beside the casket looking at the face of her dead son. The relatives crowded the room and overflowed into other parts of the house, yet Elena DaVinci seemed to be alone. For hours she stood without moving, thinking private thoughts, perhaps remembering moments no one else knew about. Once she had shared those moments with the boy who had wandered so far; and was now home again for the last time—a stranger in a coffin.

The uncles, all men of fairly advanced years sat nearby talking quietly, glancing occasionally at their sister, the dead man's mother. There was nothing they could do to console her, to ease her silent grief. Her silence was so intense that no one dared intrude, not even these men who owned great companies. In her grief there was something almost frightening. Elena DaVinci was less "American" than the others, because she had lived only for her family, for its honor and pride, yet despite the fact that she had led a sheltered life, there was nothing submissive about her. Indeed, she was the equal of any man in the room. Wealthy in her own right, she could be as daring and independent as she pleased. But even had she been poor, she would have been no less proud or self-willed.

The uncles were all busy men and their business enterprises lay untended while they gathered for the funeral. It remained for Antonio, the brash politician, to show the first signs of impatience. He was not a young man and had traveled all the way from

Philadelphia by train. Now, with all respect to the dead, he wanted to get back.

Antonio stood up and produced his big silver watch. It was an expensive watch with soft, tiny chimes on the quarter hour. Antonio had been watching the wall clock and knew exactly what he was doing. When he opened his watch it chimed and he spoke to his sister.

"Elena, don't you think it's time we got started," he said hesitantly, for she could be a woman of fierce moods. "The undertaker, the hearse has been waiting for an hour. You said two o'clock."

"Let them wait," Elena said without turning. "They're paid to do what I tell them to do. If you're in such a big hurry, Antonio, why don't you leave."

She turned then. "You can all leave. It's all right. I will stay with my son. You see, there is no hurry for either of us. Not now."

The uncles murmured their eagerness to stay. Such talk was unheard of at a funeral. They wanted to be gone but knew she would never forgive them if they left. Only Antonio, a foxy faced man, persisted. Like the others, he was puzzled by the delay.

"But why, Elena?" he asked, touching her gently on the elbow.

Elena pulled away from him. "Because I am waiting for someone. My son and I are waiting for someone."

Antonio shrugged at the others in the room. "But we are all here," he said. "I ought to know. I made the arrangements to send for everyone."

Elena's voice was cold. "There is someone you did not send for."

"Impossible, Elena. I made a list. No one was left out." Antonio smiled briefly. "Even Pasquale who drives a horse trolley in New York is here. There he is over there, eating and drinking more than he should."

201

A burly Italian in a rough black suit acknowledged his presence by holding up a glass of wine.

"I don't understand," Antonio said. "Is it a man?"

Elena nodded. "I told you to wait. Do I have to tell you again?"

"But who is this man? You must tell us."

"I don't have to tell you anything." Elena's face softened and she turned to her brother. "Forgive me, Antonio. You have been very kind and understanding. I know Benito's bad name could not have done you any good in your profession."

"He was still my nephew, part of the family. I am not so American that I forget that. The man who killed Benito will pay for this. There are ways to do it. I haven't been in big city politics for twenty-five years without learning a few things. A word in the right ear is all it takes. Benito's killer will die. It's something we must talk about after the funeral."

Elena shook her head. "No, Antonio, it can't be done like that. Where is the justice if some stranger kills this man, Buck Duane? It must be done by my son's family."

Antonio's ruddy, well fed face turned pale and his hand trembled slightly as he put away his watch. What Elena said had come as a shock. He had been prepared to engage the services of a nameless, big city killer; a man who would kill for money and slip away after the job was done. But to do it himself, to be a part of it, was unthinkable.

He turned to appeal to the other uncles, all comfortable and prosperous, far removed from death and violence. "What you suggest is impossible," he protested. "We are all businessmen, all getting on in years. I have never owned a gun in my life. I know I speak for the others."

The other men agreed in a chorus, some not as agitated as Antonio, but all nervous.

The muffled doorbell tinkled softly. It seemed

loud in the sudden hush that fell over the room. Elena didn't move from the coffin, but her eyes were bright as she looked toward the door. "He's come," she said almost to herself. "It can't be anyone else."

The elderly Negro came to the archway that separated the room from the entrance hall. Surprise showed through the practiced blandness of his face. "A Mr. Ben Davin begs leave to come in," he announced.

The man who came in was taller than anyone in the room. Maybe he was an inch under six feet, but he seemed taller than that because of his slight build. His hair, worn long, was dark blond, his face a reddish brown; and he seemed to move without making any noise, though the floor was polished hardwood without any rugs. He wore a dark gray suit of light wool and the hat he held in his big hands was the same color. A polished gunbelt without cartridge loops slanted across his lean middle. The holster and gun were hidden by his coat, but he carried with him the feeling of danger; a man always on edge, waiting for something to happen. He stood in the archway staring at them with eyes that hardly blinked.

"I'm looking for..." he started in a soft Western voice that was out of place here.

"I know," Elena said. "You are looking for your father. There he is. That is your welcome home, Benito."

The uncles rose from their chairs as if they had been pushed from behind, and for the moment the dead man was forgotten. He lay in his casket, almost an afterthought in the confusion of voices, of exclamations and excited questions.

The man called Ben Davin brushed past them without answering and went to the foot of the casket. His father lay wax faced and cold, his dead hands folded around a crucifix; and the only sound was the drip of the melting ice that preserved his body from corruption. There was no sorrow in Ben Davin's eyes, just a sort of wonder. The uncles crowded beside him, silent now.

Ben Davin spoke quietly to Elena, his grandmother. "I never knew what he looked like," he said. "When I was a boy I thought of him a lot. Pictured him this way and that. I used to think someday he'd come along and take me with him. I wanted that more than anything. Then when I got older and heard the kind of man he was, I didn't want to see him. Who killed him, Grandmother? You didn't say in the telegraph message."

"A man called Buck Duane killed your father," Elena said. "Your father and my son. That's all that matters now."

"Buck Duane the outlaw," Ben Davin said.

Elena looked surprised. "You know this outlaw, this murderer?"

"I know him by name if he's the same man."

Elena said Buck Duane was a Texan and described how he looked. "They say he never raises his voice but he's a deadly killer. He is wanted by the Texas Rangers for many things."

"It has to be the same Buck Duane," Ben Davin said. "They say he's so fast he can outdraw a striking rattler."

Elena looked at him. "Does that bother you?"

Ben Davin shook his head. "All I know is he killed my father. If a lawman killed him I'd have to think about it. If a lawman killed him in the course of his job I'd have to think about it. Now I know different. Buck Duane is as bad as my father ever was. Fact is, word got to me that my father had turned some kind of lawman right toward the end. It got to me third hand so I never got the straight of it."

Elena looked puzzled for a moment. "The *straight* of it?"

"I never heard the true story," Ben Davin explained. "What is the truth?"

Elena's eyes were hooded, then having decided to lie, she opened them wide. "Your father started out wrong," she said. "But he was young then. I think he was sorry all his life for the things he did. Oh yes, he did many bad things, but in the end he tried to change. You see, someone finally gave him the chance he never had. A decent man who believed in him, trusted him. This man's name was Joseph Bacon, a banker in a small town in Texas nobody ever heard of. Harpetown was what they called it. Mr. Bacon wanted to start a community where men like your father, men with a past who wanted to go straight, could find a haven. Mr. Bacon felt that no man was so bad that he didn't deserve a second chance. So he gave one to your father, arranged to have him appointed sheriff—and then this man Duane killed him. You might have been proud of your father if he had lived."

Ben Davin's big fist clenched in anger. "Too late for that. What I don't understand, you say this Harpetown was a place where outlaws could find a new life. How did Buck Duane get mixed up in it? He's a bigger outlaw than anybody."

The uncles remained silent. It seemed as if the threat of having to kill Buck Duane, kill him personally, had been removed. So they were ready to agree with anything Elena said.

"Buck Duane was the one man Mr. Bacon didn't want in Harpetown," Elena went on, warming to her lies, justifying them by the presence of her dead son. "Mr. Bacon sensed that Duane had come to his town with a sinister purpose. To make Harpetown into a truly outlaw town instead of a community of reformed men. By the time he moved against Duane it was too late. Duane robbed the bank with the help of a confederate disguised as a peddler and killed

205

your father when he tried to keep him from getting away. Mr. Bacon, a quiet, decent man, was lucky to escape being killed himself. This Duane is a cold-blooded murderer, Benito."

Ben Davin's smile was bleak. "Call me, Ben, Grandmother. That's what my mother called me. Not Benito, just Ben. Sorry about the money she sent back to you. She always said you were ashamed of your bastard grandson. You wanted nothing to do with us, then we'd have nothing to do with you."

Elena stared at the floor. "Forgive me. I was wrong. The family..."

"The only family I ever had was my mother," Ben Davin said. "How do you like my name, Grandmother. Ben Davin? Davin is a good old Irish name. Didn't take more than the changing of a few letters to turn spaghetti into Irish Stew. Funny thing is, after I heard what my father was, all I ever wanted was to be a lawman. My mother said I was going to be everything my father wasn't. That's usually how it goes. So I became a lawman and then a bounty hunter."

Antonio spoke up for the first time. "A bounty hunter. What's that?"

Ben Davin smiled another cold smile. "They don't have them in the city. A bounty hunter is sort of a lawman without a badge. No badge, no credentials. It's legal though. You go after a man with a reward on his head and bring him in for the money."

"Then you will make a lot of money when you kill Duane," Antonio dared to say.

Ben Davin's young face grew dark with anger. "I'll kill him but not for the money. I didn't turn bounty hunter because of money. The law was too slow for me. A killer wanted in Arizona could run free in Montana. That didn't seem right to me so I decided to do something about it. I did, especially after a friend of mine was gunned down by a gunny come

206

north from New Mexico. You know what I'm going to do with the money I get for killing Duane?"

Antonio shook his head.

"I'm going to spend it on a stone for my father's grave. My father's grave stays the way it is until Duane is dead."

The cousin who drove the trolley in New York had been drinking too much wine. "Or until you're dead, Cousin," he said, swaying on his feet.

Ben Davin took no offense, though the other men grew nervous. "Nobody's going to kill me," he said. "I've killed too many men not to be able to kill one more. I don't know who all of you are, and I don't give a damn. You never did anything for me and my mother, and it's too late to do it now. My mother worked herself to death trying to bring me up, when one kind word from you was all she needed. No matter. I'll do the killing, but I won't be doing it for you. Nobody knows me in Texas. Never even been in the state. I doubt if there's a man in the whole State of Texas knows my name. Born in Colorado and raised along the Canadian border. Never been south of Montana till now. Nobody has cause to give me a second look. Why should they? I'm a true blue American."

The New York trolley driver was drunk enough to say what he wanted to say. "You sound like you're shamed to be an Italian."

Ben Davin's response was mild, but the death look in his eyes made the sober men shiver. Whatever else Ben Davin was, he was a natural killer.

"No, I'm not ashamed to be an Italian," Ben said easily. "Far from it. It's just that not looking like an Italian is going to give me an edge. Now let's get on with it."

The lid of the casket closed on the dead face of Skiddy DaVinci.

Hundreds of miles away, in Austin, Texas, Captain MacNelly listened to the end of Buck Duane's report on the goings-on at Harpetown. He interrupted only twice to ask a question that had to be asked. Mostly he just smoked and grunted. It was a pleasure, the Captain thought, to listen to a man who knew how to state the facts without dragging them through the brush at the end of a long rope.

"Joe Bacon got away while I was busy with DaVinci," Duane said. "I wasn't there to clean out the whole town. Just to get the evidence there back to you fast as I could. Bacon sent DaVinci to stop me and got stopped instead. I warned him to throw down his gun. Being the hardcase he was, he wouldn't listen."

MacNelly knocked cigar ash into the bean can. "Did you think he would?" he asked with a sour grin.

"He got his chance and didn't take it," Duane said. "He got shot, and I guess that's the end of it."

"Looks like it," MacNelly agreed. "Too bad this Joe Bacon was able to get away. On the other hand, there ain't a lot we could have done if you'd caught the weasel. Man, I tell you I never heard of such a plot in my born days. 'Course you always have outlaws trying to band together, but that's just for protection. This is the first time they tried to start their own state."

Duane stretched his long legs. It had been a long trip back from Harpetown and he had made good time by pushing himself to the limits of his endurance. Not to mention what he had been through before he left. The Jackrabbit Kid had stayed behind to see what he could see. There were plenty of owlhooters left in that wild country up north and the Kid, being the Kid and naturally curious, elected to stay and keep an eye on them.

"You think Joe Bacon is going to start up again?"

he asked MacNelly. "He got his plans all blown to hell and gone. Maybe he'll lay low for a spell."

The Captain began to stuff the papers back in the leather bag. He handled them as if afraid he might catch the plague. The Captain said, "This Joe Bacon, or whoever he is, sounds like the kind to do just that. Lay low, crawl into his hole, lick his wounds. A plan with plans that big won't just let it go, chalk it up to experience. The point is—men like that are crazy, and when they're smart too, that makes them all the more dangerous. I figure you made yourself a bad enemy there, Buck."

Duane yawned. The long ride and the short hours of sleep along the way were catching up with him. The thought of a big solid breakfast and a big soft bed looked better and better all the time. Joe Bacon didn't press too heavy on his mind.

"I've made enemies before and I'm still around," he said.

"Not like this one you haven't," MacNelly reminded him. "You didn't just cost Bacon a lot of time and money. No siree, you did a lot more than that—you made him look bad." MacNelly slapped the leather bag. "The high mucky-mucks in here are going to be awful mad at our friend Bacon. He promised something he couldn't deliver and in the kind of circles he moves in, crawls in, that's something they don't forgive so easy. I'm telling you, old friend, you better watch yourself for a while."

Idly, Duane wondered if he had started a blood feud. Skiddy DaVinci had to have some Italian in his background, and Italians were known to harbor a grudge. In the coastal cities there was always talk of them doing in some gent, usually one of their own people, for some wrong that often went back fifty years.

"Naw, I don't expect you'll get any trouble from that quarter," MacNelly said. "It's a well known fact

209

that this here Skiddy came from a good family. Don't know that much about it. The word is they got plenty of money, every which kind of business. Ships and tobacco and so forth. Not the kind of folk to be associating with killers and riff-raff. My advice, based on what I know, is forget about the DaVinci family. Joe Bacon is the one to look out for. My guess is there's nothing right off to fret about, supposing you were the fretful kind, which you ain't. Bacon will be too busy explaining to his friends to bother you for a while."

"I'll be waiting for him when he does," Duane said.

"Confound it, Buck. You know Bacon won't try it himself. But I ain't sure that the time hasn't come for you to drop this undercover work. What you did up in Harpetown wasn't exactly the work of an outlaw."

Still thinking of a big steak and a long sleep, Duane grinned and said, "Don't tempt me, Captain. Lots of times I think wouldn't it be nice if I could be a regular Ranger like the other men. Be able to walk into a saloon and drink a mug of beer on a hot day and not have everybody staring at me. Like I had two heads with horns to match. Even the Rangers I ought to be working with stare at me, not knowing what I really am. Except for you and the Kid there isn't a Ranger I can call a friend."

"All right then, why don't you pack it in?" MacNelly asked. "There's plenty of straight law work you can do. What's the good of undercover work if they spotted you at Harpetown?"

Duane thought about it for a while. "I'm not sure they got me spotted at that. Sure, they got me down for stealing those papers and wrecking their plan. I'm hoping they'll put that down to my vicious, criminal nature. Maybe they'll think I wanted to take over and got mad when I couldn't do it."

MacNelly growled, "They won't want to kiss you,

that's for sure. Still and all, I'd hate like blazes to have you give up the work you've been doing. Seeing as how you're so vicious and criminal, not to mention a man that beats old ladies, you can go places no other Ranger can go. And that's worth more than gold to the State of Texas. In the end though, it's your decision. You want to think about it?"

Duane said, "There's nothing to think about, Captain. In for a penny, as the man said."

"We're not talking about pennies," the Captain snapped. "We're talking about a man's life, namely yours. I'd rather have you doing regular Ranger work than..."

"Than dead," Duane finished. "Well, I'm not dead yet and I don't aim to be. So I guess I'll remain an outlaw until something happens to change my mind."

"Or mine," MacNelly said gruffly. "I'm the boss here and don't you be forgetting it. If I tell you to start wearing a Ranger badge in plain sight, that's how it's going to be. Understood?"

Duane pretended to give a military salute and MacNelly told him not to be a damn fool. "And you better get some real sleep before you fall out of that chair."

Duane had an idea. "I'm on my way, Cap. There's just one favor I'd like to ask you, Captain sir."

"What is it," MacNelly asked suspiciously, grinning in spite of himself. "I can't rightly recall the last time you called me 'sir.'"

"You got everything under control at the moment. That's right, isn't it?"

"How would you know, Duane? You ain't been here. All right, there's nothing giving me any more grey hair than I got. Now what's this all about?"

"Well, Captain, you do agree that I did some fine work up there in Harpetown. Is that not a fact?"

211

MacNelly was ready to throw the bag of evidence at Duane, but thought better of it. "Listen, bucko," he growled. "Who's in charge here, you or me?"

Duane grinned at his chief's exasperation. "You are, Captain. That's why I'm asking to get two weeks off duty. No joking. I'm kind of worn out after Harpetown. I've been around too many people too long. When that mood gets on me, I have to get away for a spell. Take my horse and ride out where nobody can find me, sleep easy and late in a good dry place. Do a little hunting and fishing. Maybe not even that."

Captain MacNelly got up and walked to the door with Duane. "Why not," he said. "No man can ever say you didn't earn every minute of it. But listen to me. Two weeks is all the time I can spare. Where will you be if something real important comes up. Come on now. I ain't going to tell a soul. More or less, where will you be?"

"Up along the Mackenzie River, above the fork where the Iron Mountain stands over it. That's good country up that way. Not a soul in it, not even Indians. No people, no towns. I like that, Captain."

"Nice country for hermits," MacNelly agreed, scratching his pepper and salt mustache. "A man could get lost in there and not be found for a hundred years—if ever. I haven't been up that way since '67 when I had to go in after Cannibal Dorn. Never did find him though I sure looked long and hard enough. My guess is he died in there. All it takes is a broken leg and you're done for. But if you like that wild country, then go to it. Just be back in two weeks."

"Why don't you come along, Captain?"

MacNelly laughed. "You know you don't want me along. Better be on your way before somebody walks in here with bad news. Watch yourself, hear."

Once he left the Range captain's office, Duane

forgot about sleep. That had been his first plan, to sleep for most of a day in Mrs. Roark's pin-clean boardinghouse over on Sam Houston Street. Frank Roark's Dutch wife didn't rent to drunks or wild men, and you could sleep in peace for as long as you wanted. The food was good too, and there was a lot of it.

No, thought Buck Duane, I'll catch up on my sleep in good clean open country. For a change it would be good not to have to sleep with a six-shooter in his hand, just close by. Up there in Mackenzie Land, as the oldtimers called it, he would do nothing but take it easy. There was plenty of game in there, but he didn't want to go after it too hard. But it shouldn't be hard to kill a deer. After all that bacon and beans or, for variety beans and bacon, he had a hankering for nice young venison sizzling over a bed of raked coals. Venison and fish, fried or baked. A man knew he was alive when he could eat grub like that. Good coffee too, boiled jumping black in the pot. Forget about outlaws and killers for fourteen days. Duane grinned at his thoughts. Well, not a full fourteen days. He would have to allow for travel time, in and out.

At a general store run by a jack Mormon, he stocked up on the things he needed: Arbuckle's coffee, the best of the lot; some bacon, in case the deer and the fish decided not to be cooperative; brown sugar for the coffee. Except for some extra ammunition, that was about it.

The man who ran the store called himself Mr. Jones, and the sign over the door said the same thing, and he minded his own business with a passion that bordered on rudeness. But he was always pleasant enough with Buck Duane, and it was likely that he had ridden on the wrong side of the law, in his time. He knew about the dark side of Duane's past, his present, for that matter, but he didn't let it get in the way.

"Got your cooking gear ready for you," Mr. Jones drawled.

"Obliged to you for letting me stow it here," Duane said. That's what he did between hard assignments when a lot of cookware would just slow a man down. Sometimes he brought along the battered and blackened coffee pot. Mostly he didn't. A good part of the time, he dined on cold beans and jackrabbits or more of that blamed bacon, fried on a flat rock.

"No need to thank me," Mr. Jones said. "When you fetch out your cook iron I know you have to buy supplies."

That was their joke, their ritual. Mr. Jones wasn't a tight fisted man, though he was far from popular. He was getting on toward sixty; there was still some of the old wildness left in him. He was a wild man tamed by a nagging, affectionate wife, tied down to the store and the quiet life of the town. There were times when Duane wanted to tell Mr. Jones that he was better off the way he was. Having a wife around wasn't such a bad idea, though it seemed kind of remote to Duane, knowing that the settled life wasn't for him. The life he led suited him fine, no matter how many pretty women looked his way, and plenty of them did. In the end, a man got the kind of life he deserved; being human though, he always considered other possibilities. Maybe when he got older, Duane thought while he stowed away his supplies. Yeah sure, when he got older—if he lived that long.

Right then and there he didn't have a care in the world.

While Duane headed for the Mackenzie River, taking his time, Ben Davin was on his way to Austin. Davin wasn't taking his time, but he wasn't pushing it so hard that his horse would get a worn-out look. He had left New Orleans right after the funeral, and his uncles, one and all, were glad to see him go. They were afraid of him though they were in no danger, but fear was the response he evoked in people who met him for the first time. He could be friendly when he wanted to be. It came hard but he could do it. Indeed, there were ladies who considered him a charming young man. At twenty-two, Ben Davin could have passed for eighteen or nineteen, yet he was hardened in killing and mancatching; experienced far beyond his years.

At twenty-two he had three years of lawing behind him. A Montana sheriff, a middle-aged man who had been sweet on his mother at one time, gave him the deputy job, more from kindness than conviction that he would ever be more than a workaday subordinate. What the sheriff didn't know was that Ben Davin was fast with a gun. He roamed the hills far from the little Montana town where he had been raised, and there in the wilderness, away from prying eyes, he taught himself to shoot and to draw. Nobody helped him, nobody gave him instruction. He told no one, he never bragged. There was nothing of the aspiring gunman about him. Instead of the fancy gunrigs favored by many young deputies, he wore a single-action, long-barreled Colt .44 in a plain brown belt without cartridge loops. He wasn't there to fight a war, he told himself. He was just going to be the best deputy Montana ever saw. And he was. His first week on the job, when the sheriff had set him to throwing cold creek water on harmless drunks, he killed two hardcases chased out of Canada by the Mounties. They were on their way south when they stopped off in Davin's town and decided to rob the bank. They killed the bank manager and wounded the sheriff before Ben Davin dropped them with two shots in the heart. A shooter as fast and as skilled as he was could have shot them in the head, but that wasn't his style. The idea was to stop them for good, and that's what he did.

The memory of what his father had become rankled in Ben Davin. Come hell or high water, he was going to be different. Of course his father's notoriety hadn't spread as far north as Montana. In Texas, Skiddy DaVinci was a famous bad man; in Montana he wasn't even a name. Anyway, there was nothing to connect the dark faced DaVinci with the boyish, Irish looking Davin.

Ben Davin didn't want to prove anything to the world. His world was his mother and himself. Now his mother was dead—and that left only him. It was all he needed. It would have surprised him if anyone told him he was a killer, had a killer's deadly nature behind the shiny badge and the youthful face. But that was what he was. Like it or not, he was traveling the same hard road as his father. His killings were all legal. He never shot a man in the back, never drew first, yet he seldom brought a man in alive. The ones he did bring in could hardly be called gunmen. Some of them had killed, but they weren't killers. So he let them live.

The sheriff, an honest lawman all his life, argued with him about the killings. Ben listened and nodded and smiled. All they had to do was give up their guns, he said. But they never did. And then, impatient with the law, he became a bounty hunter. Again, it was all legal. Not a body he brought in had a hole in the back.

And now he was on his way to kill another man. Buck Duane's fame meant nothing to him. Duane was a man and could be killed like all the others.

Ben Davin put his horse in a boxcar and man and animal rode to Austin in less than two days. By the time he arrived there, Buck Duane was close to the Mackenzie, and still hadn't a care in the world.

Captain MacNelly was drinking his first coffee of the day and chasing fried eggs around a tin plate when the young Ranger who did his best to keep people out of the office now came in and announced that there was a Montana deputy who wanted to see him.

"Montana!" MacNelly raised his bushy eyebrows in surprise. "You sure that's what he said?"

"That's what he said, Captain. Wearing his badge even. Name of Ben Davin."

MacNelly set his plate of eggs aside and poured another cup of coffee. There was much you could do to ruin a couple of fried eggs, but the Ranger cookie did his darnedest. It must be a special gift, MacNelly thought sourly. "Tell the Montana man to come on in. Why not—everybody else does."

Ben Davin had thrown away the dark suit he wore to his father's funeral. Now he wore a wool shirt and pants, range boots without any fancy stitching, a wide brimmed gray hat with a Montana peak. He looked very young to Captain MacNelly, but that was before the lawman got a good look at him. The moment he did, he changed his mind. This young man was someone to be reckoned with. It showed in his hard, lean body, the thrust of his clean shaven jaw, the quiet determination in his eyes.

Ben Davin knew Captain MacNelly wasn't a man to be fooled with a few words and a ready smile. But it could be done. There were few men who couldn't be fooled, if you worked at it hard enough, and no man who couldn't be killed.

Ben Davin said his name and waited to see if it meant anything to the top Ranger. On the way to Austin he had considered using another name— there was no name on his badge—but decided against it. He was what he was. Ben Davin was his name and he was going to use it.

"You want coffee?" MacNelly asked, looking

217

around for another cup.

Davin shook his head. "Thanks anyway, Captain. I should have wrote ahead I was coming."

MacNelly said no need for that. "You're a long way from Montana. Fine country they tell me. Now sir, what can I do for you?"

"I'm looking for a man named Buck Duane."

MacNelly's eyes narrowed, then he laughed a creaky laugh with no humor in it. "You're looking for Buck Duane. Here in Ranger headquarters? I reckon this is the last place you're going to find him."

Davin smiled back. "Right you are, Captain. I know it sounds crazy, but I need Duane's help."

"Why would an outlaw want to help the law? You're talking backways, Deputy. 'Cept you don't look like a feller to do that. Suppose you say what this is all about."

"It's a special case," Davin said. "I know Buck Duane's reputation, know he'd shoot me soon as talk to me. Tell you the truth, that's about all I know about the man. I know he's tough and fast and mean."

"That about describes him," MacNelly said cautiously.

"I also heard he's pretty straight about most things," Davin went on. "I never heard him called a backshooter, did you?"

"Get on with it, Deputy."

It was a mild reprimand but Davin responded to it like any young deputy. "Here it is, Captain. Up in Montana we got a man we're holding on a murder charge. Real bad, sir. Attacked and murdered a young girl. We got some evidence against him, mostly circumstantial. I'm sure he did it. I'm the one that brought him in and on the way he all but bragged that he was the killer. But we both know that won't stand up in a court of law, not with a smart lawyer, and that's what he's got. This man arrived in Montana about a year ago. Came with plenty of money, bought himself a good ranch. My guess is he's an outlaw from Texas that moved north."

"The point?" MacNelly prompted.

"We don't rightly know who he is. Sure, he has a name but I'll be damned if it's his real one. He uses it but never got used to it. After I locked him up I called him by name a couple of times. There were other deputies around when I did it. This man—Cass Dooley—didn't react like any man does to his own name. Well, he answered to it, but not right off. You know how it is."

"That I do, Deputy," the Captain said wearily. "But what has this to do with Buck Duane?"

"Maybe nothing," Davin said. "Maybe everything. Dooley's a big drinker and every time he got drunk in town he bragged about all the famous men he used to know. Kept changing his story, the way drunks do. At times he said he was an ex-Army scout, other times a lawman. Hinted he'd been a real desperado in his day. Famous names kept popping up in his stories. The Dalton Brothers. Wyatt Earp. Hickok."

"Sounds like a drunk," the Captain agreed.

Davin nodded. "Sure. But one name came up more than the others—Buck Duane. It was like he hated Duane because of something in the past. The others he admired. Duane he seemed to hate. It was like he really knew Duane at some time."

MacNelly didn't have to check his wanted posters to know that he had never heard of any Cass Dooley. Unless this Cass Dooley was so old that he killed his first man with a horse pistol, he didn't mean a thing to MacNelly.

"That's what I mean, Captain," Davin said. "On the face of it, Cass Dooley is a hard-working rancher. Drinks and brags but pays his bills. No different from a lot of men. Can't hang him for being a loudmouth. On the other hand, if I can get Buck Duane to make a signed and sworn statement, witnessed by me as a law officer, I think I can send this child killer to the gallows. All Duane has to do is give me his real name, the things he's done in the past, then Dooley will swing."

MacNelly wasn't giving anything away, not just yet. "Other people must have known Dooley, so called. Anyhow, what good is a sworn statement going to do?"

"I have a picture," Davin said. "Got us a photography studio in our town. One day Dooley, so called, got drunk and got his picture made. Here it is."

Davin produced a tinted photograph of a rugged looking cowhand in his middle thirties. At that moment the man in the photograph was yelling at a bunch of runaway calves in the Montana hills. A man who couldn't read or write, and ate his peas on the blade of his knife, he respected women above all else.

"That's Cass Dooley, so called," Davin said, passing the photograph to the Captain, who turned it this way and that.

"Doesn't look like such a bad feller," MacNelly said, but as he knew all too well, a man's appearance didn't mean a thing. The worst killer he ever tracked down had blue eyes like a baby. "Nope. Never saw him before in my life. No need for me to check the files." MacNelly tapped his forehead. "I got their faces right in here. Dead or alive, they're all in my head."

Davin swore and apologized for it. "I was hoping somebody would be able to help. It burns me to think of Dooley walking away from this. Naturally, I came to you first, thinking you might have an idea where Duane was holed up. I mean to find him, sir,

220

but I don't know how long I've got. The county prosecutor got the judge to postpone the trial so I could come down here and try to find Duane. Lordy! You should have heard Dooley's lawyer yelling. Said he was going to appeal to a higher court. If he can rush the trial through before I get Duane's statement, Dooley is bound to get off. The hell of it is, they can't try him again, not on a murder charge. They can't try him even if he confessed after the trial. God! Captain, if you could have seen that poor girl."

Davin didn't know what he was looking for, but he knew there was something. That something was in MacNelly's face. The Ranger captain was trying to make up his mind, so Davin helped him.

"Duane's statement would change everything," he persisted. "Once he's identified beyond a doubt as a former outlaw, no doubt a killer, the jury won't believe anything he says. He'll hang for murdering that unfortunate girl. I'd give five years pay to see that. I'd give more than that."

MacNelly helped himself to a cigar. Nothing like a good cigar to help a man think. It was a touchy situation all around. He couldn't tell this young man that Buck Duane was a Ranger. He could swear him to secrecy, but that wasn't the way to do it. He knew that Duane was a Ranger, so did the Jackrabbit Kid—and that was it. He felt bad about the girl in Montana, but not to reveal Duane's real identity. A secret was like a tiny pebble thrown into a pond. No matter how gently, how carefully you did it, the ripples spread out and kept on going till they reached the other side. Girl or no girl, he couldn't take chances with Duane's life. To the world, Duane was an outlaw and must remain one. That was his decision and MacNelly respected him for it.

The Captain studied the smoldering Havana for a while. "I might have an idea where Duane is. Keeping a line on wanted men is part of my job, as you know. Last I heard from a pretty good source, an old miner, is that Duane is taking his ease somewhere up on the MacKenzie River. That's north of here a good piece. I'd say that's where you'll find him. Fact is, I was about to send a man up there to take a look, but we got a gang of bank robbers in Denby to think about right now."

"Thanks, Captain." Davin stood up and held out his hand.

"Whoa there!" the Captain called out. "You go after Buck Duane you better do it nice and easy. Don't try to sneak up on him 'cause it won't work. He'll see you before you see him. But he won't throw down on you. Not his style. If he tells you to lay down your weapons, you be smart—do what he tells you. You may think you're fast with a gun. Forget it—Duane's faster. Wait for him to make his move. He'll do it when it's safe. Then you do what talking you have to do. Mind you, I don't say Duane will turn on another outlaw. He's been hunted too long to love the law. In this case, you got a better chance than most. Duane may be an outlaw but he's all man, and don't you forget it. I reckon he'll give you the statement, if that picture looks right."

Davin smiled his thanks. "You sound like you almost admire the man. No offense, sir. It's just the way you talked just now."

"Admire Buck Duane!" MacNelly's face twisted in scorn. "Not likely, Deputy. Just giving the devil his due. Someday soon I'm going to put that maverick behind bars, where he belongs."

Davin smiled again. "Let me have him first, Captain," he said.

Buck Duane knew he was being followed. The feeling came suddenly and refused to go away, and he had spent too many years on the trail to think he was wrong. It was out there—it had to be one man—watching him. One moment he was easy and relaxed, enjoying the morning sun in his face, then he was tensed up, waiting for something to happen. There was no mistaking it. It was real as the river, as strong as the sun.

Duane was hooking the coffee pot off the fire when the feeling came out of nowhere. For a moment he braced himself for the shock of a long range rifle bullet. It didn't come but that didn't mean that it wouldn't come. He thought of Indians and dismissed the idea. There were no Indians in the Mackenzie River country. The great iron mountain that loomed over the fork of the Mackenzie and the Blue Rivers was sacred to the Indians, and they kept away from it. Had for many years. Still, the thing out there moved like an Indian, the thing he couldn't see. So it could be a renegade Comanche or Kiowa, some wandering outcast from his tribe, half starved and desperate, prowling the desolate hills for a victim. To such a man a rifle would be a prize, a horse a great treasure. It—the thing watching him—could be anything. Only one thing was certain—it was a man, a two legged predator.

Duane drank coffee and waited. Nothing happened. He knew he made a fair target, but no bullets came at him. Again, that had to mean something. Maybe the man stalking him didn't have a long gun. Was he waiting for a chance to get closer? Duane finished the coffee and began to pack up his gear. His horse, Bullet, grazed on yellow grass along the bank of the river. Maybe the man out there was after the horse and didn't mean to kill him to get it. That didn't spell outlaw or Indian renegade. But stealing and killing went together, so it made no difference, in the end.

Duane saddled up and rode north along the Mackenzie. So far it had been fairly open country.

Now it got broken, slashed across by ravines and old dry watercourses. Now and then he checked his back trail without seeming to. Still nothing moved in the harsh morning sunlight. Whoever he was, the stalker knew what he was doing. It could be the Rangers. No, that wasn't likely. Cap MacNelly told the Rangers where to go, pointed them at their targets. A bounty hunter was just as unlikely. A bounty hunter would be armed to the teeth, wouldn't give him a chance. The best of the bounty hunters, meaning the worst, all carried long range rifles, the best blood money could buy. A Big Fifty Remington, a Winchester Express model, those were what a bounty hunter would carry. The tools of their trade. Usually a bounty hunter who knew his dirty business just lay back at three or even four hundred yards and killed his man at his ease.

Duane moved on without hurry. He would lead the stalker, then set a trap for him. That was the idea. Duane wasn't altogether sure that it would work that smoothly, because only a fool thought he knew all the answers. Other men had bested him—not many—but one or two had done it. It was something you had to expect. Finally, all a man could do was make his experience work for him.

He nooned and moved on again, looking for a place to surprise the stalker. He thought he had found it when he saw a thrust of rock hanging out over the river. There was no way around it without riding up far and high above the river. Instead of doing that he rode his horse down to the edge of the river, running high in spring flood, and made his way under the overhang of rock. Another horse would have had trouble, but Bullet was too sure-footed, too well trained, to stumble or panic.

Out from under the great rock, Duane gave a quiet command to the big horse and it went on ahead. Duane slid out the Winchester and waited for the stalker to show himself. He had to come by way of the river or lose a lot of time. Duane waited, rifle ready, but nothing happened. His eyes swept up to the rock. Nothing there. Unless a man left his horse and climbed the rock and crossed it on bare feet there would have to be some sound. But the only sound was the wind and the rushing river below.

He was about to move on when a voice called out, "I got a rifle aimed at your spine, Duane. I can blow it out through your belly if you make a move. Lay down the rifle and turn around. I'll kill you for sure if you do anything else. This is the law talking, Duane."

The last words were what saved the stalker's life. An instant before Duane had decided to draw and fire even while he was being killed. He knew he could do it. His hand hadn't moved and now it remained motionless.

"All the way round," the voice ordered. "Leave the rifle and step away from that rock."

Duane turned to face the man who meant to kill him. The first thing he saw was the sunlight glinting on the deputy's badge. His eyes took that in, without deciding anything, then moved to the man's face. It was a very young face, but hard as nails. Not that the reddish brown face was seamed or sun leathered. Far from it. The hardness was mostly in the eyes, cold and pale blue, merciless eyes. This man hated him and Duane didn't know why. This man wasn't an outlaw, didn't have that wild, hunted look outlaws get after dodging too long. The badge said he was a deputy sheriff, but there had to be something more.

Duane didn't show the surprise he felt when the other man suddenly dropped his rifle and let his hands hang loose by his side. So far none of it was making sense. First, the man went to a lot of trouble to get the drop on him, then threw the best part of it away. The only thing that kept the gun in Duane's holster was the badge. Damn the badge!

"You'd be who?" Duane said, looking at the badge. The badge didn't look like a Texas badge. He had dodged enough Texas badges to know. This badge was more in the shape of a V, something like the Federal symbol. They didn't wear badges like that in Texas.

"Ben Davin," the badge toter said.

"Means nothing to me," Duane said. Something clicked in his mind, but nothing fitted together. "You think you have business with me?"

Davin's smile was cold as the river still running high with snow water from the hills. "Some business," he said. "I'm going to kill you."

"Doesn't sound like law talk to me."

"It'll do."

"You're no Texas man. What's the reason for the hard talk? What am I charged with?"

"Murder," Ben Davin said. "The murder of Benito DaVinci. You'd know him as Skiddy."

"Sure," Duane said. "You're his son. You don't look like him, but you do. Then the badge you're wearing is just a fake."

"Wrong, gunslinger. I'm still a deputy sheriff of Fairfax County, Montana. Up my way you stay a deputy, keep yourself ready for anytime the sheriff needs you. It's all legal, gunslinger."

"It's not legal in Texas," Duane said, trying to make up his mind what to do. He was in one hell of a bind, and he knew it. He knew he could outdraw Davin, or just about any other man, but how could he be sure he wouldn't have to kill him. Kill him to keep from being killed, returning fire in the fury of the moment. Or just plain kill him by accident. Not even the best shot in the world could put all his shots where he wanted them to go. Not all the time.

"A lawman is a lawman," Davin stated. "I don't have to be a lawman to kill you."

"You keep talking about killing."

"Men like you always get killed."

"Not this time," Duane said, making a decision he knew had every chance of being wrong. "You're going to have to take me in, sonny. I won't draw on you, if that's what you want."

"That's what I want, gunslinger. I could have dropped you ten times before now."

"Why didn't you?"

"Because I wanted to face you up close, get a good look at the man who murdered my father."

Damn undercover work! Duane thought. "Your father had it coming to him. He was in thick with the worst bunch of rats this State ever produced. That's not to say that I wanted to kill him. There was no other way. I warned him to leave it be. He wouldn't so he got killed."

Davin's cold eyes grew colder with sudden hate. "My father was some kind of lawman and you killed him. Maybe he was in with a bunch of rats. What was your interest? I never heard of Buck Duane doing anything to help the law."

Damn! It had to come out, it had to be said, no matter how double-dealing it sounded. One thing sure—it wasn't going to be easy convincing Skiddy DaVinci's hard-faced son. And something warned Duane that it wasn't going to make any difference what he said.

But he said it. "I'm a Ranger. That's the truth. I work for a Captain MacNelly, chief Ranger in Austin. The Captain and one other man are the only ones who know. Captain MacNelly gave me the job because I used to be an outlaw. I'm not denying that. It started with a misunderstanding and built from there. I'd probably be dead now if it hadn't been for the Captain. So I work undercover for him, paying him back the only way I know. Captain MacNelly is the best friend I have in the world."

Davin's smile was mirthless. "Sure he is. That's why he wants to put you behind bars so bad. That's what he said, gunslinger. You want me to repeat his words? That's right. I talked to the Captain. How do you think I knew you were up here."

The truth wasn't buying him a thing, Duane realized. Still, he had to keep trying. It was better than having to kill this man he didn't even know. "What else could the Captain say? That's my cover, the Captain's fake hate for me, all the wanted posters. I'll tell you something. If MacNelly really wanted to get me he'd do it. Listen to me. I had to go after your father. It was part of my job. He was part of a conspiracy to split the State of Texas. I know it sounds crazy."

Davin looked at him with contempt. "That's the first true word so far. You think I'm a damn fool, believe a crazy story like that? Why don't you go all the way with it? Say my father was part of a plot to kill the President."

"You don't believe me, then you'd best take me in," Duane said. "If I have to stand trial for killing your father, so be it. I'm ready to go any time you like. Captain MacNelly will set you straight."

"No," Ben Davin said in a dead, cold voice. "It ends here. Just the two of us. I'm a long way from Montana and who's to say what you and that old Ranger are up to. Something's going on that I don't understand, don't want to. Maybe that old Ranger sent you to murder my father. Makes no difference how it was. He's dead. You think you're that fast with a gun, go to it. You won't be taking any advantage of me, gunslinger. I know how to shoot a gun."

Duane held back, telling himself he was a fool. But Davin was still some kind of lawman and it went against the grain to draw on a badge. To Duane, the badge meant old Cap MacNelly and all the other decent lawmen all over the country. Last of all, he didn't want to kill Ben Davin, twisted though his motives might be. He had killed his father, and that seemed enough.

"You didn't backshoot me so that shows you still have some respect for the law," Duane said. "You don't believe my story—fine! But you're going to have to take me in. I'll say it again. I won't draw on you. If you want to kill me, you'll have to do it in cold blood."

"Who's to know?" Davin sneered, looking edgy at the same time.

"You'll know," Duane said. "You have the look of a man who keeps things to himself. Kill me and you'll think about it in the dark hours before first light."

"The other men I've killed never bothered me. Why should you?"

"Because you gave them a chance—your idea of a chance—and they took it. Sure you took a chance to give them their chance. No difference. It was murder just the same. It won't be any different with me. Yeah, I guess it will at that. I won't take your offer. Kill me or take me in. There's no third way."

"You're gutless, that's what you are," Ben Davin snarled. His hand streaked for his gun and it came out like a flash of light.

Well, Duane thought, looking at the cocked revolver, you made your decision and now you have to live with it. Die, more likely. It was too late to draw against a cocked gun, especially in the hands of this man.

"You've got no guts," Davin said again. "You're all mouth and no guts. A story gets started and you help it along. Pretty soon people start believing it. That's what you are, Duane—a fraud. But you're going to get dead just the same. Like hell I'm going to take you in, back to that old Ranger captain. You're all Texans here and I'm a stranger. That's all I've ever been. One last time. You're going to die so why not do it like a man. You want odds, then I'll give you odds."

"No odds," Duane said. "Kill me or take me back. Rope me if you like. That way I can't jump you on the trail."

Duane held the gun steady. "You won't jump anybody. All you're going to do is die. Here I'm the judge. I'm sentencing you to death. You admitted you killed my father, and that's all I need."

"Then do it."

Ben Davin raised the revolver. "You want it so bad, here it is."

•

Buck Duane stared into the black muzzle of the six-shooter. Then the gun moved away from his heart. It didn't move far.

"There's a better way," Ben Davin said, smiling now. If a snake could smile, that's what Ben Davin looked like. "You should have taken my offer, friend. Now it's too late. You're still going to die, only now it won't be quick and easy. You're going to run and I'm going to follow. So you still get a chance. You may not like how it ends, but you're going to get it. You're the famous Buck Duane, the terror of the West. Let's see how good you are. You're supposed to be as good as an Indian when it comes to dodging and tracking. That's right—run! No horse, no guns—nothing but what you think you know. I'll even give you an hour's start. That ought to be enough for a big man like you. Don't fret. I won't kill you long range. When it happens you'll see my face."

Davin pointed with his left hand. "Up there, gunslinger. Stay by the river, run to the hills. No matter to me. I'll find you. Now the talking's all done. Move out!"

Ben Davin moved around and behind Duane as he unbuckled his gunbelt and let it drop. Davin made him take off his boots and when he did Davin felt inside them, looking for a knife. He threw them back and Duane stomped them on. "Seems to me a sneak like you would carry a knife," Davin said.

Duane didn't answer. All he could think of was—I'm alive. So far I'm alive.

"Go on—scat!" Ben Davin said.

For an instant Duane almost tackled him, gun or no gun. No man living talked to him like that. He forced his temper back into its cage and his face was a question.

"An hour, no more," Davin said. "No cheating on the time. You have my word on that. I got a watch. He was wearing it when you killed him."

Davin snapped open a watch with one hand, but by then Buck Duane was running. No bullets chased him as he ran. A meadow dappled with flowers ran along the side of the river. On the far side of it was a thick stand of pine. He heard the whinny of his horse, surprised and dismayed at being left behind. Set your pace, he told himself as he ran. But first put some distance between you. Don't try to think of a plan. It's too soon for that. Move out, set your pace, keep to it. Then you can start to make a plan.

Duane crossed the meadow and got into the stand of trees. The pines ran uphill along the river for several hundred yards. Under the trees it was dark after the bright sunlight of the meadow. A carpet of pine needles stretched out in front of him, broken only by the tree trunks. The ground felt spongy as he ran over it. At no time did he look back as he ran. Davin had given his word and Duane knew he would keep it. Maybe the man was crazy, but he would keep his word. Why give his word and then break it, when he had had every chance to kill him.

He paced himself, knowing how far he could push

231

himself. The trees seemed to go on forever, dark and gloomy. Below he could hear the rush of the fast-flowing river. But this was no creek he could lose his tracks in. The river ran fast and wild, swollen by snow water from higher up.

Duane ran counting in his head. He kept going. Five minutes passed, then ten. Then he was out of the shelter of the trees and a long slope of broken shale ran for half a mile. After that there were more trees, stunted, clinging to rock. His boots scuffed in the sand and shale as he ran along the slope. The slope ran long and high, but his breathing was still easy. The sun was strong except for the chill wind that blew down from the hills. If he lasted till night it would be cold without a fire or a blanket.

He reached the top of the slope and on the other side it dropped into a ravine choked with rocks and brush. Thorns tore at him, ripping his clothes, as he went on through and climbed up the far side. Shifting sand kept pushing him back as his hands and feet searched for a hold. Easy, he told himself. You're going at it too fast. Pace yourself, man.

He clawed his way out of the ravine and lay in dead yellow grass sucking in breath. Above his head a squirrel ran along a branch and twittered. The squirrel had never seen a man before. You're better off, little fellow, Duane thought crazily. Let's not be thinking about men and squirrels, he warned himself. Just men—one man. A crazy boy with the eyes of a killer.

Duane pushed on. Brush and rocks ran down to the river and he had to skirt the bank of the river to get through. At times he had to hang on to twisted branches and sandy roots. In one place the river bank was nothing but sheer rock and he had to swing his way from branch to branch, ten feet above the white-frothed water. If he fell the jagged rocks and the swift rushing current would tear him to pieces.

Then he was across and both wrists were bleeding. Blood oozed from a gash in his chest put there by a broken branch. After that he made good time. He knew that Davin wouldn't push himself so hard. He didn't have to. Maybe that was Davin's weakness. Overconfidence had done for better men than Ben Davin. But for now putting distance between them was all that mattered. Already he had stretched the hours start to nearly two hours. That was what he figured, knowing that he might be wrong. But there was no time to think about anything but stretching the distance. When that was done, if he did it, he could make his plan.

Three hours had passed since Ben Davin snapped open his dead father's watch. The sun was well past the noon mark by now. Still a long way to go till nightfall. At two o'clock by the sun, he rested for fifteen minutes. He came to a wide sandy place in the river and lay there drinking water, listening for sounds. But there was nothing but the water running over rocks. One side of the river was shallow and sandy and he went through there until he was forced out by a rockfall. Back on dry ground, he followed the course of the river until a stretch of ravines ran down into the water, blocking his way. Now there was nothing to do but climb, move on up from the river, and keep going. As the day wore on, the sun began to lose its warmth and the wind from the high country blew harder, colder. Coming down from the peaks, the wind had a mournful sound. He couldn't hear the sound of the river. It was too far away.

The sun slanted toward the east and Duane moved on. He rested in a high place and checked the country behind him. There was no sign of Ben Davin. He was in the foothills of the Mackenzie Mountains. Far above him were the peaks, with snow still packed in crevices and holes. Behind him the grass of a lower mountain meadow waved in the

233

wind. All day he had been moving on nothing but a cup of coffee. Behind him, along with his horse, his guns, he had left a skilletful of firm-bodied trout, fried just right. His belly rumbled when he thought of the fish, the biscuits that should have gone with them.

He ate handfuls of choke berries, bitter tasting and hard, not ripe yet, not much of a meal. On a slope he rooted for wild onions and rubbed the dirt off with his sleeve. He rested, chewing the pulpy onions, and then moved on. Ahead there were cliffs. They looked close but he knew the fading light wasn't to be trusted. It would be full dark before he made it into the shelter of the cliffs. There were caves where there were cliffs. Usually there were. Easy now, he warned him.

He made it there just before the sun dropped out of sight. One moment the dying sun was a great glowing copper ball, then it seemed to hiss out, and was gone. The only light came from a red glow on the far side of the mountains. It faded and then it was dark.

The cliffs ran up into the dark sky, jagged and sinister, grey as death. Duane edged along the bottom of the cliff looking to find a way up. There was none that he could find, not in the dark. Bushes growing out of crevices in the rock wall rattled in the wind. He was dirty and hungry and hurt all over. It began to get cold.

It got colder as the rocks gave up the heat of the day. Duane felt the heat being drawn from his own body. He scrambled along the foot of the cliff, no longer trying to find a way up. All he wanted now was a place to sleep without freezing. It was spring in the hills and the cold wasn't enough to kill him, but it would keep him awake. Or if he managed to sleep in spite of the cold, it would be bad sleep. Years on the prod had taught Duane the value of sleep. A man, no matter how hungry, could keep going if he had sleep. With no sleep, or bad sleep, a man's mind began to wander. The mind still worked but it made wrong judgments. And if a man went too long without sleep he began to see things that weren't there. Duane knew about sleep. He had been through it before, years before on the Staked Plains when he had been tracked by Kiowa scouts. Day and night they kept after him. Not the same men. The Indians knew about sleep. Some slept and some followed, then they switched, and always the pursuit continued until he was ready to go clear out of his skull....

Easy now, Duane thought. You'll find a good place to sleep. A place with sand he could burrow into like an animal. Out of the wind it wouldn't be so bad. A few minutes later, he found it, a shallow cave. Hardly a cave, more like a hole in the rockface. He took a broken branch and poked inside to drive out rattlers. During the day the rattlers basked on the rocks in the sun. At night they crawled in where it was warm.

Nothing rattled. Duane went in and there was just room to turn around. No room to stand up or even raise up on his knees. But it was floored with fine sand and he dug into it with his hands with the eagerness of a tired man getting ready for bed. He dug until his fingers scraped against rock, and knew that was as far as he could go. It would have to do, it was fine.

Before he lay down and scooped sand around him, he stripped the broken branch until he had the closest thing to a spear. The wood was dry but there was plenty of spring left in it. Then he searched until he found a long splinter of rock. Crouched in the dark, he rubbed the splinter against the smooth wall of the cave until there was a point on it.

He lay in the dark with the stone knife in his hand, the pointed stick by his side. Outside the wind

235

whistled in the rocks. He was hungry but not so cold. God! he thought, right this minute I could be sleeping sound in one of Mrs. Roark's featherbeds. Now he knew what it must have been like in the days of the cave men. There were no giant lizards or sabertooth tigers to threaten him. A well armed killer was just as dangerous. Maybe more so.

He didn't think Davin would come in the dark. The killer lawman was too smart for that. It was possible but it wasn't likely—and a man had to go with what was likely. He hoped Davin would come, for in the dark there would be some equality of weapons, but he knew he wouldn't. More likely, Davin would try to wear him out, break him down, until he was heartsick with running. Then he would move in for the kill.

There was nothing to do but sleep. That came first. After that he would decide what had to be done—could be done. There was no use dwelling on it. Duane pushed Davin from his mind, closed his eyes, and was instantly asleep.

A mile away, Ben Davin sat with his back against a tree, a blanket draped over his shoulders, a rifle in his hand. Only once during the long day had he lost Duane's trail, and that was only for a while. That was when Duane went down into the river shallows and walked upstream in the sand. The swift moving current washed the tracks away, and there were no broken branches along the edge of the river, no flattened grass, so there was no way to be sure if a man had passed that way. At one point a rock slope, smooth and swept clean by the wind, went up from the river. A man could walk over rock like that without leaving a trace.

Ben Davin didn't climb the rock. Instead, he stayed with the river and he was right. Not far from the rock the shallows petered out and there was a broken branch that Duane had used to pull himself up on the steep, sandy bank. After that it was easy. Even so, Duane was making better time than he had figured. No matter. The big man had to be getting tired by now. Ben Davin grinned wolfishly in the darkness. That was it. Tired and hungry. Cold too.

Thinking of cold made Davin pull the blanket tighter around his shoulders. Damn near as cold as Montana this Texas high country was. Davin chewed handfuls of jerked meat and drank water from his canteen. His horse moved in the darkness on a short rein. Duane's horse was somewhere out there. It went against his strange nature to kill a good horse, so all he did was unsaddle the big animal and turn it loose after Duane started to make his run. The horse had followed and was out there. No matter. Just a horse, but maybe he'd have to shoot it after all. No, he couldn't do that. Not now. A shot would give away his position. To a man like Duane, a shot would be like pinpointing his position on a map. Maybe the big horse would give up and wander on downriver.

Chewing jerky, Davin thought of the choke berry patch where Duane had rested. The big man was down to eating choke berries. Soon he wouldn't be eating anything at all. Most likely Duane was sheltering in the cliffs up ahead. That's where he had to be, unless he decided to climb them in the dark. That wasn't what a man like Buck Duane would do. He would sleep and be on his way before first light climbed up over the rim of the eastern mountains. The trick was to be there when Duane started his climb, going up the rockface like an ant. Not as easy as an ant though. Duane would have to fight his way up, clawing for holds in the sheer rock.

Davin patted his pocket to make sure the small brass-framed binoculars were still there. They were.

Even without a gun, the binoculars would have given him all the edge he needed. Earlier in the day, he had glassed the cliffs from a long way back. The rockface looked unbroken from one end to the other. Of course, Duane could always work his way along the bottom of the cliff and try to find a way around the great escarpment without having to climb. That wasn't likely either. The great mass of rock ran for miles. Duane would try to climb. He was betting on that. In the end, it made no difference what the big man did. He would find him.

Ben Davin forced himself to believe that he was giving Duane a fighting chance. He had to believe it. That was what he lived by, the idea that he always gave the other man a fighting chance. Hell! Of course he was giving Duane a chance, a better chance than Duane gave his father. Taking Duane back to stand trial was put of the question. There might not be any trial, and even with a trial the best he could hope for was life in the state pen for Duane. The hell with that! It wasn't enough. They could put Duane behind the gray walls, but he wouldn't stay there for long. Whatever he did, it wouldn't be enough. Duane had to die. It was as simple as that. Nothing less would satisfy him.

Still, he had to admit that he liked the idea of hunting a man like Buck Duane. The man was a legend, even in Montana, and even men who hated him talked about him with reluctant respect. Buck Duane did all the things other men said couldn't be done. Duane did them, but never bragged about the doing. Never even talked about it.

Ben Davin shifted to make himself more comfortable. Well, sir, he thought, he wouldn't brag either. He would never tell another living soul about the day he killed the toughest man in Texas. No reward would be collected, no matter what he had said to his grandmother about using the money to erect a monument to his father. That was recent but now it was in the past. No, the killing of the famous Buck Duane would remain a secret. Ben Davin found humor in the thought that he would kill Duane and bury his body in a place where it would never be found. Bury him in a secret place, line the top of the grave with rocks, then cover the whole thing with dirt. Duane would disappear, vanish forever, and then wherever he went he would be able to smile when men spoke of the famous Texas outlaw. The legends would grow, as they grew up around every famous outlaw. Men would say that the great Buck Duane had gone to South America like Butch Cassidy. In time men would swear they had seen him there, robbing a bank or drinking whiskey in a saloon or a cantina.

Ben Davin smiled. He would listen and he would smile because only he knew the truth. It wasn't in Ben Davin's nature to boast. The thing that caused other men to brag had been left out of him. It never bothered him. In fact, he thought of it as making him different from other men. That was it—he was different. What was the word he had learned at school. Unique. That was it—he was unique. One of a kind. And because he was different, he was better than all the others. He made his own rules and lived by them. Life had forced him to be a loner, but instead of fretting about it, he used it to his advantage. Of what he would do after he killed Duane he had no idea. Killing Duane was all that mattered, and he wasn't ready to think past that. It was as if all his life he had been preparing to kill Duane. Duane was a challenge, the biggest he could find, the biggest he was ever likely to find. There was satisfaction in that. But not so other people could slap him on the back, say what a big man he was. The killing of Buck Duane was entirely private— between him and nobody.

Ben Davin wished he could sleep. He hadn't slept well since his grandmother had sent the telegraph message to Montana. Since New Orleans his sleep had been fitful, and for the last few days he hadn't slept at all. After it was over, he would sleep. Go off some place he wasn't known and sleep for a week, if he wanted to. That was fine, but what about sleep right now? He had to get some sleep.

He closed his eyes but they jerked open again. It was no use. He spilled water into his hand and rubbed it in his face, around the back of his neck. The shock of the cold water felt good, and it revived him for a moment. Then he found himself staring into the darkness. Always he found himself staring.

During the night he slept for an hour. Maybe it wasn't even an hour, he thought. It didn't make him feel any better. If anything, his nerves were pulled tighter than they had been. No matter. It was something he had to endure. Trying to turn his lack of sleep into an advantage, Ben Davin tried to tell himself that being keyed up would make him sharper, quicker to react when killing time came. As the night wore on and the black sky began to fade, to turn from dead black to gray, he began to feel invincible. Nothing could stop him. The next day would finish it.

He stood up and threw the blanket aside. He would get the horse and the blanket on the way back. The wind was cold at that hour, but he would have a nice day for the ride back. After it was over there would be no more need to hurry. Ben Davin picked up his rifle and moved out. It was starting to get light.

Buck Duane, stretching his long legs, crawled out of the cave and stood in the cold light of dawn brushing sand from his face. There was no more time to lose. He sensed—knew—that Ben Davin was already on his way to kill him. He was tired and hungry, but danger drove out everything else. He was tired but alert and as he breathed in cold air the tiredness left him. It would stay away until hunger brought it back. For the moment he was all right.

Moving away from the rockface he looked up. Nothing. Then as he moved along the great cathedral of stone he saw it, a split in the rock he had missed in the dark. It started higher than his head, and that was why he had missed it. As the light grew stronger he was able to see that the split in the rock went all the way to the top of the cliff. The inside of the rock was stepped and broken. That meant he could climb if he could get in there.

It had to be now. This was something that had to be done—or he would die. In the full light of morning he saw that the cliff ran away into the distance. How far? Not as far as it looked. It couldn't run that far. No cliff did. Easy, he said in a whisper. All you have to do is make that first jump. Then you have a chance. Do that—make the first jump, then hang on—and you have a chance.

Some chance! He put down the stone knife and walked away from the cliff. He looked at it, then moved back more. That would do it, ought to do it, if it could be done. Now! Duane ran forward and jumped. His fingers touched the split in the rock, then they tore free. He was falling to the ground, ready to try again, when a rifle bullet smacked into the rock less than a foot from his head. The shot sounded as if it came from a long way back. Maybe not so far back. Maybe Davin wasn't taking his time, was in too much of a hurry to aim right. Another bullet hit the rock lower down, but Duane had rolled away by then.

There was only one way out—and that was up. Bullets sang at him as he moved back for another run. If he missed this time it was all over. He steadied himself, forced himself to stand upright. Another bullet came at him and he thought he heard a wild yell in the trees that faced the cliff.

He ran and jumped and this time his fingers found a hold. Holding on with one hand, sweating hard, he reached in wth the other hand and found a break in the stone. A bullet spattered on the rock, throwing bits of lead in his face. He felt the trickle of his own blood. Now the yelling was getting closer. Slowly, agonizingly, he pulled himself up, his arm sockets ready to tear loose. Then he was inside the split with his sweating face pressed against the cold rock, sucking wind, shuddering in every muscle.

Bullets plowed into the rock split, but he wasn't hit by anything but splinters. He braced himself and began to climb. He went up and bullets followed him, but now Davin had nothing real to aim at. Davin was yelling, firing wildly. Duane didn't look down at him, didn't do anything but claw his way up. The top seemed to be a mile away.

Now he was up about halfway and he heard Davin below him, boosting himself to where the long climb began. He looked down and Davin was trying to aim a six-shooter at him. Davin fired and the bullet went wild. Then he fired again and the pin clicked on an empty chamber. Duane kept on climbing and then there came a time when he couldn't climb any more. His muscles wouldn't take any more punishment. He was close to the top, but he couldn't make it the rest of the way. Davin was still climbing, still cursing and wild eyed. He got closer, clawing at the rock, his feet slipping in places where water dripped. He kept yelling, "I'm going to kill you, Duane. On my father's grave I swear I'm going to kill you. You'll never get away from me. Run, climb—you can't get away."

It was going to be over soon, Duane knew. Here it

would end for one of them. He felt a great weariness as he waited for Davin to get even closer. Davin came up an inch at a time, the way he had done.

Davin grabbed at Duane's ankle and nearly got a hold on it. Duane kicked at him but missed. Davin began to laugh—wild, madman's laughter. It echoed in the rocks. Amplified, it boomed out over the quiet hills, and then it died away.

Davin grabbed again and this time his foot slipped and he was hanging by nothing but his fingertips. Sweating, Duane reached down and got a grip on one of his wrists. The way he was positioned, he couldn't get a grip on the other wrist. Bracing himself against the rock, trying to keep from falling, he put every ounce of strength in trying to pull Davin up after him. He knew he couldn't do it, but he kept trying. Then his hold began to slip. Davin looked up and his eyes were wild with craziness and fear. He cursed Duane and begged for help at the same time. But his yelling, his frantic struggles, only made it worse.

Then he lost his footing completely and began to swing from one side of the split to the other. Below him there was nothing but a drop of two hundred feet. And then he fell. Down and down he went, his body battered against rock, shattered on the rocks below.

Buck Duane, when he was able, began to climb down.

"What I don't understand," Captain MacNelly growled. "Is why you didn't gun him down when you had the chance. Look at you, for God's sake, you look like you been clawed by a grizzly. Answer up, man—why did you let it go so far. I have a mind to bring you up on some charges. What that charge might be I haven't figured yet. Maybe there's something listed under stupidity. I'll say it again. Why did you let it go so far?"

Buck Duane had just returned from the hills, battered and showing the signs of the ordeal he had been through. He was bone weary, ragged, badly in need of a shave.

He turned a coffee cup in his hands and looked at the Captain. "I just couldn't draw on him," he said. "There was something crazy about him. Besides, he was wearing a badge."

The Captain snorted with impatience. "What's that got to do with it? Lots of crooks and crazy men wear badges. You're a fool, Duane. You been an outlaw, but you don't have to keep paying for it the rest of your blamed life. I nearly lost a good man out there. That's you, stonehead!"

Duane said, "You know, Cap, I felt sorry for him even at the end. Yes! Yes! I know a Ranger isn't supposed to think like that. Maybe I'm not that good a Ranger."

"That's for me to decide."

"I think a lot of things we'll never know about drove Davin to become what he was."

"None of our business. Can't you ever get that through your head? We don't judge these people. They break the law and we go after them. A judge does the judging. It's not your business to have feelings one way or another."

"Does it matter, Captain?" Duane asked. "He's dead. I buried him close to where he died. Piled rocks so the coyotes won't be able to get at him. I don't know that I ever met anybody like him. Hope I never do again. I'd as soon tangle with a bunch of bank robbers than have to deal with another man like Ben Davin."

"You'll get your chance," MacNelly snorted, chewing angrily on his cigar. "Damn you, Buck Duane, I thought sure you were dead. You know you stayed three days past your leave."

That was the old Captain's way of saying he had been worried about him. "I'll make up for it," Duane said. "Now about these bank robbers? You got an idea who they might be?"

"Hang it, man," MacNelly stormed. "That's for you to find out. Soon as you get fixed up I want you to go down to Fairfax County and see what the Sam Hill is going on. So far they've busted open two nice fat banks. More to come, I don't doubt. No need to leave rightaway. I already sent the Jackrabbit Kid and two other men. I don't know which of you is more trouble to me—you or that Kid."

The Captain's face softened as much as his leathery countenance would allow. "You been through the wringer, Buck. You come out kind of flat, it looks to me, but I guess you're all right. The point I'm trying to make is this. Don't always push your luck so far. Luck is like India rubber. Push it too far and it breaks. No more taking chances with your life, hear. No more than you have to take. A good man is hard to find, like they say. You're the good man I'm talking about, ironhead."

"You expect me to say I'm sorry about the way I handled Davin. No way I can do that, Cap. I played the cards my own way and I won. If you can call it winning."

"This time you won. What about the next time? You say this Ben Davin was too friendly with death. Well, listen to me, *Mister* Duane. There's some of that in you. Maybe I had some in me when I was young. I was lucky enough to live long enough to get over it. You may not be so lucky. Don't be in such a blamed hurry to get out of here. There's something I have to talk to you about. You look all in, but what I have to say can't wait."

Duane didn't smile. "Go ahead, Captain," he said.

MacNelly settled back and lit a cigar. "You

remember that Joe Bacon we were talking about?"

Duane nodded. Here it came.

"I told you he'd probably lay low for a while before he started up again. Well, sir, I guess I was wrong. No, there's no new conspiracy that I know of. Not yet. What I'm going to tell you is much more personal. Word has sifted in here that Bacon is dead set on killing you, Buck. Don't talk. Let me finish. So far it's just rumor, but I listen to every rumor soggy or firm. Word is out that Bacon is going after you. I don't know when or where, or how he plans to do it. That's the bad news for today, and I have the feeling it ain't just saloon talk. One thing Bacon has is money. Money is what it takes, especially in his slimy line of endeavor. There are men in this state so bad they'd kill a child for a dollar. Bacon's got more than a dollar. I'd say he's got all the dollars he needs, and then some."

Duane drank what was left of his coffee and set down the cup. "You have any idea where Bacon is?"

"So far nothing," MacNelly answered, frowning. "That's the worst part of it. If I knew where he was I'd know how to handle him. He might get shot by accident on purpose, if you know what I mean. Don't look at me that way, sonny boy. You just been through the legalities, and see what it got you. I got every lawman, Ranger and otherwise, trying to get a line on Bacon. The minute I hear something I'm going to send the boys in after him. Meantime, you get on down to Fairfax County. Leave Joe Bacon to me. That's an order. Now git!"

Leaving Ranger headquarters, Buck Duane thought about Joe Bacon. Watch himself, the Captain said. That was good advice, but how did he go about applying it? For Buck Duane knew better than any man that there was no way to walk away from death. There was no way to know the time or place. No matter. It was out there waiting to make its

246

claim. You could fend it off for a time, but it never went too far. In the end, it made not one whit of difference.

And, thought Buck Duane, I wouldn't have it any other way.

THREE DEATHS
FOR BUCK DUANE

The man behind the big mahogany desk in the library of the mansion in San Antonio, Texas, had worn many names in his time. In Mexico they thought he was the devil himself and called him by variants of that title.

He had carved a bloody trail across the Argentine Pampas and in the silver towns of the Bolivian *altiplano*. They knew his face in the *apache* dens of Paris and on the London stock exchange.

Many names. Many lives. Always hated and never loved wherever he went.

In the booming frontier town under the shadow of the Alamo, the name he gave himself was Joseph Bacon.

He lived in a four storied and towered stone mansion on the edge of town. Outside, were wide lawns and trees, a fountain and a cast iron deer. Inside was heavy, expensive furniture, dark oil paintings, oriental rugs, and many works of sculpture. There were deft, soft footed servants, there were wines and liquors and rare works of art.

Joe Bacon leaned back in his chair and looked at the three men who faced him across the desk.

"I brought you here," he said, "to kill a man." He said it quietly, but the evil fires of hell seethed in his breast and behind the smooth mask of his face.

"I thought as much," said the tall, swarthy, mustached man slouching by the window. "That's mostly what men want me for. I'll kill him if the price is right."

The man was called Durango. If he'd ever had another name the world had long forgotten. He was known along the border as a fast and deadly gun, a ruthless killer for hire.

"The price is right," Joe Bacon said. "For this man's death I'm willing to pay one hundred thousand dollars in United States gold coin."

In spite of themselves the three before him drew in their breaths in greed and astonishment. It was like a very soft hissing of deadly snakes.

No snakes could have been deadlier than these three.

Next to Durango sat a small, fearsome man garbed in the height of New Orleans creole fashion. His spare frame was raw boned and his face made pink and white by the deadly fevers of tuberculosis. His eyes were black and hard and unblinking. He wore the frock coat and tailored trousers of a gentleman. His shirt was freshly laundered white linen—and all the buttons were diamonds set in gold.

Along Bourbon and Dauphin Streets, and in the back street dives and houses behind the levee, he was known as St. Pierre. "He holds the keys to heaven and hell," the gamblers and pimps and the robbers said of him.

The third was a big, quiet ruddy faced man wearing conventional western townsman's garb, newly bought. He came originally from the Five Points slum in New York City. At the age of ten he'd cut a man's throat with the razoredged glass of a smashed beer bottle. He'd gone on from that to become a lieutenant in the "Dead Rabbits" gang of thieves and killers and a terror in the alleys and slums.

They called him Irish Pat, or sometimes just the Irish Death.

All three were specialists in sudden death and tops in their porfession.

"I'll kill him for you," Durango repeated. "You'd

249

no need to send for these others here. There's no man I can't kill for you by myself."

"You haven't even asked his name," Bacon snorted.

"That's true," the Creole said. "I assume that this is someone special—someone hard to kill."

The Irishman leaned back in his chair and began to clean his finger nails with the point of a long, folding bowie knife, hilted in horn and nickel silver from Sheffield.

"The man I want killed," Joe Bacon said, "is the Texan they call Buck Duane."

He said it flatly, tonelessly as if he were naming a brand of wine or a favorite race horse. He kept his face a mask and watched the three merchants of death.

"If one of you kills Buck Duane for me," he said, "I'll pay him a hundred thousand dollars in gold. If you do it together the money will be split between the two or three who are actually in at the death. If you hire others to help you, that comes out of your share."

He waited a long moment, watching the greed shine in their eyes. "It's the biggest price ever paid for a killing in Texas," Bacon reminded them.

"But the man is Buck Duane," Durango said.

"He's a tough man to be up against," St. Pierre said, "and how do we know you will pay us? We risk our lives, but what is our guarantee?"

Irish Pat and Durango nodded. "Yeah," said the slum-toughened Irishman. "What is our guarantee?"

Joe Bacon reached over and picked up a silver dinner bell. He rang it three times. The trio of gunmen turned to see three figures enter.

Leading the trio was a Mexican known to the public only as Don Andres. He had been banished from his native land since the death by firing squad of the Austrian Emperor Maxmilian. Don Andres

250

was a royalist, and now he could never go home. But he was known to have friends and relatives, connections and many sources of wealth below the border.

The second man was an Englishman who went by the name of Mr. Will Hadley. He spoke for and was agent of a certain London pool of entrepreneurs, speculators in dubious but potentially profitable schemes, and exploiters of the fringes of the world. He was plainly and simply dressed, a soft spoken man with gamblers' eyes and an air of command that came from the great wealth and power of his backers.

The third was a woman, tall and beautiful and dressed in the height of fashion. Bacon introduced her to the others as his wife, Helen, though in reality no marriage had ever actually taken place. She played the role of mistress of the house and played it well.

"Gentlemen," Bacon said to the gunslingers, "Your guarantee. You know us all for wealthy men." The trio nodded as one man. "So what's the plan," Durango asked.

"I've arranged it all," Joe Bacon said over the rim of his fragile great bubble of a brandy glass. "The first step of the many that will give us control of Texas once and for all."

"We have agreed to put up the money," Will Hadley observed, "but for myself I am still not convinced of the need for such indiscriminate killing. Through our friend Don Andres here we have the connections and the market to move all the cattle we can steal out of Texas into Mexico. You have put us in touch with the bandits ...uh...rustlers, you call them, to do our work here.

"We can sweep the wealth out of this State as a broom sweeps sawdust off the floor of one of your saloons. My bankers and backers will supply what capital we need to buy up the ranches after we have stolen the owners bankrupt. We can buy protection from the law."

"Exactly," Don Andres agreed. "Why must we guarantee these moves which will deliberately provoke the most dangerous arm of that same law? To me it is putting our head needlessly into the jaws of the lion." He spoke flawless, unaccented English.

"We have to do it," Bacon insisted. "You aren't familiar with local conditions, Mr. Hadley. As long as the Texas Rangers exist our heads are in the lion's mouth. What's more it is absolutely certain that those jaws will close on us, unless we soften their bite first."

"I don't understand," Hadley repeated. "You assured my principals in London that your frontier law could be bought, corrupted to protect and even further our aims. Are you reversing yourself now?"

His tone left little doubt as to what his backers would feel about any such reversal.

"Not that," Bacon assured him. "Not at all. Enough of our legislators, judges and sheriffs can be bought exactly as I explained to your people. The only law agency we cannot buy is the Rangers. They are skilled and very dangerous and have a statewide jurisdiction. They can harass our raids, kill our men and hamper our plans in many ways, and they..."

"And they are incorruptible," Don Andres said. "I begin to see your point. The Rangers are our greatest danger. Still there must be a way to deal with them besides declaring open war. We can buy the legislature you say? Then let them hamstring the Rangers. Let corrupt Ranger officers be appointed, their budget cut, their best men assigned to posts where we do not operate. Surely that is the best way to deal with these men."

Joe Bacon leaned back in his chair and pulled at his long, Havana cigar. Only the woman, who knew him really well, could see how much of an effort he made to appear calm. The trio of hired killers watched him for any signs of uncertainty. There were none.

"You may be right," he said to the others. "Perhaps it could be done that way, but you forget the one prime factor in our plans. That factor is time. The methods you suggest would take months if not years. These Rangers are exceptional men. In months they could shatter our whole operation. The only way is to kill them one by one until enough are dead to destroy the prestige and morale of the others. A half dozen of the most dangerous will do it I think."

"I see," Hadley said.

"And what has Buck Duane to do with this," interjected Durango.

Bacon smiled. "To kill a snake, you kill the head. Few men, and I am one, are aware that Duane is a Ranger." The announcement startled the trio, who looked at each other. "I assure you, it's true," Bacon continued, "He is their best man. When I have destroyed the best of the Rangers, beginning with Duane, Texas will be ours."

"If you can have them killed," Don Andres said. "As you say these are terrible and dangerous men. If they detect your plan—I would not give a peso for the lives of any of us."

"They won't detect," Joe Bacon said. "I will hire men who can kill Rangers. As many as I need I will hire. The border is full of desperadoes. We kill Rangers one by one—beginning with the best of them."

He spoke with authority and all the confidence he could put in his voice. It was evident that the other men were fully convinced.

Joe Bacon smiled. He knew these men were his, now. With the financial backing of the two foreigners, and the deadly guns of the other three men, he knew his plan would work.

No one else in the room, except for the woman he now called Helen, knew the real motive behind selecting Duane as the first victim.

Had the men heard her whispered words, they might have had second thoughts about joining Bacon's venture.

"Revenge for Harpetown," were the unheard words.

II

Buck Duane rode into the little town of Bandera on his way to San Antonio. He was coming in from an assignment up in the Panhandle country close to the Llano Estacado, the fearsome Staked Plains where the Indians and the renegade Comancheros rode.

Bandera was nothing more than a way stop, an opportunity for brief rest and refreshment of steak and potatoes and canned tomatoes and a loaf of sourdough bread in the combined restaurant, saloon and general store.

It was the last place in the west where the big Texas Ranger would have expected anyone to be waiting for him.

He tied his big horse, Bullet, to the hitching rack and slapped the acrid, alkaline trail dust off his woolen pants before going into the place.

Duane stood over six feet tall, and his powerful frame made him a very big man indeed. His steel gray eyes saw everything and revealed nothing, like those of an Indian. His shoulders were broad and tapered to narrow hips and the long, muscular legs of a horseman. There wasn't an ounce of fat on his body and he was tanned a mahogany brown by wind and sun.

He wore the broad brimmed felt hat, the wool

shirt and pants of the frontier, and a pair of beautifully tanned, high heeled horseman's boots.

Two Colt forty-five revolvers in tied down holsters were suspended from a filled cartridge belt. A lever action hi-wall Winchester repeating carbine hung in the saddle boot on his mount.

Duane wore no badge or other insignia as a lawman. An undercover agent for the Rangers, most men knew him only as a former outlaw, one whose exploits and wild escapades were told and retold in the towns and camps.

His face was well enough known that the seedy old bar fly lounging on the wide, unpainted porch near the hitching rack, recognized him at once.

The old fellow got out of his chair and hurried off down the street to report: "It's him, mister. Buck Duane has come into town." And pocketed the silver dollar his report had earned.

Inside the saloon, Buck Duane ordered his meal. He had one glass of rye whiskey straight at the bar while the Mexican cook fried up the steak. One glass to cut the trail dust, and no more.

When he ate, he picked a small table at the side of the big room where he could put his back to the wall and watch the two entrances to the room. It was a gesture of long ingrained habit, the involuntary response of a man who had been on the run for most of his life.

There were only three or four men in the room, none of them bearing any sign of the gunman. Duane watched them casually as he ate. Equally casually, his glance flickered to the window and the two doors.

That's how he saw the kitchen door begin to open, not pushed open suddenly as the cook and barkeep would do, but parted very slowly, as if by someone who didn't want the movement to be noticed at all.

Duane froze and was suddenly totally alert.

The door came open a little wider. There was the barest flicker of light where the lamps in the saloon reflected off metal.

Buck Duane threw himself off the chair to the floor. He lit on his left side and shoulder. By the time he hit the floor his right hand cradled a big forty-five and his thumb had the hammer all the way cocked.

The movement was too sudden for the man behind the kitchen door. He jumped and triggered off both barrels of the sawed-off shotgun he held. He fired too fast without giving himself time to change from the original point of aim. The two loads of buckshot went over the table, passing through thin air where Duane's chest had been a split second before and splintering the boards of the wall behind the table.

Buck Duane fired one shot from the floor. His heavy slug thudded into the solid oak of the door as it swung shut. Over the triple thunder of the three shots there was the sound of running feet across the kitchen floor.

Even before Duane could scramble erect horses hoofs thudded and drummed away down the alley behind the saloon.

They found the Mexican cook unconscious on the floor of the kitchen. When they revived him with cold towels he still wasn't able to help much. He'd been pistol whipped by someone who had come up quietly behind him.

"I don't see hees face, senores. I don' see heem at all. Only hees boots as I start to fall down. I see only the new boots."

"That does it," the bartender said. "Only one man in this town has new boots. That's the eastern dude rode up from San Antone three days back. We wondered why he'd stay in this place. Seems like he was waitin' to bushwack you, mister."

"Seems so," Duane agreed. His mind was racing.

He knew of no reason why an eastern dude would try to kill him or even how the man had known he would be riding to town by this road.

Hasty inquiry at the town's one rooming house confirmed the fact that the stranger was missing. His horse was gone from the livery stable.

Duane finished his dinner, had one more drink for the road, and took Bullet to the livery stable for a feed. It was pitch dark by then, but he decided against spending the night in Bandera. He doubted that the man who wanted to kill him would return that night, but no sense in giving him a target to shoot at if he did.

The big Ranger knew this country well and he pulled an old outlaw trick to make sure of a good night's rest. He rode out of town on the road to San Antonio, then cut off the road for a clump of cottonwood a little way up the course of the first small stream he forded. Here he made a fireless camp and slept soundly, secure in the knowledge that not even an Indian could track him in the dark.

He was awake long before the first crack of dawn and making his first plans for the day.

He thought like an outlaw, like a man whose life depended always on his ability to outguess the deadliest of trackers.

Duane still had no real idea why an eastern stranger would want to kill him, and unlike most other men in his situation, he wasted no time in trying to solve that riddle. Time enough for that later on.

Right now, the important fact was that a man who did want to murder him was alive, loose and armed—and somewhere nearby. That much was fact. That, he must deal with. Many times in his life Duane had faced this kind of a situation. He felt supremely confident of his ability to deal with it successfully.

He put himself in the mind of the man who was hunting him. The stranger had set himself in ambush in Bandera and waited until Duane rode in. That meant that he was no casual bandit. His target was the Texas Ranger.

Whoever he was, he wouldn't give up with this one try. He'd set a second ambush and, apparently knowing that the Ranger was headed for San Antonio, it would be somewhere on the road to the City.

Since he was a city type from the east, he wouldn't really know the country. He couldn't stalk or hide like a frontiersman. That would limit his course of action.

That would make Duane's own task all the simpler. His first step was easy.

"Where would I hide out if I was a stranger and a dude?" he asked himself.

The answer came almost immediately.

"Pipe Creek crossing," Duane told Bullet as he saddled the big horse. "It's the natural place for a man like him to choose. The only question is, will he lie up on the west bank or the east? Better scout both sides to be sure."

He checked his two Colts, loosened the Winchester in its boot and swung up into the saddle.

The road from Bandera crossed Pipe Creek at a spot where the little stream ran between high, steep banks. The road dipped down through a narrow slash worn by cattle, and, before them, by buffalo making the crossing. It then climbed steeply to reach the open plains on the east.

It was no Grand Canyon of course. At the most, the steep banking walls were only some thirty feet high from the bottom of the creek. The banks were steep enough, though, so that a horse and rider had to use the road or make a detour of several miles.

There were cottonwood trees on the east side of

the stream. That was the San Antonio side. A bushwacker could hide himself among them and gun down a rider crossing towards him from Bandera.

"That's what I'd do if the man I wanted had no reason to suspect I might be there," Buck Duane told himself. "On the other hand, this ranny tipped me off when he tried for me last night. He knows I figure he'll set an ambush someplace. If I come riding down to Pipe Creek he can bet I'll be watching the cottonwoods. If it was me in his place, I'd lay up on the west side which he figures I won't be watching because it looks so open. That's where I'd be—so I better figure that's where he will be."

Just north of the road where it dipped down to Pipe Creek there was a small knoll, not much more than a swell in the ground, with the grass growing waist high on its crest.

Buck Duane tied Bullet in a little scrub thicket half a mile north of where the road crossed Pipe Creek. The first gray light of dawn was spreading across the flat land.

Duane made the last half mile to the crossing on foot, with a care and precision that only an Apache or Comanche could have equalled, taking advantage of even the slightest dip in the ground or the scrawniest mesquite bush for cover. He moved as silently and unnoticed as the shadow of a cruising hawk far overhead.

Within three hundred yards from the knoll overlooking the crossing he knew that he had figured right. The bushwacker was there, clearly visible in the early light.

He was a city man, all right. The fool had even been smoking a cigar as he waited, which no plainsman would have done. Duane followed the rank smoke right to where his man waited. He made the last stretch on his belly in the grass.

When he knew he was almost on top of the man,

Duane stood up, still without making a sound. He wanted this man alive for questioning, and now he had the drop on him for sure.

The stranger was a big man wearing a new Stetson hat and riding boots, and his suit was city-cut. He lay slightly back of the ridge of land where he could look over and down at the road by moving the tall grass a bit. A rider on the road below would be at the mercy of the double barrelled shotgun on the ground close to his right hand.

Duane eased one big Colt into his right hand. "Just freeze," he told the man in quiet tones, "I can put a slug in your spine."

A westerner would have lain still, knowing that whoever could stalk that close could also kill him at will.

The man on the ground should have obeyed the order, but he didn't. Stupid or just a fool, he took the desperate long chance. He snatched at his shotgun and rolled in the grass.

Duane didn't dare let him pull trigger on the shotgun. At that range nobody could miss. He shot for the man's right shoulder. He wanted to cripple his gun arm so he could hold the man and question him.

The fellow was rolling too fast though, and the heavy forty-five soft lead slug took him in the throat instead of the shoulder.

On the way out it broke his spine, and he was dead before the sound of the shot had ceased to boom across the prairie.

Duane grunted. Despite his fearsome reputation, this big, quiet man hated to kill. A prisoner would have been valuable to him right then. A dead man was simply a corpse.

He searched the body carefully. There was a wallet with money but no identification. In the pockets of the suit were a set of brass knucks and a switch blade knife. Hung in a holster under the left shoulder was a cheap revolver of the "English Bull Dog" brand.

He found the man's horse and recognized the brand of a well-known San Antonio livery stable where the beast had been rented. Still no identification.

Buck Duane had no way of knowing he had killed the famous New York "Dead Rabbit" known as Irish Pat.

III

Late that evening, Buck Duane rode into San Antonio by back streets. He had the body of the man he'd killed wrapped in a tarp over the back of the fellow's led horse, and he didn't want to attract attention.

He left both horses in the stable used by the local Texas Ranger detachment. In the office which fronted on the street, he found his commanding officer and close personal friend, Captain MacNelly of the Texas Rangers.

The Ranger Officer was a small man. Lean and wiry and tough as whipcord and rawhide, MacNelly knew the trails and the hidden ways of the nation's biggest state as another man knows his own front yard. He could track like an Indian and use any one of a dozen frontier weapons to the admiration and awe of his own Rangers.

He had a fine mind, a hair trigger reaction to any problem, and a genius for command. His men loved and trusted him. They would have followed him into Hell itself at one word of command.

Tonight he sat behind a desk that was little more than a big pine table in an office lit by a single kerosene lantern. The table was piled high with maps and papers, routine reports both finished and half finished, pens in a glass tumbler, ink in a Mexican silver well, a bottle of sour mash Bourbon whiskey and a couple of plain glass tumblers.

The office itself, so small and cluttered, would have been scorned by any merchant, lawyer, saloon keeper or politician in San Antonio, yet these men came at times to this same cramped cubby hole to see MacNelly and to ask for his advice and help.

As Buck Duane came in, the Captain nodded him to a chair and a glass of the sour mash and went on reading the paper in his hand.

He looked up finally at his friend. "I hear you brought in a body, Buck. Anyone I know?"

Buck Duane tossed down his drink. "Captain," he said, "I don't know if you know him, but I can swear I don't. I never saw his face before in all my years. What's more, I never saw that fellow on a wanted poster or heard him described."

"Then why did you kill him?" the Captain asked.

"Because there was nothing else I could do," Duane said bluntly. "He was waiting for me at Bandera. Fired a shotgun through the kitchen door at me as I ate.

"Then he laid up for me at Pipe Creek crossing. Waiting for another crack at me. I back stalked him and put him under the gun. I had to shoot or die. I brought him on in to see if any of the boys could put a name to him for me."

"That fits," Captain MacNelly said. "Here, take a look at this." He took a piece of paper off the desk and handed it over.

It was a single sheet of white notepaper. The handwriting was a woman's. The note said:

"Take good care of Buck Duane, Captain. There are men hired to kill him. The price of his life is one hundred thousand dollars in gold."

The note was unsigned.

"I figured as much," Duane said. "I'd never

tangled with the man, so I knew he didn't have anything personal against me. Question is, who hired him, and who is he?"

"Let's take a look," the Captain said, pushing away from the table desk.

Captain MacNelly got up and took the lantern. Quietly the two men walked to the stable where the body lay on the floor. Duane turned back the corner of the tarp.

"I've seen this one," MacNelly said.

"He rode into town on the stage from Dallas a couple of weeks back. Registered at the hotel as Pat Riley of New York. He made no trouble here."

"Well, he made plenty of it for me," Duane told his commander. "I never saw him or heard of him. I never been to New York. Don't know of any enemies there, let alone one would want to kill me."

"This one wanted to kill you," MacNelly said as they went back to the office and sat down. "And he had a hundred thousand dollars worth of motive. You won't be safe, Buck, till we find the man who's behind this."

"Well," Duane said wryly, "I've made enemies like a dog collects fleas. Half of West Texas wants me dead."

"That's true enough." the Captain said. "One thing though. Half of West Texas doesn't have the money or the connections to send all the way to New York City for a gun to kill you. That took a man who knows the East—a man who can go to a lot of trouble and expense to make sure he gets you. I'd say a man wealthy and crazy enough to hold blood feud. A brave man, but a crazy man, too, and a man of influence and power.

"Who do we know like that, Buck, that would want you killed and could pay for it."

"There's only one name that comes to my mind right off, Captain; trouble is, it isn't even a name."

"The boss of Harpetown," MacNelly said.

"That's him. The one they called The Mask because nobody saw his face, not even the people who knew him best. We don't know his real name, but I guess I caused him plenty trouble."

"You can bet your boots you did. You stole his papers for the plan to split Texas apart. You shot and killed his best gun, DaVinci, and blew up his bank so his own killers looted his money. When you were through with Harpetown, man, it wasn't even a town any more.

"We never found him, because he wasn't in town when you struck it. We never got closer than a guess as to who he really was—but we know his whole scheme was ruined and broken up, and there's many a man and woman in Texas has good reason to thank God and Buck Duane for that.

"There's a man has reason to want you dead. There's one is familiar with the East and has the ways to find killers and money to hire them. I agree. He's our man, Buck."

"Right," Duane said, leaning back in his chair and lighting one of the Captain's long Cuban cigars. "Still . . . it don't help where we need help. This man could be anywhere at all. We don't even know his name. If we did, we couldn't arrest him unless we had proof of something. That won't be unless we take one of his guns alive and make him talk."

"If we can get one of them before they shoot you." MacNelly said somberly.

IV

By noon of the next day the news was all over San Antonio. And there were different versions depending upon the section of town in which the story was told.

The merchants and responsible citizens heard only that a man had been ambushed on the Bandera road, but had killed his attacker and brought in the body.

The gamblers and rustler bosses and the leading figures in the criminal element had a more accurate version. Some dude had brought in an Eastern killer to bushwack Buck Duane. Duane was alive and the gunman dead.

In the bars and stews they said drunkenly that Buck Duane, who could outdraw a rattler's strike, had been bushwacked by a dozen bandits and killed ten of them.

The news was out.

It reached the mansion some miles out of town where Joe Bacon heard, and knew who had died, and kept the information from his partners but not from the ear of the woman called Helen.

It was talked of in the lobby of the expensive hotel where Laurent St. Pierre had engaged a suite of rooms. He slept late, and heard the news from the black waiter who brought up his breakfast on a silver tray.

He listened without comment, but within his mind was quite content. There was one less rival for the hundred thousand dollars which he meant to have all for himself.

By noon, a rider was pounding south along the back trails towards the Rio Grande where the man called Durango was gathering some trusted friends to help him with the kill.

The least troubled person of all those who got the news was the big Texas Ranger Buck Duane himself.

He, too, slept late, but not in an expensive hotel. He took a bunk in the Ranger barracks back of Captain MacNelly's office. It was the safest spot in the city, and Duane slept long and soundly.

When he got up at what for him was the

exceptionally late hour of eight in the morning, he got breakfast from the barracks cook. Beans and a beefsteak, hot coffee, biscuits and the city luxury of a half dozen fried eggs vanished like snow before a summer sun, along with a big bowl of grits and sockeye gravy.

After lighting another long cigar, a luxury in which Duane rarely indulged and then only when in town, he went into the office again looking for Captain MacNelly.

The lithe Captain was there—quite as busy as he had been the night before.

"Morning, Buck," he said. "Sit back for a minute. I swear we need ten men for every one we've got, and a dozen clerks to boot to take the paper work off my hands."

A few moments later he leaned back and pushed the papers away. "Now that you've slept on it, what can you tell me about that note I showed you last night? Has it come to you yet who wrote it?"

"Not rightly," Duane said. "I don't recognize the hand and I don't know for sure who wrote it."

That was true enough as far as it went. He hadn't recognized the neat, feminine script and he wasn't certain what woman would both want to save his life and feel that she had to act anonymously. Not absolutely certain, that is.

He did have a notion, though. There was a woman he had helped when she was just a girl. At Harpetown he had met her again as "Lady Nell," owner and operator of the town's big saloon and gambling hall and practically queen of the gamblers, rustlers and hired guns who swarmed in that capital of Texas crime. That time they had each helped the other.

Duane hadn't seen her since, but if she had kept up her connection with the mysterious "Mask," and if he was the one who was hiring men to kill Duane, then she might well have written the note of warning.

Until he was certain, though, Duane had decided to keep his own counsel. "I don't know who wrote it," he said again.

"That's as may be," MacNelly said. "If you can find her though, it would help. What are your plans? I could send you out on a long patrol where you'd be hard to find until this all blows over...?" He left that as a question rather than a statement and looked for the big man's reaction.

It was what he had known it would be.

"I'll stay right here in San Antone," Duane said. "We both know blood feuds don't blow over, Captain. If I stick around, he'll come at me again. I reckon I can be ready for him, and sooner or later I'll back track whoever he sends. To kill a snake you kill the head."

They were the same words that Joe Bacon had used when he talked of Duane's own death.

Captain MacNelly nodded in agreement. "I was hoping you'd say just exactly that, Buck, though I wouldn't be about to give you such an order. I think it's about the only sensible thing you could do. Running from a killer doesn't work. You have to stay and take him sooner or later.

"There's another reason I'm glad you're staying too. There's plenty of wild talk going around town. In the dives and the alleys people say the Rangers are going to be killed off one by one, till there aren't any Rangers left. They say somebody will pay twenty thousand dollars for every Ranger killed."

"So it's not just me alone," Duane said thoughtfully. "Sounds more and more like it is the Mask. He's the only one I know crazy enough to try such a scheme. And the only outlaw who would connect me with the Rangers."

"You and I both know it's a scheme," MacNelly said seriously, "but this border riff-raff might get to believing it, because it's what they want to believe. It might encourage someone to make an independent try."

"We won't give them a chance," Buck Duane said. "I'll find the sidewinder behind this, and put a stop to him and to these rumors."

"I'm counting on you, Buck," the Captain said.

Buck Duane left Ranger Headquarters shortly after his talk with Captain MacNelly. He took his usual room over a hardware store in the downtown section of San Antonio and put up Bullet in a livery stable down the block. The owner of the store was a longtime personal friend and rented to the big man whenever he was in town.

After putting his saddlebags in his room, Duane checked his guns, washed up and went down onto the street. It was still early afternoon and the business section of town was crowded.

Many men recognized the big quiet man with the steel gray eyes and the sun-bronzed face. A few nodded to him or touched their hat brims in salute, but only one or two stopped him to shake his hand.

His way of life had made him widely known, but it was a life that had room for few friendships.

He wanted to let himself be seen, though, and to let it be known that he had no intention of leaving town. The people who would be most interested were unlikely to be stirring at all before darkness. By then the word would have reached their haunts.

Buck Duane strolled about for an hour and then headed back for his own room.

To his surprise the hardware store owner stopped him on the way in and handed him a sealed envelope engraved with the letterhead of the town's most fashionable hotel.

"Boy from the hotel brought this by for you, Buck," the man explained. "He said he wasn't told to wait for no answer."

Duane thanked him and took the envelope up to his room to open. It was addressed simply to "Mr. Duane", and contained a single sheet of notepaper. The writing was in an elaborate copperplate script, full of flourishes and elaborate capitals. He had never seen that writing before. It said:

"Dear Mr. Duane: I am a stranger in town and we have never met. However I have information that can be of utmost importance to you in your present difficulties. Like anything of value, my information is for sale—but this time not for money. I'd be honored to buy you dinner in the excellent dining room of my hotel. Be in the lobby at eight tonight, and I will introduce myself."

It was signed, with a flourish, Laurent St. Pierre.

Buck Duane folded the envelope and letterhead carefully and put them both in the back pocket of his trousers.

He decided to accept the strange invitation. He considered dropping by first to see if Captain MacNelly knew anything about this man, but then rejected the idea. The fellow was a stranger in San Antonio. Besides Duane had a shrewd idea that the Captain would keep track of where he went and who he saw.

Duane took off his boots, stretched out on the bed and slept as peacefully as if there was no single cloud in all his personal sky.

It was a habit learned in his outlaw days and never forgotten. Never waste an opportunity for safe rest. You just don't know when another chance will come.

V

At eight that night, Buck Duane was in the lobby of the large hotel. Crowds of well dressed and prosperous men and women moved back and forth around him on business of their own.

269

Duane recognized some of these people from other days and far different places, but his impassive poker-face showed no sign that he did.

It wasn't long before he was approached by Laurent St. Pierre. The creole was a small man by Western standards, a good six inches shorter than the big Ranger, and yet he gave a subtle impression of standing very tall indeed. It was partly the aura of a man accustomed to command and be obeyed, and partly the intangible vibration of menace within which he walked.

The impassive, chalk white face, all the more noticeable in that town of suntanned men, and the black obsidian eyes radiated a deadly presence so that men and women unconsciously made way for him as he advanced in a perfectly straight line across the lobby.

He wore a plain black suit of New Orleans cut, a white linen shirt with diamond and gold studs and cufflinks, and Eastern half-boots designed for walking in muddy streets rather than rough riding in the scrub. Duane was certain that the man must have more than one weapon hidden on his person.

There was no menace however in the chill smile with which the little man greeted his guest. After a brief greeting he led Duane to a table for two in the hotel dining room and ordered dinner for them both.

They exchanged trivial remarks until the food had arrived and been eaten. Then St. Pierre leaned back in his chair and looked at his guest over a glass of excellent wine.

"Now, Mr. Duane," he said with his odd Creole French accent, "I think it's time I set your curiosity at rest. I'm sure you know I didn't ask you here purely for the prestige of being seen at dinner with one of the most—notorious—men in the West."

Buck Duane said nothing.

"No," Laurent St. Pierre continued, "this meeting

stems from an impulse that I don't quite understand myself. An impulse to show mercy, Mr. Duane. An impulse to warn you of a real and very terrible danger of death."

He paused, but once more Buck Duane said nothing and showed no emotion.

"I don't think you are taking my warning seriously, Mr. Duane," the Creole said intently. "You should. I assure you that it is quite genuine. Would it shock you to know that I myself was offered a truly incredible sum of money to bring about your death? Would you believe that?"

Buck Duane smiled at him. "Of course it wouldn't shock me. You were offered a hundred thousand dollars to kill me."

Now St. Pierre looked startled, his acid gambler's mask was pierced for once.

Duane smiled again. "The only thing that puzzles me, Mr. Laurent St. Pierre," he said, "is why you haven't tried to collect that fortune. Or are you going to try now?" Duane was tensed for any move the other might make.

St. Pierre spread out both his hands upon the table top. "I assure you . . . no. I am not . . . and for the same reason that I refused the offer to begin with. You are too good with your guns, Mr. Duane. I do not go against impossible odds. Evidently you are also good with your brains and your source of information, since you already know about our friend and what he plans for you. I congratulate myself at not having fallen into the trap of underestimating you."

Duane held his peace again. The one thing he did not know, although St. Pierre apparently assumed that he did, was the identity and whereabouts of his enemy. He desperately wished that he could ask without giving away an advantage to the deadly little man. He could not.

"Since you already have the gift of the knowledge I intended to give you, it places me at some disadvantage. I had intended to trade my warning to you," St. Pierre said.

"Now you'd like me to take your good intent for the fact," Duane said. "Why not try me? What was it that you wanted from me?"

Now it was St. Pierre's turn to smile. He let it grow as close to a laugh as he was capable.

"I am sure you will see the irony in this." he said. "I planned to trade a life for a life. I would save your life with my warning and ask you in return to save mine."

"How could I do that?" Duane asked.

"By killing a man who will otherwise kill me if he can," the little Creole said. "I am sure that it would be no problem for you. This man is a border ruffian. You will know his ways and how to fight him—which I admit that I do not."

"Why does he want to kill you?"

"He came to New Orleans and lost a great deal of money to me in a gambling house. A very great deal of money, I assure you. He will not believe that I did not cheat him, though I assure you that I did not."

"And now he wants revenge," Duane said. "I can understand that. What is his name?"

"They call him Durango," the Creole said. "He heads a gang of rustlers and thieves. Will you kill this man for me?"

"I'm not a killer for hire," Duane said.

"Not even when the price I pay is to save your life?"

"You haven't saved my life." Duane said coldly, "you gave me a warning yes, but what does a warning amount to? Give me the man who wants me dead. Then you will have accomplished something of value to me, my friend."

"Aha," St. Pierre said. "So you don't know who

272

he is or where to find him. I don't say that I do of course, but just suppose I did. You kill Durango for me. When I hear that you have done that, I'll tell you where to find your man. Is that a bargain, friend?"

Buck Duane made no sign.

VI

Buck Duane parted with Laurent St. Pierre without committing himself in any way.

The little man's proposition puzzled him. The warning could have been only an elaborate hoax to enlist his help against Durango. It was no secret by now that someone wanted Duane killed. Many sums had been named as the promised price for his life.

On the other hand why should the little man admit that he himself had been asked to do the killing? Was that another ruse to gain confidence?

If not—then what was it? Was it supposed to send Duane against Durango who would be ready and waiting with his gang? Had Durango himself sent the little man?

Certainly Duane didn't trust the man from New Orleans, and in any case he had no intention of making a deal to kill Durango for any price that might be named.

Duane spent the rest of the evening moving from one bar and gambling house to another, letting himself be seen for a few minutes in each. As was his custom, he neither smoked nor drank more than an occasional mouthful of beer, and kept on the constant alert for any hostile move.

It was easy to see by the way men turned to watch him in every room he entered that the word was out in San Antonio. People knew that Buck Duane was marked for death and watched avidly to see what form that death might take.

No one actually made an overt move against him,

however. They weren't fooled by his calm and apparently disinterested manner. The two big Colt revolvers swung at his hips and the ruffians and bar flys and their women knew the deadly speed and accuracy with which the big man could use those guns.

Many a man who watched that night would gladly have traded his soul for the sums of money rumored to await the killer of Buck Duane—but to trade a soul was one thing, and to face certain death was another.

If the game had not been such a grim one, Buck Duane might well have been amused by the conflicting emotions he saw on men's faces.

It was well after midnight when he returned to his lodgings above the hardware store. From the street he could see that a lantern had been lit behind the closed blinds of the window.

He went up the stairs slowly and very alertly. He made no sound at all to warn anyone waiting for him.

The Ranger paused in the hallway outside the door to his room.

Inside the room, someone was strumming a guitar very lightly. The melody was an old border tune, and after a moment Duane recognized the distinctive fingering of the player.

He called out: "Open up, Kid, and let an old friend in."

Inside the room he heard the scrape of a chair being pushed back and the thud of booted feet on the bare wood of the floor. A moment later the door was flung wide and Duane was shaking hands with his young friend and companion, the rookie Ranger called the Jackrabbit Kid.

The Kid was young, wiry and slender, with the stamp of the border in every line of his face. He pulled Duane into the room, picked his guitar off the bed so the big man could sit down, and took the single chair for himself.

"Where have you been?" Duane asked.

"And what am I doing here?" the Kid finished for him. "I've been listening to talk of you, old wolf, down along the border. I'm here because you're going to need somebody you can trust to watch your back for you. What in blazes have you been up to that brings the pack down on you?"

"I've done nothing," Duane said, "and I'm not totally convinced all this is more than the wind in a tumbleweed."

"I stopped to see Cap MacNelly when I hit town," the Kid said seriously. "I'd been hearing jawbone all the way down to Eagle Pass and San Pedro Springs. It all said death for my old pal Buck. I figured then I'd better come up and see for myself, so I did.

"The Captain said one man had already made his play for you and died. He told me of the talk here in town. He gave me this for you too."

He handed Duane an envelope similar to the one the Captain had given him the night before. The note, in the same feminine hand, said only:

"Durango coming by the lower Presidio Road. Send word ahead to bring Buck Duane out to him, to trap and kill."

Again the note was unsigned.

"You know who wrote that don't you?" the Kid asked.

"I can't be sure," Duane said. The Kid had been with him at Harpetown, and he wanted the youngster's reaction. He got it right off.

"Of course you know," the Kid insisted. "MacNelly says you both think that guy they called the Mask could be back of all this. There's only one woman who was close to him at Harpetown and could still be with him. That's Lady Nell and we both know it."

"It could be," Duane admitted. "I'd thought of that myself, but I can't be sure. Besides, I haven't the least idea how to find her. She'll have to find me if she wants to see me. That should be easy enough. I can't take a step out of this room without eyes on me since this started."

"I can," the Kid said. "Nobody knows I'm in town except Cap MacNelly. A woman like Nell is hard to hide too. She stands out from the rest of womenfolk like a palomino in a herd of scrub ponies. Meanwhile you watch out for Durango."

"What about him?"

"He came down to Eagle Pass on the river a few days back. He has lots of friends there and he let it out he means to kill you, Buck. He didn't say for money or for why, just that he's a better gun than the great Buck Duane and he means to prove it to the world."

"He knows where to find me."

"Sure he does, but Durango's not the type to come and challenge you in the open. Just like he's not the gun to beat you in anything like a fair stand up and shoot it out. He's recruiting friends to help him and making plans to give himself the edge when the time comes."

"He knows the word will come up the trail to town," Duane said. "Will he come with it, or will he wait for me to come down to the Grand River and smoke him out?"

"I don't know," the Kid said. "What's your guess?"

"I think he'll try a little of each and all," the big Ranger said thoughtfully. "It's his way. He'll make sure I know he's coming after me and dare me to come out and meet him on the trail. If I do, he'll bushwack me for sure. He'll have friends riding well off the road to close in on me at his signal. It'll be like taking minnows in a draw net.

"If I don't take the bait and come out, then he'll bring his pards on into San Antone and try to pull the same trick here. Either way I fight him on his terms."

"That's what he thinks," the Kid said. "But you can out-think him."

"If I don't," the big man said. "I won't live long enough to care."

"At least you've been warned," the Kid said.

Big Buck Duane got up and paced the length of the small room before turning to face his friend.

"I've been warned," he said then. "I been warned and warned again till the taste of warning is too sticky in my mouth. Everybody in this here town is busy warning good old Buck about Durango.

"I don't like it, boy. It's just too good to be true, and it makes me wonder who else I should think about besides Durango. They set him up with me like the tar baby for Br'er Fox . . . and while I fight the tar baby where is my real enemy?"

VII

Buck Duane was not a man to let himself be troubled very long by doubts or indecisions.

Within the hour, he and the Jackrabbit Kid had gotten their mounts from the livery stable and were quietly making their way out of San Antonio by back streets under cover of the darkness and the very late hour.

They did not go unnoticed.

A man who had been watching the livery stalked them a few blocks till he knew which road they would take. Then he went back and got his own horse and rode hard out to the other side of town to the big mansion where Joe Bacon lived.

It was dawn when he arrived, and the master of the house was still abed, but the rider spoke urgently to several servants. Within a matter of half an hour Bacon came down in robe and slippers. They conferred briefly by the stables out of earshot of the big house. Then the messenger rode back to town, richer by a handful of silver dollars.

Joe Bacon walked slowly back to the mansion with his hands in the pocket of the purple velvet dressing gown he wore. His brow was creased in thought.

Once there, he sent another messenger to town to summon Laurent St. Pierre, and went himself to the woman he called Helen and whom Buck Duane knew as Lady Nell.

An hour later St. Pierre, Helen and Joe Bacon sat at early breakfast in the dining room of the big house. Don Andres and Will Hadley were still asleep in guest bedrooms on the second floor.

"We can be sure he's not running away," Joe Bacon said. "Buck Duane's not the man for that."

"If he's going south to the border," St. Pierre said, "It's exactly the thing I'd do in his place. He knows the way this Durango will act, and he's gone down to stop him while Durango still feels perfectly safe in his own country and before he's ready to move."

"I think he's right, Joe," Lady Nell said. "It's exactly what Duane would do. Attack before he can be hit by his enemy."

"There's humor in it at that," the little Creole said. "there sits our scoundrel assassin plotting all sorts of treachery and trickery, and all the time Death coming down the trail for him as fast as a horse can run. That's one to make the Fates come back out of their ruined temples to laugh."

Joe Bacon turned on him. "You may think this is a laughing matter," he said. "I don't. For sure I don't. Durango has to be warned—and before Duane gets there—and I don't have a man here I can trust with a message like that."

"You can trust me," St. Pierre told him, his smile gone. "Give me a couple of your ruffians as guides and to cook for me. I can ride."

"He might make it," Lady Nell said. "He can cut across to the upper Presidio Road. Give them a couple of changes of horses. If they ride hard they can make it ahead of Duane and the Kid. They'll want to bring their mounts in fresh."

"That's right," Bacon agreed. "Besides, Mr. St. Pierre can help Durango with the kill and cut himself in for half the reward. If we get busy with this now, he can be on the road within the hour."

It was settled.

Laurent St. Pierre was a tougher man than he looked, and rode as if he'd been born in the saddle. Bacon's men had to guide him and cook for him, but they soon recognized that here was no helpless Easterner.

They left San Antonio on Tuesday morning and were within sight of the lights of Eagle Pass before midnight on Thursday. To make it they'd worn out three horses each and left the beasts exhausted by the road to die or be stolen as the case may be.

Now they drew up on a little hill looking down on the distant town.

"That's it, Mr. St. Pierre," one of the rustlers said. "That there is Eagle Pass."

"Alright," the Creole said. "Let's get off the road now. I want to go into town by a back way so I won't be spotted. You know such a way?"

"Sure we do," his other guide said.

Twenty minutes later, in the dark, the little man drew his revolver and shot both of his guides dead. One shot in the back of the head for each. They never knew what struck them.

He left them where they fell, but he didn't go all the way on into Eagle Pass that night. Instead, he made a dry and fireless camp in the brush.

He slept quite soundly and peacefully.

The next morning, he rose early, and watched the trail. Not once that day did he leave his hiding place.

Buck Duane and the Jackrabbit Kid didn't sight the ramshackle buildings of the town of Eagle Pass until early Friday evening. As Bacon had guessed, the big man wanted to come into town with both himself and his mounts rested.

There was a fight ahead, and whether they won or lost that fight, there might be a chase at the end or a great deal of hard riding ahead. Long years of experience on the owlhoot trail had taught Duane not to waste his strength at any time. That extra burst of energy he hoarded had saved his life on more than one occasion.

Unaware they were being watched, Duane and the Kid pulled about a mile off the trail and stopped under cover to rest and cook a meal.

It was dark by the time they finished making camp. A desert bird rustled the mesquite, then all was still.

"What do you reckon to do?" the Kid asked as they finished a hearty meal of bacon, beans, sourdough biscuit and coffee.

"Do the only thing I can do," Buck Duane said. "I figure to ride into town after dark. Knowing Durango, he'll be drinking and talking in the biggest saloon in town. I'll face him down there before he has time to gather help, and while his boys with him are caught unaware. Won't give em time to drink and jaw their courage up."

"You going to gun him down right then and there?"

Duane shrugged. "You should ought to know me better than that, boy. I'll kill him only if he forces me to it. I came down here to keep him from killing me."

He got up and kicked sand and dirt over the embers of the small, hardwood cooking fire they had used until it was completely extinguished and they were in a dark broken only by the blazing stars high above.

The wind which had come up with the day's ending blew away the last traces of the smell of fire and food. A little way off Bullet stamped and snorted softly, but not in alarm.

"I aim to get the drop on him so fast and hard he knows I have him dead to rights," Duane said. "Then I'll arrest him. Plenty wanted posters out on him for that. If he gives in, and I think he will, we take him back to San Antone and ride him into town handcuffed in broad daylight. That'll stop the loose talk going round for sure. If he won't throw in his cards . . ."

The big, steel hard Ranger stopped there, but the Kid finished for him.

"It'll be him decided to commit suicide," he said.

They sat for at least two hours more before they got up and caught their horses. Duane had been asleep. The Kid had heard him snoring softly. He wondered again, for the thousandth time, at the iron control Buck Duane had over his nerves.

The big man rode easily and relaxed in his saddle. That was the surface for anyone to see. Inside his stomach there was a hard, icy knot. It came whenever he rode to a meeting with death. He did not like to kill, but he was a practical man. There were times when Death, like Life, had to be met face to face. Buck Duane rode to such a meeting now, and the cold knot within him was the sign.

VII

Durango was having a late dinner of steak and potatoes and whiskey in the Golden Eagle saloon and gambling house.

As befitted his standing in this wild border town,

he ate on a special table in the office of the owner of the saloon instead of in the crowded main room of the place. Later on he would take another table on the main floor to drink, gamble and entertain his cronies. While he ate he preferred the safety of the private room.

It was here that the boss of the five men who tended the forty foot bar in the big room located him. It was typical of the fear in which Durango was held that the man just came in and stood by the table waiting to be spoken to.

"What's bothering you, Mac?" Durango asked finally through a mouthful of fried meat and bread.

"Sorry boss," the bartender said. "There's a little Eastern dude out here claims he has to see you right away. Just rode in off the Upper Presidio Road. Says his name's Larry St. Pierre or something and he has a real important message."

"It's alright," Durango said. "I know who the little varmint is. Bring him in."

A moment later the little Creole gambler came into the room. Unlike the bartender, he acted perfectly at home, pulling a chair up to the table and sitting down opposite Durango. He even helped himself to the whiskey bottle and poured a drink into a small telescoping silver glass he took from his pocket.

"What's the matter," Durango scoffed. "You too good to drink from the bottle or something?"

"I don't have to drink from any man's bottle," St. Pierre said. "I've got a message from Mr. Joe Bacon."

"If it's about Duane backshooting that Irish slob, I've already heard the news."

"Too many people have heard about that," St. Pierre went on. "That's what worries Bacon. Everybody's heard that and about the price on the Ranger's head. Bacon doesn't like it."

282

"Who cares what he likes. He's just putting up the money, not risking his own neck. I don't see no harm in how much folks talk."

"Bacon cares, and since it's his hundred thousand dollars you and I had better care too, friend Durango. He wants you to come on up to San Antonio and make your play right now. He says if we give the Rangers time to think they'll cook up a way to foul up our plan. Give them time too, and they might find out it's him back of things. If that happens his deal with us is off."

"I don't think of it that way," Durango admitted. "Well, maybe I should move. I've got a dozen boys lined up to help me. We can start north sometime tomorrow. Hell, just as soon now as later."

"I think you're wise," St. Pierre said. "What time will we start?"

"*We* won't," Durango said. "Me and my boys will light out when we're good and ready. Since you come to Eagle Pass, you can stay right here. I got plenty muscle without you, and that way the whole hundred thousand is mine. You savvy?"

St. Pierre drank the last of the whiskey from his silver cup, wiped it dry on the tablecloth and put it back in his pocket.

"I suppose I should have figured that," he said without emotion.

"Sure you should." Durango laughed. "If you was as smart as me, you would have."

"Yes," the little man said. "I suppose that if I was as smart as you are I would have figured it exactly that way."

The irony in his voice wasn't entirely lost on the border gunfighter.

"Just don't try outsmarting yourself right now," he said. "This is my town and the people in it are my people. You just set around here and take it easy till I'm long gone up the trail to San Antone. That way

283

you keep your health."

A moment later, he got up and went out into the big room, leaving Laurent St. Pierre alone with the whiskey. The little Creole poured himself another glass and gimaced at the taste of the raw liquor.

"There's only one way a man like Buck Duane can be killed," he told the glass and the empty room. "It has to be by treachery. By someone he trusts absolutely because he feels he has reason to trust that person. Friend Durango doesn't know that. It's just a bit beyond the level of his intelligence. That's why—here or in San Antonio—when Durango goes against Duane he goes to his own death."

He raised the glass and drank the last dregs in a silent toast to the empty room. Then he looked at the remains of steak still lying uneaten on Durango's plate.

"The condemned man enjoyed a hearty last meal," Laurent St. Pierre said. Then he too got up and left the office of Golden Eagle Saloon. He went by the back way into the alley.

At eleven o'clock that night Buck Duane and the Jackrabbit Kid rode into the little border town of Eagle Pass, Texas. The streets were deserted. Honest citizens were long abed. The rest were in the gambling joints, saloons and houses of ill fame.

The largest and most elaborate of the gambling dens was the Golden Eagle, well patronized by citizenry of dubious virtue. Mostly they were lined up at the bar, though one faro table was getting a play, and five men were playing poker at the right side of the room from the entry.

At the left side, Durango sat with two of his lieutenants, Nero, Weld and Clubfoot Al. They were drinking whiskey and making plans to gather the rest of their crew and ride north to San Antonio the following morning.

When Duane and the Kid pushed through the

swinging doors from the street the clubfooted killer looked up at them casually and then glanced away again.

He had seen Buck Duane once, years before, but the big Ranger was the last man he expected to see come through those doors. It just plain didn't register with him what had happened.

The instant they got through the door, the Jackrabbit Kid took several quick steps to his right to get his back against the wall. There he could watch the faro and poker table and the men at that side of the long bar which stretched along the far wall. He didn't draw either of the big Colts that he wore, but let his hands swing easily close to their butts, ready to get into action at lightning speed.

It was the silent menace in his look that caught the eye of the faro dealer. The man froze, cards in hand. Then the men at his table turned, and a moment later one after another of the men at the bar began to realize that something was amiss.

Durango, who should have been the first to spot a danger to himself, was the last.

He was leaning over the table talking to his men until he suddenly noticed that the big room had fallen silent.

When he finally looked up it took him a moment, through whiskey-blurred eyes, to recognize the big man who stood silently just inside the door.

Duane started to walk quietly towards the table where his enemy sat. Like the Kid, he left his own guns in their tied down holsters within easy reach of his hands.

Durango and his two men watched the big man come with horror and hate in their eyes. They were caught bent over the table with their hands on its top. Not one of them was in the position for a quick draw.

They saw death across the room with easy strides.

"What do you want?" Durango called out.

Duane stopped in his tracks. "I've come to take you back to San Antone, Durango," he said. His voice was quiet and contained, but every man in the room heard him without trouble. "There's a warrant out to bring you in for trial."

Durango said nothing at all.

"Push back from the table," Duane said. "Put your hands on the top of your heads and stand up. Then walk around the table where I can see you all the time. One at a time unbuckle your gun belts and let them fall to the floor. All nice and easy like I say. That way there'll be no trouble and no killing needed."

The three at the table braced themselves while every man and woman in the room watched them. Even the Kid let his eyes flick over their way.

The men were under the gun for sure, and knew it. Without a miracle they were doomed.

They got their miracle.

The instant Jackrabbit Kid turned his eyes towards the three men at the table, the bartender, Mac, slid his hands under the bar. He came up with an old, sawed off, ten gauge shotgun with both barrels loaded with buckshot. It was a percussion gun with caps already on both nipples and the two big iron hammers already cocked. The two barrels rested on the bar and pointed right at Duane.

With that steady hold and at the short range inside the room, he couldn't possibly have missed. The buckshot would have torn the life out of Duane before he ever knew what happened.

Mac meant to fire, but he never got the chance.

Laurent St. Pierre stepped through the door which led from the kitchen to the area behind the bar.

He had a gun in his hand, and he shot Mac once through the back of the head. It sounded like a cannon being fired in that otherwise silent room.

Durango and his two men made their play.

The rustler boss kicked the table away from in front of them and came out of the chair pulling his guns.

The men in the room were all watching, but none of them could actually say later on that he had seen Buck Duane make his draw. One minute the big, quiet man's hands were empty.

In the next split second each hand held a forty five, and the two guns boomed together.

Durango and Nero Weld each took a single bullet in the heart. They died with their guns drawn but unfired on the dirty floor of the Golden Eagle Saloon.

Clubfoot Al was wiser, if not quite as brave. He left his gun in its holster and put up his hands.

The gunfight was over almost before it began.

Buck Duane started to drop his two guns back in their holsters.

He never knew what instinct warned him. It might have been a flicker of movement reflected in the long mirror behind the bar or just the quick telepathic alertness of a man who had been hunted after for years without end.

He twisted his right wrist and pulled the hammer back on the big gun even as his own eyes flicked over behind the bar. What he saw made him drop to his knees even as his finger tightened and his own gun fired.

Laurent St. Pierre pulled both triggers of the shotgun he had taken from the dead bartender's hands. The two charges of number one buckshot tore the air where Duane's head had been a bare instant before.

Then Duane's single shot took the Creole in the forehead and blew out his brains.

It was four days later before Buck Duane and the Kid rode back into San Antonio. Fast riders had taken the news before them by back trails. They could see by the faces of the men in the streets that the fight at the Golden Eagle was known all over town.

Captain MacNelly knew. He was waiting for them in the Ranger office.

"There's no more talk of killing off the Rangers one by one," he said in greeting. Then: "Could you get any of Durango's men to talk?"

Buck Duane said: "Not a one. Most of them blew town the same night. Clubfoot and a couple of others would have talked alright, but they didn't know what we wanted. Durango hadn't ever said who he was working for."

"Too bad you couldn't have kept the little New Orleans man alive. Rumor has it he was the third man hired to kill you."

"I'm sure of it," Duane said, "and he was the deadliest of the lot because he was clever. Did you hear he tried to hire me to kill Durango to take suspicion off himself? He figured after he shot that bartender I'd trust him, and I did. Another second and he'd have had me."

"If he'd lived we could have made him talk," MacNelly said. "Now we don't know for sure who backed this play.

"But I can tell you now, talk says a certain very wealthy man left town in a hurry. And this was delivered to me this morning." The Captain handed Buck Duane a note.

The message in the familiar feminine hand was brief. "You have won, Buck Duane," was all it said.

Duane grinned.

"I think we can drink to that," MacNelly said and got the bottle out.